A RECKLESS RUNAWAY

JESS MICHAELS

PROLOGUE

I t should have been the happiest time in Anne Shelley's life. That was what everyone around her said, from her maid to her friends to her sisters. The happiest time, for she was just one month from her wedding to an earl. And not even one of the older earls who circulated through parties and drooled over the debutantes. A young one who, Anne supposed, was tolerably handsome if looked at in the right light.

She was just weeks away from her wedding and she should have been happy. But she wasn't. Not in the slightest. Panicked? Yes. On the edge of breakdown? Always. But *happy*…not at all.

"Are you Miss Anne?"

She squeezed her eyes shut at the sound of her intended's voice. Slowly she turned to face him, the Earl of Harcourt. His dark brown eyes flitted over her briefly, then away as he held out a glass of wine for her.

"Yes," she answered. Harcourt never knew who she was. He couldn't tell her apart from her sisters Juliana and Thomasina. They were triplets and she'd spent her life correcting those around her about her identity.

But somehow she'd always dreamed that the man she'd married

would see her just for...for *herself*. That he would instinctively recognize her in a crowd even if she were standing in between her sisters wearing the exact same gown.

Harcourt didn't. And it was disappointing. As was the silence that now rose up between them while they stood overlooking the ball.

"How do you find Harcourt Heights now that you've been here a few days?" the earl asked.

Anne barely held back a sigh. It was a reasonable question. After all, this shire and Harcourt's manor in its center, Harcourt Heights, were to be her home now. She wanted to like it.

"It's very...fair," she muttered into her glass. "A bit remote for my taste."

Harcourt's mouth thinned. "Well, I'm certain you will find plenty to tempt you back to London, since your sisters will be there."

He glanced across the room where Juliana and Thomasina stood with their father. There was something in the glint of Harcourt's eyes as he looked at them. Some little flash of the passion Anne had longed for all her life. But then it was gone. Anne had imagined it, of course. Harcourt never displayed passion, after all. She doubted he had an ounce of it in his body, nor humor, nor anything but strict responsibility and rules.

He would have been better suited to either of her sisters. But here they were. She knew why her father had chosen her to wed first.

"I find myself a bit warm," Anne said with a glance over her shoulder to the terrace doors. "I think I'll step outside for a moment."

Harcourt nodded. "Of course. But when you return, I think we should dance. This gathering is for us and those at the assembly hall are our neighbors, friends and tenants. They would like to see us exhibit."

Exhibit. Yes, that's what it was, after all. This entire marriage was an exhibition. Not driven by emotion or desire, but a union of a far more practical bent.

She nodded, barely holding back the tears that suddenly choked her throat and blurred her vision. As he turned away, just as disinterested as she was, she fled, making her way to the terrace before anyone could stop her and see the truth in her eyes. The utter misery.

She shut the door behind her and glanced around to see if she was alone. When she found she was, she rushed to the farthest corner from the door and bent her head. The tears came then, hot against her cheeks.

"There is no escape for me," she whispered, to remind herself of that fact as much as anything else. "I must accept this. I…I must."

"That sounds very dire."

She jolted at the masculine voice that came from behind her. Pivoting, she faced its owner and jolted to find he was standing just two long steps behind her, watching her. He was an exceptionally well-favored man. He was tall, with broad shoulders, dark hair that was a little too long and rakishly mussed. His eyes were what drew her in, though. They were blue. Shockingly blue. Ice blue.

She realized she had been staring at him for who knew how long, and she turned her face to gather herself, even as she quickly glanced at the stranger from the corner of her eye. "I beg your pardon, sir. It is very rude to eavesdrop."

He arched a brow and grinned, popping a dimple in his cheek that was just as attractive as anything else about him. "*Can* someone eavesdrop into a conversation a lady is having with herself?"

She frowned and worried the cross necklace she wore. "I think someone can eavesdrop on any conversation that he isn't invited to be a part of."

His lips thinned a little, hardening as if he was irritated by that answer. But then the expression softened and he shrugged. "I suppose I should apologize."

She paused, waiting for him to do so, but he didn't. Instead he sidled up to her without invitation and placed his hands on the terrace wall next to hers. She jolted at the sudden invasion of her space, at the heat this man seemed to emanate. She'd never felt anything like it. She inched away as she turned to look out over the garden behind the assembly room.

"You are Miss Anne Shelley," he said matter-of-factly.

She glanced at him out of the corner of her eye. "I-I am, yes." She wrinkled her brow. "Did we…did we meet earlier tonight?"

She didn't think they had. One wouldn't so quickly forget the handsome hulk of a man standing beside her. One who was watching her from the corner of his eye with a bit more directness than was proper, especially if he knew her name and the fact that she was engaged to someone else.

"We didn't exactly meet," he said with another one of those dimpled smiles.

She faced him now. "I see. It seems you will play a little game with me by not telling me exactly how you know who I am."

He tilted his head. "Playing games is my specialty."

There was a flutter of something in her belly. Something she hadn't felt for a very long time, not since her engagement to Harcourt. This flirtation, for that was what she had to call the exchange, brought her back to London and the *fun* she used to have when she was carefree.

She found she liked returning there, if only for a brief moment.

"Am I to guess?" She placed a finger to her lips as if to consider. "I saw you in a shop in town? Or perhaps you are a friend of a friend I met in passing long ago? Oh…wait…are you a highwayman? Have I seen your picture on wanted posters all over the countryside?"

He laughed, and her cheeks warmed with pleasure. It was in her nature to make little jokes, but Harcourt *never* laughed at them like this man just had. He was far too serious a person in general.

"You are close on one of those counts," the stranger said. "But I won't tell you which one."

"That hardly seems fair," Anne said.

"Life isn't fair, my lovely lady," he drawled, and her heart fluttered again at the improper endearment. "I *will* tell you my name, though. Ellis Maitland, at your service."

She bobbed out a playful curtsey. "Miss Anne Shelley, but you already knew that."

He nodded. "I did, indeed. Perhaps I'll give you a hint as to which guess is right if you agree to see me again."

All the playfulness left her body as she stared up at this stranger, this Ellis Maitland. "I-I am engaged. You must know that."

"I know that fact very well." He stepped a little closer, and once again she had the sensation of her personal space being invaded. She ignored the instinct to step back and held her ground as she stared up at him.

"Then you know I cannot meet with you," she whispered. "It would be wrong."

"Wrong and right are slippery things, Anne," he said. "Now, is it wrong to meet with a friend?"

She swallowed at the question, which wasn't a fair one, and they both knew it. "Of course not."

"Then I'd like to be your friend. Your Harcourt has a pretty little pond on his estate, west of the main house. Meet me there tomorrow at two. I know a young lady like yourself would be able to figure out how to escape all the barriers put in place to keep you from what you truly want. You can call it a game if it soothes your conscience."

She worried her lip as she turned away. "I don't know," she whispered, thinking of the scandal. Thinking of how wrong his suggestion was.

He was quiet a moment, long enough that she faced him. His face had hardened and he shrugged. "Very well then, Miss Shelley. Just go ahead and accept that there is no escape for you."

She turned her face as her own words returned to slap her. That was what she feared, wasn't it? No escape. This interesting, clearly dangerous man was offering her a brief moment of just that. What was the harm in one last taste of freedom? Once she was wed, she'd never see it again.

"I-I will find a way to meet you tomorrow," she whispered.

He smiled, somewhat smug, as if he'd always known he would bend her to his will. And then he tipped his hat and strolled away into the darkness of the corner of the terrace. She tilted her head. Where was he going? There was no entryway back into the ball from there.

She moved toward the darkened corner and blinked. He had vanished! She stared down below at the garden ten feet down. There was the faintest flash of movement toward the woods.

He had jumped over the terrace.

A thrill worked through her as she turned toward the ballroom. Inside she could see Harcourt speaking to her sister Thomasina, whose hands were fluttering around her like a nervous little bird.

To meet another man behind her fiancé's back was wrong, so very wrong, no matter what Ellis Maitland said about the fluid nature of such things. But she was going to do it anyway because it was her last chance to have an adventure. A last chance to have a little fun.

And she would stay in control of herself and the situation. So what could go wrong?

CHAPTER 1

One month later

Rook Maitland smoothed the edge of his blade along the wooden block, cutting away the unwanted splinters as he transformed the piece into a carving he could be proud of. It wasn't the original purpose for his knives, but he had adjusted in the last year. In more than one way.

"What a waste of your talents, cousin."

Rook froze at the voice behind him. It was familiar, despite his not having seen its owner for many months. He slowly rose to his feet, setting down the knife and the wood fragment before he turned to face his very much unwanted guest. The one who had been so silent in his approach that even Rook's trained ears hadn't detected him. But then, Ellis Maitland had always been deadly like that.

Part of why Rook hadn't seen him for so long.

He looked his cousin up and down. His appearance was exactly the same. Somehow that was both frustrating and comforting. Frustrating because he felt like Ellis should have aged as punishment for all he'd done in the not-so-distant past. Comforting because at least the man was alive.

"What are you doing here, Handsome?" he asked, reverting to Ellis's street nickname. One earned from years of seducing unassuming women out of fortunes and smallclothes.

Ellis had been smiling, but now the expression fell and a dangerous glint lit his gaze as he stepped farther into Rook's workshop. "That's some welcome for your partner."

Rook shook his head. "Former partner," he corrected softly. "I'm out of your game, Handsome. You know why."

Ellis took another long step toward him and Rook stepped back out of habit, shifting his weight in preparation for an attack. Ellis stopped advancing and looked at him like his motion was a betrayal. For a moment his entire life led at his cousin's side flashed through Rook's mind. The good and the very bad. And he mourned all that could have been and would never be.

"You're out of the game but still benefitting from it," Ellis said softly.

"I suppose I am," Rook agreed, and ignored the twinge of guilt that accompanied the admission.

Yes, his ill-gotten gains, saved up for years, now paid for the life he led here in the wilds. He hated himself for it. And yet he didn't stop. He didn't give it away. So perhaps he deserved Ellis's censure.

"Why are you here?" he repeated, sharper than the first time he asked the question.

"I need your help," Ellis said.

Rook arched a brow. There a slight desperation to his cousin's tone, even if his body language remained cool and unaffected. That never led to good. Ellis was uncontrollable enough when he wasn't desperate. "No."

Ellis lunged forward and caught his arm before Rook could dodge the motion. He supposed it was done to prove Ellis could get to him. But it was also to plead. To beg.

"No one will get hurt this time, I swear to you," Ellis said.

Rook thought of the life the two of them had led on the streets. He remembered no other, in truth. Robbing, swindling, lying and cheating had been his life since he was old enough to understand the meaning of hunger.

"I'm not sure that was *ever* true, Ellis," he whispered.

Ellis's gaze narrowed. "Don't get noble now, cousin. Not when you have as much of a past as I do. I *need* your help. I'm your blood —are you really going to turn your back on me?"

Rook yanked his arm free of Ellis's grip and paced away, running a hand through his hair. His cousin's desperation was dangerous, indeed, but at least if Rook helped him, perhaps he could temper it. Make sure his promise not to hurt anyone was kept this time.

It wasn't as if Ellis would leave him alone anyway. Once he had a plan, there was never anything that could stop him. One way or another, Rook would be dragged into it. At least this way he could set his terms.

He folded his arms as he faced Ellis and met his gaze evenly. "What is it you want me to do?"

"Nothing difficult," Ellis said with relief on every line of his face. "Just meet me in Beckfoot in three days' time."

"Beckfoot?" Rook repeated with a tilt of his head.

"It's just across the sea. You'll only be gone from Scotland and your precious island for a day at most." Ellis shook his head. "Don't you hate it here?"

"I do not," Rook said with no further explanation. "How do you think I'll get there? It's over a week's ride in the best of conditions, and in Scotland it's *never* the best of conditions."

"I've hired a boat for you to come and to go back. It's all paid. It's a few hours across the inlet. You just have to board it in three days when he comes to your little dock." Ellis eased forward. "Please."

"There's obviously a great deal more to do than what you're explaining. What's your angle, cousin?"

Ellis hesitated a moment, more of that desperation entering his gaze. He opened and shut his mouth, like he was struggling with the explanation. Then his face hardened. "I'm just trying to get back something that was taken from me. That's all. I need your help in Beckfoot. Will you come?"

Rook sighed. This was his cousin, a man more like his brother. Ellis could be a rabid dog, but he had once been more. Once he had been Rook's hero, by action and by reputation. And it was for that reason that he nodded. "I'll do it. But you listen to me, Handsome. This is the *last* time. I don't want to see you here again asking me for favors."

Ellis swallowed. "It's the last time. I swear on my life. If I manage this deal, I'll settle down like you have. You won't have me darkening your doors again, I swear it." He reached out a hand. "See you in Beckfoot."

With great reluctance, Rook shook the offered hand. "In Beckfoot. Three days."

His cousin gave a half-hearted salute as he ducked his way out of the workshop. Rook didn't have to follow to know Ellis would have already vanished into the trees.

He sighed as he retook his seat in front of the whittling materials. He no longer felt like using his knives. He was too concerned about what he'd just agreed to. Because it could lead to no good.

Anne stood at the fireplace in her future husband's fine parlor, watching anything but the man beside her. She couldn't look at Harcourt, not when her mind was spinning with such wretched choices.

She had *tried* to care for this man. She truly had. But in the past month it had become perfectly clear how impossible that would be. Since she met Ellis Maitland, with his big laugh and certain words and seductive smiles, well...it had been perfectly plain to Anne that she could *never* be happy with the Earl of Harcourt.

And now she was just a week away from her wedding and the

crushing weight of all of it rested heavy on her chest. Heavier still when she thought of the letter she had received from Ellis that very morning. A shocking, impetuous letter where he declared he couldn't live without her and asked her to run away with him.

He would be waiting for her that night, hoping she would escape and be his.

She could almost see his words dancing before her and her eyes blurred with tears at the choice they represented. A life led with honor…or one with at least the *possibility* of love and passion. Certainly Ellis Maitland was an adventure to be had, if nothing else, as opposed to the years of mundane indifference she was sure to face with Harcourt.

"May I fetch you something?" Harcourt asked, interrupting her thoughts.

"Hmm?" Anne said with a shake of her head. "No, no thank you."

He stared at her a moment, and it was almost like he was seeing her for the first time. Then he turned his face. "This is our future, Anne," he said softly. "This wedding and the marriage that will follow is what we planned and what we *must* do. For propriety's sake if nothing else."

She wrinkled her brow at his…well, it was almost an admonishment. She folded her arms. "I am well aware of what propriety dictates, my lord. You and my father have made it very clear."

She waited for him to respond to her statement. To show her any emotion, anything at all. Instead he inclined his head and said, "Good. I'm glad we're both clear. Excuse me."

With that he pivoted and made his way across the room to where her sisters were standing together. He left her alone, and for a moment she saw the entire span of her future fold out in front of her. Alone, if she remained here. She would always be alone.

But if she went with Ellis… Certainly she liked him so much. And he liked her—more than liked her, if his passionate letter had been written with any truth. He was *fun* and they would share a life of laughter.

Wasn't *that* the better of two evils? To choose a life with any kind of happiness over one so empty?

She gasped at breath as the thoughts overwhelmed her. The room was busy, each person in conversation with another, and she took the opportunity to rush to the door and sneak away. She stumbled through the fine corridors, ones that would be hers if she refused Ellis's offer of escape. He would ask her only once, he said. Wait for her only once.

If she didn't go tonight, she would be *forced* to embrace this life.

There was an open parlor door at the end of the hall and she fled to it. She raced to the settee, threw herself onto it and flopped her forearm over her eyes as the reality of her situation washed over her in great, unfightable waves.

What could she do? What *should* she do? To abandon her engagement was a terrible thing, especially so close to her wedding day. Harcourt would be damaged by the scandal, something the man avoided at all costs.

Worse, her own family would also be harmed by her escape. She wasn't so selfish to not be aware of that. Thomasina and Juliana, her beloved sisters, would be painted with the same brush she was. Reckless. A bad bargain. Their being triplets was already seen as an oddity, a mark against them on the marriage mart.

Could she hurt them like that to avoid her own heartbreak and misery? Could she?

Before she could think of an answer, she heard the door to the parlor shut a second time. She froze, praying it wasn't Harcourt come to find her, or her father to harangue her about more wedding details. Mr. Shelley had delighted in managing this whole affair from the beginning. Certainly *he* didn't care about her happiness. He never had.

"You need to *stop feeling this!*" the voice of the person who had entered the room said. Anne realized it was her sister, Thomasina.

She sat up, distracted from her own worries by the sound of her sister's panicked tone. "Stop feeling what?"

"I, er—" Thomasina murmured, gaping at Anne like a fish that had been flopped out of the water. "I didn't—"

"Oh gracious, you are turning purple!" Anne said, getting up and crossing the room to her. She caught her hands and drew her toward the warmth of the fire. At least here she could help someone, even if it wasn't herself. "Take a breath, Thomasina, before you fall over! I'm certain whatever you are feeling, it cannot be so bad as that."

"You would be surprised." Thomasina shook her head and sucked in a few breaths. "Wait, what are you doing in the parlor? I only just saw you at the luncheon."

Anne swallowed hard. She hadn't realized she was being watched so closely in the other room. And Thomasina and Juliana were very good at reading her. It was a triplet matter. Could they see her panic and misery? She hadn't told either of them about her feelings or about Ellis. She was too afraid.

"Oh, I needed a moment away from it all," she said, waving her hand as if none of it were that serious. "I swear, ever since we arrived weeks ago, it's been one thing after another. This never-ending march to my doom."

Thomasina shook her head slightly as Anne paced away so her sister wouldn't see the truth in her eyes. "Well, it *is* your wedding celebration, isn't it? You must have expected there would be much to do."

"I suppose," Anne said, plucking at a loose thread on the back of a chair on the opposite side of the room. "I just thought it would be more...more *fun*. There has only been one fun thing here and it—"

Anne broke off. God, how she wanted to tell her sister everything. She wanted to weep into her shoulder and beg for help. For an answer she couldn't find herself.

Thomasina stepped in her path and caught Anne's cold hands in hers. "Dearest, I realize that marrying must be a rather overwhelming idea. After all, it is pledging your life to one man for the rest of your days. But you will be happy. Harcourt will make sure of it."

Anne shook her head as the desperation became too much to bear. She had to tell Thomasina some of it. Just some of it. "Oh, Harcourt! Harcourt, *Harcourt*. That I would marry such a man as *that*."

Thomasina drew back and her shock was evident. "What—what do you mean? A man such as that? What is wrong with the earl?"

"He never smiles, Thomasina. *Never*! And laugh at my quips or jokes? No! He only stares at me like I've carried something unpleasant into the parlor."

Thomasina opened her mouth, but Anne couldn't stop now. It was as if the floodgates had opened and she could do nothing but spill out her heart and her blood until she was empty, depleted.

"His finances must be in a *terrible* state," she continued, "even worse than rumor has named, for he is always hunched over some ledger, utterly distracted. He likes the country over London, so that means I shall be forced to stay here on this dreadful estate with him and his mother, who always seems so nervous and never meets my eyes. Almost as if she has something to hide. Probably that her son has dead wives stacked up in some locked room somewhere and I shall be next."

Thomasina straightened and a rare flash of anger flared in her green eyes. "Anne, that is ridiculous—you've been reading too many French fairytales. Harcourt is a good and decent man and to accuse him, even in jest, of something so terrible is not right."

Anne tilted her head and stared at her sister. Thomasina was very defensive of Harcourt. But then, she always tried to see the best in people. To please them. Anne could admit she had used that desire against her sister a few times over the years.

Not her finest moment. But *extremis malis extrema remedia*, wasn't that the saying? Today was her most desperate hour. And a rather desperate plan was starting to form in her head in response.

She pushed it away and sighed. "You are right, of course. Harcourt is nothing but *decent.*"

Thomasina let out a huff of breath. "You say that as if it were a curse."

"It's just so boring!" Anne said, flopping back on the settee. "My life will be endlessly, ceaselessly, lovelessly *boring* and I shall wither up and die from it."

Thomasina's lips parted as she sat down on the edge of a nearby chair. "You really think your marriage would be loveless?" she asked. "You don't think you could come to love Harcourt if you tried?"

Anne froze. She had always imagined she would make a love match. She'd read many a romantic book to prepare herself for that moment. She'd looked forward to it.

And yet here she was. And she couldn't love Harcourt. Now, granted, she hadn't had the thunderstruck feeling she'd expected with Ellis either, but at least he sometimes made her stomach flutter when he looked at her a certain way. That was *something.*

She peeked over her arm at her. "And you say I read too many fairytales! What one have you spun for yourself about my future life with this man? That I will find deep and abiding love for him hidden somewhere in the larder?"

"You could—"

"No, my dear," Anne interrupted. "*That* will not happen. And *I* am not the problem. I have love and passion to share in abundance. The problem is *him.* He is…he's incapable of love, I think. He's made himself so cold to the world, so dedicated to propriety and naught else, that he could not allow himself to melt even a fraction for any woman. And that is what *terrifies* me."

There. She had said the words out loud, shocking as they were. She had said them and now they hung between her and her sister. Hung in the air where they made her tremble in pure anguish.

She would never love Harcourt. And she didn't want to marry him. Which left her with Ellis and his shameless offer to run away with her. The best option. The *only* option if she didn't want to be truly miserable for the rest of her life.

Thomasina was quiet, just staring at her for what seemed like an eternity. When she spoke again, her tone was gentle. "Anne, you may be correct that Harcourt's nature is not the perfect complement to your own. Father should have thought of your temperament before he made the match, but your engagement has been announced, the bannes read, and your wedding is happening in a week's time. There is no other answer than to make the best of it."

"No other answer," Anne repeated softly. But she knew it wasn't true. She did have another answer. Another option.

"I wish for your sake that there was, for I hate to see you so unhappy and so certain that your future will be bleak," Thomasina continued. "But I do believe that Harcourt is a good man. And if you were just to… to try a little, perhaps you would find more to connect yourself to him than you think. In time you might even be happy with him."

Anne sat up slowly. Here was Thomasina telling her that she wanted her to be happy. She didn't understand the truth of what would bring that outcome, but Anne would take that permission regardless. Only she needed her sister's help.

"Perhaps you are right at that," she said slowly, being purposefully vague. Thomasina would never be a willing partner in what she was about to do. Nor should she be. There would be less trouble the fewer the people who knew her plans. "Perhaps I *should* regroup and make the best of it."

Thomasina nodded, though her face was pale and a little sad. "It's for the best, I think."

"I only need one thing to do so," Anne continued, hating herself as she said the next words. "One little favor from my best and truest sister."

"What do you need?"

"A break," Anne said, clasping Thomasina's hands in hers. "Oh, Thomasina, how I need a respite. Since we arrived it's been hectic, and perhaps that's part of why I feel so overwhelmed. But if you could just help me take a little time away, I'm certain I could return to my duties refreshed and ready for my future."

"A break?" Thomasina repeated in confusion. "What do you mean?"

This was it. Her last chance to stay the course. To keep her promise. Anne drew a long breath. And then she made her choice.

"The ball tonight. I cannot face it in my current state. But if you were to take my place—"

"Anne!" Thomasina gasped. "You cannot be serious!"

"Why not? We have traded in the past!"

"The last time we did that we were fourteen," Thomasina said. "And the larger problem is that tonight is the final ball to celebrate your engagement. It is the ball to introduce you to the society of Harcourt. It is important to your future."

"It is," Anne agreed with a nod. "Can you imagine my partaking in my current state? I am in no condition to do so and make a good impression. But you could easily—you have always had more tact that I have."

"The *cat* has more tact than you do!" Thomasina interrupted, and Anne flinched even though she knew that observation was probably true. "Anne, this is ridiculous."

"It is only one night." Anne let her voice fill with true desperation. "Please, Thomasina, I am begging. I am *pleading* with you. I need your help—will you not provide it?"

Thomasina stared at her, and for a moment Anne let her true feelings show. Thomasina wouldn't understand them, but she would recognize Anne's fear and pain and desperation. She would want to please her, to soothe her, to fix her. Her sisters had always been better people than she was. What she was about to do proved they always would be.

Thomasina let out a long breath. "Do you *really* think you will feel better if I grant you this boon?"

Anne nodded. "You would be saving my very life and ensuring my future."

Thomasina stole her gaze to her clenched hands in her lap. Her expression was unreadable as she pondered the shocking request. Anne held her breath, waiting for the response, waiting to know if her life would be saved or if she would be condemned to an eternity of emptiness.

At last, Thomasina cleared her throat. "I-I would do it if you think it would help."

Anne let out a yelp and launched herself from the settee and directly into Thomasina's arms.

"Oh, Thomasina, yes! Yes, you would be helping me more than you know." She kissed Thomasina's cheek hard and squeezed her. Then Anne stepped back and looked her up and down as the pieces of a plan came into her mind. "You will pretend a headache, that will be your excuse for not joining us and why everyone will leave you alone tonight. Your maid won't help us play this trick—she's as concerned with propriety as you are. But that's fine. You'll just sneak through the adjoining door from your chamber to mine and I'll have Nora assist. My maid has more discretion, after all. But we cannot tell Juliana. God, she would ruin everything!"

Thomasina nodded, her gaze cloudy and unsteady. That look gave Anne pause for a moment, but she pushed it away. Yes, she would hurt her sisters with her reckless decision. But wouldn't they also be hurt by watching her in misery for the next forty or fifty years of her life? Wouldn't they rather she be happy in the long run?

She'd find a way to make it up to them. She had to. Later. Once her future was set.

18

CHAPTER 2

There was a light knock on Anne's door a few hours later, and her heart jumped as she smoothed her gown and called out, "Come in."

She expected Thomasina to enter, so they could prepare for the ball tonight, but it was Juliana who entered instead. Her sister paced into the room and looked around with a frown. "About to ready yourself for the ball tonight?" she asked.

Anne followed her gaze to the red ball gown she had laid out across her bed. The one she would never wear, probably never again. She felt a little regret about that, but not enough to keep her from her plans.

"Er, yes," Anne said, glancing at the door with worry. If Thomasina came in, Juliana was too sharp-eyed not to recognize something was going on between them. And then Thomasina would succumb to overly active honesty and everything would be ruined.

Juliana stared evenly at Anne. "I'm worried about you," she said softly.

Anne jerked her gaze back to her sister. "You are?"

Juliana nodded. "How could I not be? Your unhappiness is...well, it's obvious."

Anne blinked. "I-I suppose it has been."

"And yet you haven't turned to me." Juliana clasped her hands together, fingers stroking each other in a self-comfort she had done since she was a child.

Anne bent her head. It was true. She hadn't turned to either of her sisters with her feelings or with her connection to Ellis. Neither one of them would understand. She had always been the wild one, the naughty one…even the bad one. *They* were good.

"Have you lost all faith in me?" Juliana whispered, her tone taut with fear and hurt.

Anne gasped as she moved toward her sister. "No! Of course not. I could never lose faith in you, Juliana. It is far more likely that you would lose faith in me!"

Juliana shook her head. "You think I would? I could never. Please, won't you let me help you?"

Anne hesitated, and in that moment she wanted to tell Juliana the truth. Just as she'd longed to tell Thomasina the same. But then she thought of her sister's response. She knew Juliana wouldn't approve of her running away. She would feel responsible, she might even try to stop her.

Anne drew a shaky breath and then took her sister's hands. "You cannot help me. You'll understand soon enough."

Juliana pursed her lips. "You mean when father matches me with my own unwanted husband."

Anne shuddered. They were all so powerless to their father's whims. It had always been a shared terror between them. Now it was coming true. Except she could stop it. Perhaps her scandal would even help her sisters in the long run. If their father couldn't benefit from their matches, he might allow Juliana and Thomasina to marry for their hearts.

And then her running away would be almost noble. Not selfish.

"You should go ready yourself," Anne said with a quick kiss to Juliana's cheek. "I promise I'll be well and happy tonight."

Juliana let out a long sigh and nodded. "Very well."

She squeezed her hand and slipped away. Anne sagged with relief as she shut the door behind her sister and leaned against it. But before she could gather herself, there was another knock, this time from the adjoining chamber that led to Thomasina's room.

She smoothed her skirt and took a long breath to calm herself before she moved to let her other sister in. She had to forget her hesitations. She had to focus on her future.

That was what mattered now. *That* was what she was working so hard for.

～

Anne watched Thomasina glide from her room an hour later, wrapped in the red dress, looking stunning. Her sister was nervous. Thomasina was always nervous, but seemed especially so around Harcourt. The man brought that out in people. Would Thomasina be all right?

Of course she would. Harcourt wasn't unkind, even if he was stern and boring. And he had so little interest in Anne that it was highly unlikely he would even recognize the switch had been made.

Either way, now it was done and the plan was set in motion. There were only a few steps left to perform and then she would be free. Or at least tied to a new future. Perhaps there was no such thing as being free.

"You look troubled, miss," her maid Nora said as she straightened up the table where she had prepared Thomasina.

Anne forced a smile for her, for she knew as little about the truth as anyone else. "Oh, just tired."

"Of course you're tired after all the excitement of sending your sister off to pretend to be you. Well, let me help you out of your gown and get you into bed." Nora was beaming as she spoke, clearly thrilled to be in on the secret.

Or as much of it as Anne chose to share. She held up a hand. "You know, I think I'll just stay in my gown. I'll lie down a while, but

I might want to go peek in on the ball and make sure my sister is well."

Nora tilted her head as if concerned, but then shrugged. "As you wish, miss. Ring when you're ready."

Anne smiled as her maid left the room, but the moment the door was closed behind her, she leapt into action. She had packed a small bag earlier in the day and she pulled it out from under the bed. It only contained two gowns and a few other items, but she tossed her brush and some pins in with the rest and fastened it carefully.

She moved to the pillows and pulled out the letter she'd written for Thomasina a few hours before. God, how she had labored over the note, trying to strike a breezy tone that would tell her sisters that she was happy with her choice so they wouldn't worry too much. She knew she was leaving them with a mighty mess to clean up. Still, she would return once she was married, and then she would help them all and take the brunt of whatever punishment her father or Harcourt chose to dole out.

She pushed the note back under the pillow, with only the corner sticking out, just in case Nora came back first—she didn't want to the maid finding it. But once she was missing, certainly Thomasina and Juliana would tear her room apart for clues and then one of them would uncover it.

She let her fingers rest on the note for a moment, as if she could pour some of her love onto the page and transfer it to her sisters in their anger toward her. Then she grabbed her bag and moved to the door.

She peeked out. There were no servants in sight, not that she expected it. With the ball going on, everyone would be busy in the hall and belowstairs before they started to prepare chambers for their occupants to sleep. That gave her the best chance of escaping without detection.

The servant stairway was at the end of the hall and she crept down it, leaning against the wall at every curve so she wouldn't be seen. But at last she made it to the back exit of the house, where the deliveries were made, and stepped out into the cool night air.

All the carriages for the visitors had been parked around this side of the house to keep the drive and stable uncluttered. Ellis had said he would meet her amongst them, and her heart leapt as she glanced back at the house one last time.

She regretted that this was her only choice. She regretted the trouble she would cause her sisters. She regretted the embarrassment she would bring down on Harcourt. But she couldn't bear the emptiness of her future with him, nor picture a way she could be happy with him.

Truth be told, she had a bit of a hard time picturing that happiness with Ellis, either. But that was just nervousness talking. He was certainly a better match to her than Harcourt and—

Her thoughts her cut off as a person stepped from between the carriages and caught her arm. She gasped and turned, crashing headlong into Ellis's broad chest. She looked up at him in the moonlight and sucked in a breath, not in joy, but in fear. The light hit him just so and he was no longer quite so handsome as she remembered, but intimidating. His brow was drawn low and his eyes had an intensity that didn't make her comfortable.

But then he smiled and lifted his head and the light hit him differently, and it was fine again. She laughed nervously and pulled her arm from his.

"You came!" Ellis breathed as he took her little bag. "I thought you might not. I wondered what I would have to do if you didn't."

"You had plans to do something if I refused you?" she asked.

He smiled and the dimple popped in his cheek. "I always have plans, my dear. Now come, we have no time for foolishness. We must away before we are caught."

He grabbed her hand again and began to weave amongst the carriages, dodging the lounging footmen and drivers as they smoked and laughed in the dim light from the house above.

Ellis was pulling her, almost dragging her as they made their way out of the main crush of vehicles and down a little hill toward the main stable. A phaeton was parked there, old and rundown, with a skinny, rather sad-looking horse grazing in the high grass by the pathway.

"Here we are," Ellis declared.

She glanced up at the rickety phaeton. "We'll drive to Gretna Green in this?" she asked as he secured her bag to the back of the rig. "Days away?"

He glanced up at the rig and back to her. "Er, no. No, of course not. This was simply the easiest method of retrieving you tonight. We'll stop along the road and switch to a far more comfortable... and private...carriage."

He lifted his eyebrows and then winked before he clasped her hand and helped her into the seat. She settled in, smoothing her skirts around her and drawing her wrap a little tighter around her shoulders.

He climbed up onto the opposite side and gathered up the reins.

"But Ellis—" she began.

He cut her off by turning, grasping her cheeks and pressing his mouth hard to hers. She recoiled slightly. Their relationship had never advanced beyond holding hands, and now he was kissing her. His tongue swept across her lips and he tasted of strong whisky.

She drew back and he smiled at her. She supposed she should have felt something now that he'd finally claimed her in a more physical way.

But there was nothing. No flutter of desire. No need to do the same again. Nothing like her books or her dreams. She felt...nothing. Except for nervousness. An ache that said perhaps she had made a mistake. Only Ellis had already shaken the reins, urging the poor pony to trot toward the gate at the bottom of the drive.

"Ellis—" she began again.

"Hush now," he said, his tone a little harder than it had been before. "It's a long few days of adventure ahead of you. Of us."

She nodded. Yes, the adventure. That was what she wanted, after all. She just had to put herself in the right mindset for it. She was setting off on an adventure with this man. Once her nerves faded, it might even be fun.

"Why don't you shut your eyes and try to sleep if you can?"

She wrinkled her brow at the idea that she could *sleep* when her mind was racing and her regrets were rising up with her supper from hours before. She had run away from a man she felt nothing for. Toward a man she thought she could feel differently about. She wanted to feel those other feelings right now so that this wouldn't all seem like a mistake.

But she wondered if it was just that she was incapable of feeling connection or desire. Was it *she* who was the problem?

And now that she was on the road, ruined for the world to see, would she have any chance of ever feeling anything but regret again?

Anne jolted awake, sitting upright from her slouched position against Ellis's arm, and stared around herself in confusion as the phaeton came to a slow stop. She didn't know how long they'd driven, but it must have been hours, long into the early morning of the next day if the waning moon was any indication.

She blinked. They were in a town, surrounded by bright lamps that burned through the dark. People chattered and laughed, bawdy language unlike any she normally heard ringing through the air. And there, just in the distance, she saw a dock and smelled the sea through the fog.

That wasn't right.

"Where are we?" she asked as Ellis shot her a look and climbed down from the driver's seat. He didn't come around to help her down from the vehicle, but spoke to a boy, handing over a coin before the lad went racing up toward the dock in the distance.

"Ellis," she snapped, and carefully inched herself down from the high rig. Her legs shook as she got her feet on steady ground, but she ignored that as she paced around the phaeton to where Ellis stood looking off into the distance.

"What is it?" he asked, his tone gruff and cold. Hard, unlike the jovial tone he'd always used with her when they spent time together in the previous weeks. He was no longer the playful and flirtatious man who had drawn her near with effortless charisma. Now he was something else. "I told you we were going to stop at a town along the route."

She shook her head. "But this cannot be a town along our route to Gretna Green," she insisted. "You would have had to go away from the sea, not toward it, and I can smell the salt air even now and see the fog from the water up there by the dock. Ellis, we could not have gone in the right direction."

He glared down at her. "Why don't you leave the planning to me? I know what I'm doing."

He moved to turn away and she reached out to catch his arm. He jerked it away and she staggered back at the dismissive action. At the coldness to him when he glared at her.

"Just stand there," he said through what were obviously clenched teeth. *"Please."*

Her lips parted and the fear that had begun to bloom in her chest at the house flowered into a full garden. This was wrong, so wrong. Not just the direction they'd gone, but more than that. She took a long step back.

"I'm sorry," he grunted with a shake of his head. He tossed her half a smile that didn't reach his eyes. "It's been a long night and I'm tired."

She nodded and tried to accept that explanation, but right now she wanted to run. Run away...only she didn't know where she was and the town looked rather rough. She had no money, no way to reach her family and alert them of her plight.

"Oh God," she whispered.

"Ah, there he is," Ellis said, and moved toward the docks and a man who was coming up the long walkway in their direction.

Her breath caught as she shifted her attention. The newcomer who was now shaking Ellis's hand was even more handsome than her intended. Tall and lean with short-cropped brown hair and eyes darker than the richest cup of chocolate. Eyes that turned on her, flitted over her from head to toe. His full lips pursed and he said something to Ellis. Ellis slapped his arm and motioned her closer.

She took a step toward them with hesitation and swallowed hard.

"Miss Anne Shelley, may I present to you, Rook Maitland."

"Rook?" she repeated, staring over at the man a second time. He shifted a little, like he was uncomfortable. Which made her all the more uncomfortable in return.

"Yes, my cousin," Ellis said, arching a brow toward Mr. Maitland. "My *family*." He smiled at her. "And soon enough, *your* family."

"Good evening," she managed to squeak to the other man.

He said nothing, but inclined his head slightly and folded his arms as he looked at Ellis through narrowed gaze.

She turned toward him, as well. "Ellis," she said, trying to remain calm. "Please, won't you explain what is going on?"

Ellis nodded. "Yes. You see, I have something I need to take care of before we can be wed. It cannot wait. You will go with my cousin and I will come to fetch you in not more than a few days."

Her mouth dropped open in shock and she stared at him, then his cousin, then back to him as the reality of this nightmare situation became patently clear.

"Wait, are you saying you are going to abandon me? Alone? With this stranger?"

CHAPTER 3

Rook's stomach turned as he watched the woman beside his cousin digest what was happening. The extremely beautiful woman, if he was honest. His heart had actually stuttered when he saw her as he walked up the dock toward them and realized his cousin's game was much the same as it had ever been. Seduction, betrayal, payment.

She was tall, with thick, dark blonde hair and the greenest eyes he'd ever seen, ones that perfectly matched the emerald cross necklace that was clasped around her slender neck. She had kissable lips, cheeks made pink by the brisk night air, and a flash to her, a snap that said she wasn't often out of control of any situation.

But she had obviously underestimated his cousin. Not that she was the first.

"Ellis, why don't you let me go with you?" she said, stepping toward his cousin.

Ellis smiled, but his gaze was flat and emotionless. He cared nothing for this woman, Anne Shelley, whatever he had convinced her. And if he told her he would come to retrieve her, that was certainly not true. He might call for her as a bargaining chip in whatever game he was playing with her father or brother or husband…but he wasn't going to take her to Gretna Green.

Rook hated himself for getting involved in this nonsense. Yet again.

"You are going with my cousin," Ellis snapped. "And that is final."

Rook expected Anne to bend her head and nod and maybe cry. But she didn't do any of those things. Her hands lifted to her shapely hips and that snap he'd seen in her face multiplied.

"I shall not," she argued. "Ellis Maitland, I was convinced to run away from my family and my future in order to be with you. I will not just go away with some strange man I've never met while you go off to take care of some errand I don't understand. I will not, and that is final."

Rook almost smiled at what a spitfire his cousin had found, but before he could, Ellis stepped forward and caught her arm. "You have no idea what you are asking," he growled.

Rook narrowed his gaze. He'd seen his cousin play these cards often enough that he could guess the next move. But this? This flash of anger? This hardness? That wasn't Ellis, not normally.

Whatever his cousin was involved with…it wasn't good.

"Enough," Rook said softly as he pushed Ellis's hand away. Anne backed up as she stared at Ellis, tears brightening her gaze. Reality was hitting her now.

"You are going with him, Anne," Ellis said, soft but clear. "And there will be no further arguments. You are ruined by running away. I would suggest you don't give me a reason to not keep my promises."

Her lips parted and she lifted her chin slightly. Rook saw her running calculations in her head, trying to find a way out of this. When she realized there was none, all the emotion left her face and she shrugged. "Fine."

"The boat is ready," Rook said, more to her than to Ellis, but it was his cousin who answered.

"Excellent. I'll be back in a few days."

Rook didn't believe him, but he nodded as he took Anne's small bag from Ellis. Not enough clothing for any extended stay. The bag of a woman who thought she was romantically running away to elope and would return to her family soon enough.

"Lead the way, Mr. Maitland," Anne said as she turned her back on his cousin.

"Rook," he corrected as he motioned toward the end of the dock.

"Anne."

She froze at Ellis's voice behind her. Slowly she turned and he stepped toward her. Rook saw her tense, he did the same, but Ellis only took her hand. He lifted it to his lips and Rook glanced away as Ellis kissed it.

"Forgive me, my love," he drawled, all practiced and controlled seduction again. "I'll make it up to you."

"You will," she declared softly, then removed her hand and followed Rook up the long walkway toward the small boat waiting for them at the end of the dock.

Anne's hands shook, but she gripped them into fists as she reached the end of the dock and what seemed like a very small boat. An older gentleman was sitting in the back near the oars. He had a glowing lantern on a hook mounted beside him, and he was glaring at her and her new companion through the fog as if he had schedules to keep and they were intruding upon them.

"Good evening," she squeaked in his direction.

He glared harder and she dipped her head as terror overcame her. She was in danger. That was clear. She had been in danger from the moment she slipped from the warmth of her fiancé's home and took off on this madcap adventure.

Perhaps she'd been in danger even earlier than that, when she'd first agreed to meet with Ellis even though she knew it was wrong to do so.

And now here she was in God knew where, watching a handsome stranger with an odd name get onto a rickety rowboat. He set her bag down none too gently and then pivoted back to stare at her. He extended a hand slowly to help her on board.

She glanced back down the dock, where she'd last seen Ellis. Somehow she'd thought to find him in the milling crowd, watching to determine she'd safely gotten on the craft. But he was gone.

She shuddered and turned back to the boat, staring at Rook's extended fingers for a moment. That rough hand, big and calloused from work, could be attached to a murderer for all she knew. He could be a great many terrible things and have a great many terrible plans in store for her. And yet what choice did she have but to go with him?

"Stupid girl," she admonished herself beneath her breath as she took the hand he offered.

She wasn't wearing gloves, she'd forgotten them in her excitement to escape on this adventure gone wrong. When her palm touched his, she felt a thrill of something, a hiss of awareness that shot up her arm and through her body.

She stepped into the boat and snatched her hand away as she settled onto one of the hard benches in the middle of the boat. Rook Maitland took the one facing her. He was so big, his knees pushed into her space and their legs almost touched no matter how far back she tried to tuck them. She huffed out a breath at this new invasion and tried with all her might to make her mind go somewhere else. Anywhere else but here.

Only it wasn't so easy. Not when her mind kept taking her back to her family. She had to assume that Thomasina would have returned to her chamber after the ball. She would have found the letter Anne had left. The one filled with hopes for a future with Ellis that now seemed so faded and far away and foolish. What would her sister have thought? What would Juliana think? Would they be able to manage their father's outrage together? Would Harcourt's fury lead to untold punishments against them?

She bent her head as the consequences of her selfish action washed over her like the bouncing waves that occasionally crested over the edge of the boat as they rowed farther into the heart of the Irish Sea. In the dark.

She lifted her head and found Rook Maitland watching her. He was hardly more than a shadow outline in their captain's lantern light, but his dark gaze glittered as he held it on her.

"How far must we go?" she asked as the sea bobbed heavier.

He was silent for what felt like an eternity, but at last he grunted, "It will be a few hours, yet. It's a long row to Scotland."

Her eyes widened. *Scotland?* She had thought that idea was abandoned when Ellis sent her off with this man. But if they were crossing the sea after all, perhaps that meant Ellis wasn't the villain he had seemed to be. Perhaps he would return for her after all and this could be resolved just as she'd planned from the beginning.

She clung to that hope and nodded. "What town?" she asked.

"You have a great many questions," her companion said softly. "Why didn't you ask Ellis about his plans for you, as he is your love?"

She bit back the retort that she didn't love Ellis and shrugged. "I thought I knew the plan," she said. "So I didn't ask. And here we are."

He nodded slowly. "Yes. Here you are."

She realized he hadn't answered her question about the town, but she was too exhausted to ask again. She would find out soon enough, she supposed. And if he was reticent to share with her, perhaps that was for the best. He wasn't going to be her companion for very long. It was probably best that an unmarried lady didn't attach herself too strongly to a very handsome cousin of her intended. People would talk, wouldn't they?

God, people would already be talking. She knew that. Her running away was too big a secret to keep, especially with the wedding planned for less than a week from now. When she didn't appear for it, when it was all canceled, there would be no stopping the tale that would rip through Society.

"You look like you have some regrets, Miss Shelley," Rook said.

The little boat careened into a wave and Anne gripped at both sides of it, clawing to retain purchase. "No," she lied. "Of course not. I know what I'm doing."

But she heard the lilt in her tone, the terror and the pain. His expression didn't change. If he heard it too, it was clear he didn't give a damn. But why would he? He'd been sent here to collect her, and he didn't seem particularly pleased by that.

She wouldn't give him any more reason to be annoyed, nor to judge her more a fool than he clearly already did. She sat up as straight as she could and did her best to focus on a point just behind him rather than at his handsome, frowning face. Of course that point was the disappearing light of the distant town, of England vanishing into the fog.

And she gritted her teeth as moments bled to almost an hour of rowing through the endless night. At last she shivered as the air pierced her thin wrap and tugged it harder around herself. The boat rolled endlessly on the waves as their captain rowed on, seemingly unfazed by the cold splash of the seawater or the blowing wind that caused the spray to soak her face and hair and clothes.

She would not cry. She would *not*, even as the fog swirled around her, making her colder than ever.

Rook had been silent during the time they rowed, his gaze fixed behind her, toward whatever their mysterious destination was. But now he suddenly moved, shrugging out of his great coat in one smooth motion. The action revealed a white linen shirt beneath that seemed to strain against broad shoulders and chest.

He held the coat out. "Here, you'll catch your death otherwise."

She blinked at the offering. His coat, which had just been around him. It seemed very intimate to accept the offer. Too intimate.

His brow wrinkled. "Take it before it loses its body heat."

Body heat. She inwardly groaned, but it was too cold to argue.

She took the woolen coat, sliding her arms into the sleeves and fastening it around her waist. It dwarfed her, for he was far bigger than she was. The sleeves came over her hand by at least a few inches and it was more like a shapeless cloak around her shoulders than a fitted coat like it had been on his.

But it was warm. He was right about that. She felt his body heat curl around her like his arms were there. And his scent lingered on the woolen fabric. It was a nice scent. Something woodsy and clean and masculine.

Once again her stomach clenched with an awareness she shouldn't have felt, and she bent her head as she muttered, "Thank you."

He didn't respond, but nodded, and his focus shifted away from her again. She glanced at him now that he wasn't looking at her. He had a hard line to his very defined jaw and an equally tight quality to his clamped lips. They were full, though. She could tell that despite the annoyance that lined his face.

He didn't seem troubled by the roiling of the boat. Her stomach rose and fell, but he didn't even have an increase in breath. Damn him. She really didn't want to make more of a fool of herself than she already had, but nausea was rising by the moment as the sea grew heavier and wilder away from the coast.

It had been such a long night, filled with such disappointment and fear. She had hardly eaten anything since afternoon tea, and now all she could think about was that food and how much she hated everything she'd ever put into her mouth.

Rook cocked his head and looked at her. "Miss Shelley?" he said softly.

But she didn't answer. All she could do was lean over the side of the boat and cast up her accounts as she cursed every decision she'd made since three o'clock that afternoon. Including the ones that had put her in the boat with a stranger, vomiting in front of him.

~

Rook had to give it to Anne Shelley. She looked like a fragile lady, but she had certainly held her own with an iron to her that was attractive. Yes, she'd vomited up everything she'd eaten, probably things she didn't even remember eating, but she had said nothing about it when it was all over. She'd sat without complaining or whining or crying, staring straight ahead, her gaze reflecting none of the fear and embarrassment and pain that he was certain burned in her heart.

As the sea grew calmer when they edged into the tiny outer islands of Scotland's southern coast, she had stopped being sick. Now she peeked over her shoulder, peering through the dim light of dawn as their destination grew larger in the distance. Their captain expertly drew them into the still waters of the island before them.

Miss Shelley shifted and turned fully as she stared into the wild, tangled woods just past the rocky beach and the rickety dock where their captain was securing the boat.

He glared at Rook in expectation, and Rook let out his breath as he got up, climbed over Miss Shelley carefully and grabbed for her little bag. He tossed it up onto the dock and grasped one of the posts to pull himself up. She had risen and was balancing herself precariously.

"Come then," he said, crooking his finger at her.

Her pupils dilated a fraction, but she did as she'd been told, picking her way closer with tiny steps through the bobbing boat. He held out a hand and she stared at it, just as she had when he helped her into the boat hours before. This would be a much bigger step. He was already calculating if he'd have to lift her. She clasped his fingers at last, but the step was too big for her to make, even with his support. He bent partially, slid his hands beneath her arms and pulled her up. As he set her on her feet, she staggered a little, resting her hand on his chest to steady herself as she stared up at him.

He released her and she moved away a few steps, her cheeks flamed with color. He refused to acknowledge any of his own reactions to that brief, glancing touch. It had just been a long time since any woman put her hands on him. He had no interest in the one his cousin was swindling.

"Thank you, Captain Quinton," he said to the still-waiting old man. "May I get you any refreshment before your trip 'round to the mainland?"

"No, but ye can get me my blunt," he grunted.

Rook blinked at him. "My cousin was to pay you."

The old man shook his head. "Yer cousin paid for yer trip to Beckfoot. But I haven't gotten a farthing for the trip back."

Rook pursed his lips. Under any other circumstance, he might have argued with the captain. He might have pushed to determine if he was lying to double collect on his due. Only, when it came to Ellis, there was always a cheat. Rook had no reason to doubt there had been one this time, too.

"Donkey's arse," he grumbled to himself, angrier than ever at Ellis for dragging him into his horseshit yet again.

He dug into his pocket and drew out what little money he had on him. "This will have to do," he said. "It's all I have."

The captain took his offering and pawed through it. He glared at Rook before he untied his rig and rowed off into the rising sun of morning. There was one man who would never transfer him to England again. If Rook was unlucky, Quinton would tell the tale of being swindled all over the nearest towns and no one would be willing to take him across the sea. His own boat was far too small to make the trip.

But he could think of all that later. For now, he had to focus on the matters at hand. The problem at hand. The one who was standing behind him at present. The one he didn't want to look at when he knew she was starting to realize how far she'd strayed from the good life she once had.

Finally he turned. She had picked up her little bag and was clutching it in front of herself with both hands. His big coat was still draped around her, making her look smaller and more fragile. He ignored the faint tug in him to help her, take care of her. He was no hero. He was a man who'd been tricked into this situation and he had no more duty to help her than he did any other human on this earth.

He cleared his throat and strode past her on the dock. "Come on, miss."

She scurried after him, switching her bag from hand to hand as they moved up the sandy pathway to the house on the little rise ahead of them. "Can you tell me what town we're in, Mr. Maitland?" she asked.

He flinched at her use of his last name. So formal. "Rook," he grunted.

She let out her breath in a sound of annoyance. "Please, if you just tell me where I am, perhaps I can find—"

"We're not near a town, Miss Shelley," he said, stopping on the path.

She careened into his chest at the sudden movement and staggered back, staring up at him in confusion. "What?"

"I said we're not near a town. We're not even on the mainland of Scotland. We're on an island. My island."

She wrinkled her brow. "*Your* island?"

He smiled despite her incredulity. "It's no one else's and I live here, so I call it mine."

Her lips pursed. "I don't think that's a valid claim of ownership, Mr. Maitland."

"Rook," he corrected again. "And if someone wants it, they can come get it. Come on now, it's been a long night for us both, I think, and I'd like to get inside before that storm coming in behind us breaks."

She glanced back at the thick, gray clouds that were rolling in from the sea. Her cheeks paled and she nodded. "Very well." She motioned toward him. "Lead the way."

He inclined his head at her permission and finished the slow climb up to the cottage above. He'd always been proud of the place.

In the past year since he'd washed himself up on these shores, he'd worked hard at building himself a home that could be more... permanent. He'd never had that and now he wanted it.

But looking at the place now with its simple construction, he was certain his...guest...would see it as trash. She had to be accustomed to palaces and marble halls. But she said nothing as he opened the door and offered her a respite from the cold breeze that preceded the coming storm. Scotland was like that. Fall and spring and winter were never far from summer's shores.

He lit a few candles and loaded kindling from the bin into the fireplace to light it. He turned back for flint and found that Anne Shelley was standing beside the settee in the big main room of the cottage. She had removed his coat and draped it over the back of a chair. Now she stood, arms folded, hands gripping against her forearms, and she was shaking.

Her face was pale, her eyes wide, and all the bravado and calm she had exhibited in the long boat ride were gone. He stepped toward her and she stumbled just as long a step back. At that he froze and held up a hand to her.

"Miss Shelley," he began.

She shook her head. "Please don't."

"You're afraid," he said, trying to find the calm she had lost.

To her credit, she shook her head firmly and straightened her back with what was a good amount of bravery. "No," she lied.

He smiled a little at her spark. "Of course you are. You're clearly a sensible person, this nonsense with my cousin aside."

She flinched at that assessment, but didn't argue with him about it further.

He continued, "Let me try to reassure you: I have no intention of touching you. I don't want to hurt you in any way."

Her gaze narrowed and he could feel her reading him, trying out her intuition on him since she had no other evidence to go on when it came to his promise.

"All you're going to do is wait here for my cousin," he said, choking on the additional words that would tell her what folly that was. She'd figure that out on her own—not his responsibility to help her get there. Anyway, maybe he was wrong. Maybe his cousin really had fallen for this beauty and would do the right thing in the end.

"He knows this place," she whispered.

Rook nodded. "He does. You can sleep here." He moved carefully toward the door just to her right and watched her track the movement like a deer tracking a wild dog or a lion. Prey and predator.

He pushed the door to his chamber open and motioned inside to the big bed within those walls. "It's my room and the bed is comfortable."

She tensed again at that statement. "I won't—"

"I'll sleep out here," he added, flicking his head toward the settee, which was fine for the purpose God had intended it to serve, but he doubted it would make a good bed. He was too tall for it, for one thing. "You can lock the door."

She glanced at the room behind him and he saw her exhaustion wash over her face at the sight of a bed. "I doubt you couldn't get into any room you desired to enter, strong as you seem to be."

He arched a brow at the backhanded compliment and shrugged. "Perhaps not, but you'll have to take my word since I have no other proof to offer you to the contrary."

"I have little choice," she mused, he thought more to herself than to him.

She wasn't wrong, of course, so there was no comfort he could offer her. She had no idea of his character or his intentions and she wouldn't until he proved them.

"May I make you a plate?" he asked.

Her brows lifted and she glanced at the small kitchen through a door at the back of the main room. Then she shook her head. "No. Just sleep, I think. I want to sleep."

"Of course," he said, and nodded as she moved through into his chamber and shut the door behind her.

He heard her turn the key on the other side. After a moment he heard the harsh screech of wood on wood, the feet of the dresser, he assumed, scraping the floor as she positioned the furniture in front of the door for an extra layer of protection. He had to hand it to her, she was very intelligent.

It was quiet for a moment and he sat down on the settee and tugged off his boots one by one. As he settled back onto the cushions, lamenting momentarily the loss of his very comfortable bed, he heard Anne in the other room.

She was crying. The door was so thin, he heard every hitch of her breath as she wept. His heart hurt for her, even though none of it was his fault or doing. Still, she didn't deserve what his cousin was doing to her.

None of them ever had.

He rolled on his side, closed his eyes and tried to ignore the sound of her heartbreak. But he couldn't block it out and he listened to it until she quieted, probably sleeping. Only then could he find rest himself. But his dreams were troubled, as he deserved them to be, by images of bright green eyes and a soft hand against his chest before they were both cast into the rolling sea.

CHAPTER 4

It had been three days since she had been abandoned on the dock in Beckfoot by Ellis Maitland, and as Anne opened her eyes and stared at the same ceiling above her on the same bed, her entire being filled with frustration. She knew this room so well, she could likely sketch it with her eyes closed if asked to do so.

She hadn't left it, after all, since she entered it days ago. At first, it had been a protective instinct. Rook Maitland had addressed her fears about his intentions directly when she dared to voice them that first horrible night here. He had held her gaze and made her promises to leave her alone, but how many men had said the same thing to women over the millennia and then taken advantage anyway?

Only he...hadn't. He'd made no effort to bother her, beyond polite knocks on her door to offer food or other comforts. Once he'd entered the chamber to fill the tub in the corner with water for her bath. He'd been all but silent as he did so and hardly looked at her. That was the only time she'd seen the man since her arrival.

On the second evening, she'd moved the dresser away from the door because she no longer felt like he would burst in to harm her.

She'd been alone for days, and that meant she'd had plenty of time to think about what she'd done.

To think about how *this* was her punishment for behaving a fool and running away with a man who was practically a stranger. How did her sisters feel now? Even her father? Were they worried about her well-being? Had they chased after her to Gretna Green only to find she'd never arrived?

"Stupid girl," she muttered as she flopped the covers back and got up.

Each day she woke and hoped that Ellis would return. Each day she went to bed without knowing what was happening. If he would ever come back.

No. He would. He'd said he would. He'd said he loved her. Hadn't he? Sometimes it was hard to remember. It seemed like he had, but perhaps that was her imagination. He'd certainly said he cared for her. He'd said he was coming back. Even if he were using her, a thought that had taken root two days before, he couldn't do so without marrying her to obtain her dowry.

God, these thoughts. These horrible thoughts.

She glanced at the book on the nightstand beside the bed and sighed. She'd finished it two days ago and read it twice since. She was *bored*.

One more punishment. After all, how many times had she lamented being trapped out on Harcourt's country estate instead of in London with all its excitements? And now she would pay ten pounds for the joy of walking those musty old halls and green grounds.

Of course, there was nothing stopping her from doing the same thing here. Just her pride. Her humiliation that made her not want to meet the eyes of Rook Maitland and see his pity.

She shook her head. This was ridiculous. She wasn't going to be so foolish as to leave herself in this room one more moment. She pulled her nightrail over her head and exchanged it for her chemise.

She'd have to wash some of her things anyway—that would be the excuse if Rook was difficult about her escape from self-exile.

She dressed, happy she had chosen gowns that fastened in the front so they were easier to manage on her own. She'd done that for modesty on the road before she and Ellis reached Gretna Green.

At least that was *something* she'd done right.

She quickly pulled her hair back, pinning it in place in a rather lopsided bun at her nape. She had never really known how useless she was at taking care of herself until the past few days without Nora.

Nora. Her poor maid would have been as shocked as the rest at her escape. Had she been punished for it?

She pushed those thoughts away with all the other guilty ones that stole her sleep, drew a deep breath and stepped into the main room of the cottage. It was quiet with only the faint click of the clock on the mantle and the clinking of dishes in the kitchen area across the way. She followed the sound and the delicious smells that accompanied it, and stepped into the small room.

It was very much unlike the big, dark kitchen in Harcourt Heights or even the one at her father's home in Kent, but it was warmer and more inviting than either of those two rooms. With a washbasin along one wall and a hearth beside it, and a table in the middle of the room for preparation and, she thought, eating.

There were three large windows on each side of the room, which let in the light to make the space more inviting. One was cracked open so that steam and smoke could evacuate the chamber.

Rook stood at the table, his back toward her. A fresh loaf of bread was on a plate beside him, steam coming from its crust as if it had just been removed from the pan. He was plating bacon from a skillet, and eggs sizzled on another over the fire.

The smells hit her all at once and her knees went weak.

"She has come out of her hibernation at last," he said without turning toward her.

She jumped at the idea that he'd known she was there, staring at him for the entire time she'd been in the room.

"Good morning," she squeaked as she inched into the room a bit farther. "I-I did not expect to find you here cooking."

He glanced over his shoulder, one eyebrow crooked in question. "You might have been hiding away these past few days, but the rest of the world turned on. How did you *think* you were being fed?"

She bristled at the word hiding, though it was entirely accurate. Shifting, she picked at a thread on her sleeve. "Er...I...I suppose I didn't think of it at all," she admitted at last.

He nodded and put his attention back to his work as he crossed to remove his eggs from the cooking fire. He met her stare as he walked to the table and slid two onto each plate, perfectly cooked with bright yellow yolks cheering up the room like the sun.

"I guess you wouldn't," he said.

She folded her arms. "What do you mean by that comment?"

"Just that a lady like you probably never thinks twice about those who serve her. She just expects to be served."

She wanted to argue, but again, his words weren't wrong. Damn him. She had led what now felt a very sheltered life. She didn't ask questions because it had never occurred to her that she had to. As a result, she struggled to do anything for herself. Certainly she couldn't have cooked the meal Rook now set on the table. He motioned for her to sit at one of the chairs and then turned to collect an extra set of cutlery and a napkin, which he handed over with a shrug.

"I didn't think you would join me this morning," he explained. "I thought I'd prepare another tray for you."

She bent her head. "While I was hiding, you mean," she said.

He nodded as he took his place at the head of the table. She was at his right hand and it felt very close. He felt very big and very close in that moment.

"I understood why you'd want to hide," he said before he took a bite of eggs. As he chewed, he cut two slabs of bread off the loaf and handed one over, along with a crock filled with butter flecked with something else.

She arched a brow at him in question.

"Cinnamon," he explained. "It makes everything better."

She wasn't sure of that, but spread her bread with the seasoned butter and passed it back to him so he could do the same.

They ate for a while in silence, and Anne found herself itchy with it. All it had been was silence for her in the last few days and all her thoughts seemed to be getting louder and louder. She needed something else to fill the space of them, to push them out so they wouldn't cloud everything and anything.

She needed to say *something* so that she didn't feel like she could read the pity in her companion's mind. She forced a smile for him and said, "This is delicious."

He didn't smile, but she thought the apples of his cheeks got a bit pink at her words. He took another bite and grunted, "Thank you."

More silence and she felt her foot begin to twitch under the table even as she ate a few more bites of the food. Would he not help things along?

"I-I fear I'm putting you out," she said. "By being here so much longer than anyone could have expected. Surely Ellis will come soon, though, and take me off your hands."

Rook froze in eating at those words and his dark eyes lifted from his plate to meet hers. He held there for what seemed like forever, making her a prisoner to that even stare, to the words he never spoke.

She swallowed hard. "We *will* be married," she whispered.

"Yes," he said at last. "That was your plan, after all."

She noted he said *your* plan, meaning her. Not including Ellis, she didn't think. Like he knew her to be a fool but was too polite… or perhaps too uncaring about her situation…to say it. He was so hard to read. He didn't seem to be annoyed that she was here, despite having to sleep on the settee instead of his bed, despite having to share his food and his fire.

Why couldn't she read him? Probably because she didn't know him at all. She'd made sure of it these past few days. But he was her intended's cousin, wasn't it? *Family*, Ellis had reminded her days ago. It was wrong of her to separate herself so much, especially now that she'd decided he was no threat.

Or she thought she had. Sitting next to him, it was hard to recall that decision. He still felt dangerous, though in a different way than he had the first night they met.

She shifted. "You know," she said, switching tactics, "I never asked your name."

He lifted his eyes again. "You know my name. Rook Maitland. And you keep calling me Mr. Maitland, and I keep telling you it's Rook."

She pursed her lips. "But *Rook* cannot be your real name."

His gaze moved back to his plate. "Rook is the name I go by, Miss Shelley. There isn't any other anymore."

She clenched her napkin in her lap and drew a few long breaths. He really was determined to make this difficult, it seemed. But they were both almost finished with their breakfast and it offered her an opportunity to fill her mind and her time.

"Since you have provided me with my bed and board these past few days," she said, rising and picking up her plate, "why don't you let me help you by cleaning up?"

He took the last bite of his bacon and stared at her, wide eyed, and she thought perhaps a little fearful as she collected the plate before him.

"Certainly," he said, leaning back as she took the items to the washbasin and stared at it.

Once again, she realized she had no idea how to do this. And now he was sitting there watching her be a spoiled brat like he'd all but accused her of being.

And she felt a sudden, strong urge to prove him wrong about everything. To be better than he thought she was. Right now.

Rook had to give himself credit. He had not laughed at Anne once while she staggered her way around his kitchen and he had only interfered in her work once, when she tried to wash his cast-iron skillet. Perish the thought she would destroy *that*.

He also had to give her credit. It was patently obvious she had never put a slippered toe into the kitchen, let alone tidied up after a meal. But she was trying. And that was more than some people would have done.

She had cleaned up the cookware and the plates, wrapped the remaining bread in a cloth so it wouldn't get dry, put things away, mostly in the wrong places, but still...

She turned back to him after she found a random drawer where she put his silverware and smoothed her hands over her now wrinkled and slightly damp skirt. Her cheeks were flushed and her eyes bright, and for a moment his breath caught. By God, but she was a beauty. He wasn't supposed to notice that, he thought. She belonged to Ellis in theory, though he didn't think that was true in practice. She certainly didn't belong to or with Rook.

But facts were facts, and the fact was that this woman likely turned heads in any room she entered. When she was a little undone the effect was multiplied. It made him think of better ways to muss her hair and pinken her cheeks.

Thoughts he pushed aside as he jerked his chair back with a shriek of wood against wood and stepped away from her. She jolted at the loud sound, but didn't seem defensive against him. If she had feared him at first, that had faded. But she didn't know his thoughts, thank God. If she did...

"Do you think I might take a look at your island?" she asked.

He blinked at the question and refocused himself. "You aren't a prisoner, Miss Shelley."

She bent her head and her regrets were plain on her face before she swept them aside. "Perhaps not, though I've made myself one these past few days when I felt...well, it doesn't matter how I felt."

He found it did matter, though. More than it should have, even when he tried not to give a damn. He had to show her he didn't, and shrugged. "You're free now, at any rate. You may take in the island if you'd like."

"Will you...will you show me?" she asked.

His brow wrinkled. Show her his island. Now why did that feel like an intimate exercise? But he knew why. No one save Ellis had ever visited here. And his cousin hadn't given a damn about his home except to drag him away from it.

So this woman...this stranger...would be the first to see the place Rook had come to love over the past year. The place he'd run to in order to forget, to heal...to forgive himself for the unforgivable.

He cleared his throat to refuse, but she took a small step toward him. "Please?"

He sighed. "I will, but it's not very big. You'll surely be disappointed there's so little to see."

"It's more to see than there's been in the bedchamber," she said with a short laugh.

He let out his breath slowly. "Come along, then."

He walked away from her, not waiting for her to follow, even though he heard her do so. They exited the cottage into the cool, gray day and he sucked in the fresh air in a deep, calming breath. Well, it should have been calming, except that when Anne stepped up next to him it felt anything but.

"It looks to rain again."

He shot her a side glance. "It *is* Scotland. There's a reason why their favorite word is dreich."

She shook her head. "I'm not familiar. What does it mean?"

He stepped out onto the path that led through the woods toward the dock where they'd come to the island days before. "Gray, cold, wet, foggy. A combination of the four, I think."

"Then it isn't quite dreich today," she said, looking around. "There's no fog."

"There likely will be," he said as they reached the dock. "There's another storm coming in."

She looked out at the rocky beach and the inlet beyond it with a sigh. "It is beautiful."

"I don't think you thought so a few days ago," he said with a small smile.

"I was too exhausted to think anything a few days ago," she admitted. "But it's lovely, despite it being *almost* dreich."

He forced himself not to laugh at her quip, though he felt his mouth twitching. He wasn't about to go liking her. He needed to feel nothing for her at all, except perhaps annoyance that she was here in his space. He had to cling to that.

She stared off in silence toward England, too far away to see. She let out a small sigh. "Could the bad weather these past few days have slowed Ellis's return?"

He held his breath a moment at the lilt of hopefulness to her voice. She was determined to keep faith in his cousin, it seemed. Rook had to believe she loved him, even if he didn't return the feeling.

He ignored how irritated that fact made him and shrugged. "Could be," he grunted.

She glanced at him after a moment and smiled. "This is the most you've talked to me since we met."

He couldn't help but smile back. "You've been hiding away since almost the first moment we met, haven't you?"

She shrugged and turned away from the dock, looking back up at the green, wooded expanse of the small island. "Is it all rocky beach like this, then?" she asked.

He motioned up the shore and they began to walk together along the sandy grass at the edge of the rocks. "No, there's softer beach just up the coastline."

She was silent for a moment as they walked, taking in the beauty around them. Then she said, "I can see why you'd choose a place like this to live. It's so quiet and beautiful."

He nodded. "Aye. I lived a busy life in London and other cities my whole life. I got so used to the noise, I couldn't be silent even with myself. But then it got to be…" He trailed off and looked at her. He hadn't meant to say so much to this stranger. This woman who wasn't his.

She leaned a little closer. "It got to be…?"

He shook his head. "You don't want to listen to me ramble."

"I asked the question," she said softly. "I wanted to know the answer."

He flexed his hands at his sides, suddenly wishing he had something to busy them with during this uncomfortable conversation.

"It just got to be too much," he finished, trying not to think of the horrible moments that had led to this end. This place. This sanctuary.

She nodded. "I can understand that. Things getting to be too much and wanting to run away. It seems you have found a way to do it right. I suppose I only made a muck of things my way."

He looked at her, watching her expression grow sad and empty as they crossed the last few steps to the windswept, white sandy beach around the tip of the island. Ellis had been a way for her to escape whatever was too much.

And it had landed her here. With him.

"Oh, the sand is lovely," she said with a smile that erased her pain for a moment. She gathered up the hem of her skirt, flashing her ankles as she hurried down the little embankment that separated green from sand. As the water came up toward her, she laughed and scurried back so her slippers wouldn't get wet.

He stared, stock still as she danced along the sand with an effortless grace. Her loosely bound hair scattered down out of the bun as it was whipped by the wind and for a brief, powerful moment he wanted to pull the rest down. Tangle it around his fingers as the sea rolled in around them.

He needed to get away from her. That much was clear. He'd been without a woman too long if the first one he met inspired such lustful urges. Especially one so far out of his sphere, who was in love with his own cousin.

"You wanted to help," he called out, recognizing how hoarse with desire his voice was.

She pivoted and came farther away from the water as she gazed up at him on the bluff. "Yes?"

"Have you ever dug for clams before?" he asked.

She shook her head. "Never."

He sighed as he came down to join her on the beach. "It's easy. See those little air bubbles on the sand?"

She squinted as she looked down by her feet. "Where?"

He leaned in closer, trying to ignore the soft scent of her skin, the warmth that came from her body. He pointed to the tiny bubble in the sand. "See?"

Her eyes lit up. "Yes. What is that?"

"A clam," he explained. "It's an air hole. If you dig…" He punctuated the word by driving his hand into the sand and pulling out a few handfuls before he caught the tubular creature and tossed it out onto the flat sand.

"Oh!" she cried, glancing in his direction in wonder.

"Do you like clams?" he asked. "They make a fine supper with a wine broth."

She nodded. "I do. Would you like me to dig for them like you did?"

"Yes. If it isn't too unladylike for you."

She snorted out a laugh. "I don't think I have any way to argue for ladylike behavior given what I've done the last week of my life. And I need to wash some of my clothes anyway, so I suppose this is the time to get sandy and salty."

His mouth went dry at the mention of her flavor. "G-Good. I'll get you a bucket and leave it on the bluff. Give the clams some seawater in it to keep them alive so they don't spoil," he explained.

She was quiet a moment, and then she nodded. "Yes. I'll do that."

"And I'll leave some things up at the cottage so you can wash up later. Do you know how to do that?"

"No," she admitted with a shrug. "But I suppose I can learn a great many things."

She turned away then, focusing her attention on the bubbles in the sand. He walked up the beach as she drove her hand into the dirt, digging down to find the escaping clam beneath. She squealed with what was clearly joy as she caught it, and he turned. She was tossing the tube on to the sand. Her face was lit up with triumph and she stared at the clam with a wide smile.

Then she backed up to the bluff and surprised him by lifting her skirt up. His throat closed as she rolled her stockings down and kicked them away, along with her slippers. She tied her skirts up her calf a little, then strode back toward the water, free to get wet without ruining her shoes.

He shifted at the uncomfortable hardness in his trousers, hating himself yet again for what he coveted. Then he walked away to the music of her hoots and hollers of success as she dug again for her supper.

He was *not* going to like her, he reminded himself. He certainly wasn't going to want her. He just had to keep himself in control a little longer and pray that Ellis would come back soon and take her away.

CHAPTER 5

A nne swung her bucket at her side as she whistled a triumphant tune. She was grimy and her nails were worn down and dirtied by work, but she'd never felt more useful in her life. Her bucket was brimming with clams she'd dug out from the beach and with mussels she'd found clinging to the underside of a rock on the cove. She and Rook would have quite the feast tonight and she couldn't wait to show him her bounty.

She stopped in the path and wrinkled her brow at that errant thought. She shouldn't care what Rook, a man whose given name she didn't even know, thought of what she did or didn't accomplish. She was just being foolish, probably because she was tired.

That didn't seem like the answer, but she ignored any questioning that lingered in her heart and continued up a path to the cottage. This was a different route than the one she'd taken from the dock a few days prior, but then she was learning that Rook's island was full of paths. All of them seemed to lead home, as if he always wanted a way to get to the little house on the hill above.

She turned and twisted through the wooded beauty around her as the rain began to fall at last. It was a light rain, but steady, and she picked up her pace so she wouldn't be utterly soaked before she reached the house. Scottish rain was cold no matter the season, and she didn't want to freeze while she attempted to wash out her things.

She saw a building in the distance and hurried toward it as the wind picked up and stirred her now-wet hair. But as she reached it, she realized it wasn't the cottage, which she could see beyond through the fog another few hundred yards, but some kind of outbuilding. The door to the place was cracked an inch and she stepped up and pushed inside for a moment's respite from the rain.

She caught her breath as her eyes adjusted to the darkness within, for there was no fire in the small hearth and the light from the windows was dim and gray. It was a small space with a large table in the middle. The ground and tabletop were covered with wood shavings and dust. Knives were mounted by leather straps to the walls and there were dozens of intricately carved pieces on the table and shelves and floor.

She set her bucket by the door and eased up to one shelf to take a closer look. A little carved squirrel caught her attention, his face so perfectly sculpted that she might have believed he would come to life with the right words spoken. Another was a rose, delicately detailed with even a drop of dew on the wooden petals. Each piece was lovelier than the next. She was stunned by it.

These couldn't have been carved by Rook. That hulk of a man who grunted more than he spoke? At least normally. Could *he* be so delicate with his hands as to create these magical pieces?

It *had* to be him who had done it. There was no one else on the island.

She shook her head at this revelation.

There was a sound at the door and she pivoted in surprise. She found the man himself standing there, staring at her. The light behind him framed him mostly in shadow, but she saw a hint of a frown on his handsome face, a shift in his posture that told her how uncomfortable he was that she had pried into his art.

He said nothing, even as she moved toward him. She opened her mouth to speak, but the light caught his face in that moment and her breath was stolen. His expression wasn't one of anger or embarrassment as she'd first thought. It was something different.

There was a possessiveness to his expression as he stared at her, their eyes locked. Something intimate and heated that made her legs clench against each other and her hands shake at her sides. She knew that feeling. She sometimes felt it at night in her bed when her hands slipped between her legs. She'd felt it when she and her sister Juliana had found a hidden book in her father's study back in London that contained pictures of men and women doing shocking things together.

Now she felt it as she stood frozen in the circle of Rook Maitland's regard. She swallowed.

"I—" she began on a shaky breath.

He turned his face and stooped to take the bucket she'd left by the door. He was silent as he stepped away, leaving her alone, gaping after him. She watched through the window as he lumbered toward the house at a fast clip. He never looked back.

She staggered away, leaning both hands on his worktable as her heart raced and she panted out the breath she had been holding since the moment she saw him standing at the door.

What was *wrong* with her? What kind of a person was she? A few months before, she had been resigned to marrying the Earl of Harcourt, loveless as that union would have been. A month before, she had told herself she was beginning to have feelings for Ellis Maitland. She had thrown away everything to be with him.

And now she was staying alone on a deserted island with Rook and feeling a powerful sensation of longing through every part of her body when she looked at him.

What did that make her?

She knew what people would call her if they saw what was in her heart. A wanton. A scarlet woman who was so mad with desire that she would covet any man who crossed her path. In novels she was written as the villainess, a woman who would grasp for men, not caring about the consequences to anyone around her.

She rubbed her eyes as she tried to find purchase again. Her whole life she'd known she was viewed as the wild one of the Shelley Triplets, the omnibus name that she and her sisters were called by to their faces and behind their backs, along with worse ones. She supposed she might also be called the "bad" triplet. Her father sometimes said that.

She'd never believed that to be true. Even now, when she could see how wrong her thoughts were, she couldn't accept that she was a villain. But then again, most villains never did.

"Everyone is the hero of their own story," she mused.

She pondered the troubling thoughts for a while, sitting in the discomfort they gave her. At last the tangle cleared. It wasn't that she was bad, she decided as she smoothed her skirts and sucked in a few long breaths. It was just that she was questioning everything. How could she not when she had been abandoned by the man she'd sacrificed so much to be with? It made her uncertain and of course she clung to anything solid.

Rook was definitely that.

She pushed the thought away and left his workshop, closing the door firmly behind her as she made toward the house. This time she hardly noticed the cold rain as she trudged up the slope to the cottage.

Tomorrow Ellis would come. He had to. And once he was there, she wouldn't have these questions anymore. Once he was there, her path would be clear again and she wouldn't think about Rook Maitland ever again.

R ook lay staring at the ceiling, filtered moonlight casting a sliver of light on the floor beside the settee that pointed toward his dying fire. It was late, after midnight, but he couldn't sleep. It had been too trying a day.

He and Anne hadn't shared the supper of her bounty of clams and mussels. She'd locked herself away in his room to wash her clothing and had taken her bowl of food with her because she'd told him they'd have to dry by the fire.

Which had only left him with thoughts of her naked in his bed.

He shifted on the settee as his hard cock screamed with sensation. Damn these thoughts. Damn these needs for a woman he couldn't have. Shouldn't have. Would never have.

And yet he had those thoughts. Thoughts of how her pupils had dilated with telling desire when he found her in his workshop. The way her breath had caught. The way her nipples had grown hard, outlined under her damp gown that had clung to her curves.

And now she was five paces away, through a thin door he could rip off the hinges if he wanted to, and fantasy was impossible to deny. Fantasy of what would have happened if he had come into the workshop like he'd so wanted to do, instead of walked away in silence. What if he had shut the door behind himself? What if he had kissed her?

What would she taste like if he claimed her lips? What would it have felt like molding her body to his? Would she have resisted if he lifted her up onto the edge of his worktable, pushed her legs wide and tasted her there, too?

He let his hand slide beneath the blanket and found his naked cock there. Already rock hard thanks to those wicked thoughts, he stroked himself. Once, twice. Pleasure lurched through his body. A pleasure he couldn't deny. If he allowed it, maybe the tension would fade a little. Maybe he could control himself just a tiny bit.

He removed his hand and spit on it for lubrication before he returned to stroke again, this time harder, faster as he pictured tearing that damp, flimsy dress from Anne's shoulders. Of cupping her bare ass as he ground against her and then delved deep inside of her as she sank her fingernails into his shoulders and rode him.

He could almost feel the hot, wet grip of her body around him, hear her soft moans of pleasure. He stroked faster and faster, wishing it was her he was driving deep inside, that the ripples of her orgasm were milking him rather than the stroke of his own fingers.

He stiffened as the pleasure arced through his body, sensation so taut and focused that it bordered on pain. His balls tightened and he came with a soft grunt. He rested back on the thin pillow and stared up at the ceiling as he panted with release and pleasure...and a tiny bit of guilt that he'd imagined doing such lewd things to a woman who claimed to wish to marry his cousin.

As he moved to flop an arm over his eyes, he caught a flash of movement from the corner of his eye. He glanced over to find Anne's door shutting softly. His eyes went wide. Had she seen him jerking his cock?

"Fuck," he muttered, even as that same cock got a little hard again in response to the idea.

It seemed that the longer Anne Shelley was in his life, the more he caused himself problems. And all he could do now was hope that Ellis would come back before Rook did something none of them could take back. Something that would change everything forever.

R ook felt a strong sense of circumstances repeating themselves as he entered the cottage the next day for his midday meal. It was as if they'd gone back in time to the first few days Anne had been there. She was nowhere to be found. She hadn't joined him for breakfast, so he'd left her a tray beside the door. She wasn't out for lunch, either.

And he couldn't help but wonder, yet again, if she'd seen him pleasure himself last night. A woman like that? Proper, protected? If she had seen him, she must hate him and be terrified of his intentions all over again. She would be doubly so if she knew his heated thoughts of her.

He sighed and set his gloves aside on the table beside the door. He'd been working on clearing a patch of heavy tree roots that morning, trying to make way for a place for a larger dock. If he ever had the money to build it. He had to be careful now, for he was spending the funds he'd saved and had no plans to bring more in though ill-gotten gains.

He sighed and was about to go into the kitchen to find himself food when he heard a sound from his bedroom. Banging. Loud banging. And the occasional sound of a musical voice. Like Anne was muttering to herself. Or talking to someone else.

God, was it possible Ellis had returned without stopping to find Rook? That he'd come in here and now he and Anne were…

He pushed the thought away and the streak of jealous heat that went with it. He would have seen Ellis if he'd come to the island. There was only one path from the sea he could have taken.

The banging came again and this time it was accompanied by a loud gasp of "Ouch!"

He moved to the door in a few long steps and knocked.

There was no response, just more of the banging and muttering, which he could now hear more clearly through the door, though the specifics of what she was saying were less clear.

He knocked again. "Miss Shelley?" he asked. There was no ceasing of the banging, and so he pounded a bit harder. "Anne!"

She stopped doing whatever she was doing then and there was a long pause. Then he heard her soft footfalls and she cracked the door. Her cheeks were pink, he wasn't sure if that was from exertion or embarrassment. Perhaps both, if the way she wouldn't meet his eyes was any indication.

"Oh, it's you," she said.

He arched a brow. "Who else would it be?"

She turned away in a huff and he pushed the door open wider to look into the room. Her little bag was on the bed and her clothing was strewn about in piles, some in the bag, some out.

"What are you doing?" he asked, trying not to look at the thin pink silk chemise draped over a chair by the fire to dry. Trying not to picture it draped across Anne's body. Or on the floor after he removed it.

"Packing," she snapped without looking at him, as if that should have been obvious by the state of her chamber. "I'm packing."

"I see," he said. "Have you had some indication that Ellis will return today?"

She froze in what she was doing and glanced at him over her shoulder. Her green gaze held desperation. He knew it far too well not to recognize it.

"He must come, mustn't he?" she said, not really asking despite the question she spoke. "He *will* come. It's been almost six days. He *must* come today."

He bent his head and stared at the ground beneath his boots. He'd been waiting for the same thing, the return of his cousin, but knowing more than Anne did about the reality of the situation. The reality of Ellis Maitland and his life and character.

Still, Rook had hoped for better for her. Almost from the first moment he met her. But now he had to address this.

"Anne—" he began.

She jolted, perhaps at his tone, perhaps at the improper use of her given name, perhaps both. She pivoted to face him fully and lifted a hand to silence him. As if that would change things. "No," she interrupted.

He took a long step closer, too close in the small chamber. "Anne," he repeated.

She shook her head. "No. *No.*"

He was silent then, but he refused to back away. He stood there, a foot away from her, and he held her stare to show her what she would not allow him to say. They held gazes as they had in the workshop the previous day, only this time there was no heat between them. At least, the heat wasn't the prominent exchange in that moment.

They looked at each other and her shoulders rolled forward with the truth she had to see.

"He—" she began, her voice so soft it almost didn't carry in the quiet room. She swallowed hard and clasped her hands before her. "He isn't coming back, is he?"

"No," Rook said softly, firmly, he hoped gently. "Probably not."

He waited then for the howl of pain, for the possibility that she would faint with great drama or burst into hysterics. But she didn't do any of those things. She stood there, stock still for what felt like a lifetime. Then she pivoted and grabbed the closest thing to her, a small clock on his mantel, and threw it with all her might, shattering it against the back wall of the room.

CHAPTER 6

The moment Anne released the clock for its final flight into the wall, she regretted it. It wasn't her clock, for one, and when it broke she realized the man who did own it could easily be enraged she would disregard his personal effects so rudely. But oh, the sound that clock made when it shattered against the wall.

It was just the tiniest release of tension, of anger, of heartbreak, of humiliation. And she wanted to clear the room of everything, smashing it all as she screamed out the tangle of feelings that resided in her chest.

Instead, she turned and looked back at Rook. If she expected anger as his response, she was surprised. He was grinning. She'd never seen him show anything but the barest hint of a smile and her breath caught. He was…beautiful. Not as obvious and showy as his cousin, with his perfectly straight teeth and dimple, but Rook's smile was better. It was a little crooked, but it was bright, and made his face shine and look years younger.

"I'm sorry," she stammered, trying to find words and breath again.

He cocked his head. "Why? That was a good show, I think. Although I don't have the blunt to afford much more of it."

She shook her head at her outburst and rushed toward the shards of glass and broken wood in the corner of the bedroom, but before she could reach them, he caught her wrist.

She sucked in a sharp breath. He hadn't touched her since the first night they'd arrived, when he'd helped her from the boat. Now his strong, tanned fingers closed around her flesh and her heart rate leapt. She couldn't help but picture those hands somewhere else.

Like slipping beneath his blanket as they had the night before. When he'd touched himself as she secretly watched from the bedroom behind him, her legs clenching and wet heat pooling between them. How many times had she touched herself since, burying her head in her pillow so he wouldn't hear her?

He drew back instantly, his bright smile fading a fraction as his dark gaze grew stormy. "Come on, I have a better idea."

He walked away and she followed in foggy confusion. He moved to the door, where he stopped and slung his greatcoat over his shoulders. At last he looked back at her.

"Do you have a wrap of any kind in that suitcase you half-packed?"

"Just the one I had the first night," she said. "It won't be very useful against the rain."

"No," he agreed. He pointed at her to stay where she was and went into the chamber she'd been occupying. She heard him going through his wardrobe, and then he returned with a woolen jumper in hand. One that seemed to be made to fit her perfectly.

"It's a bit tiny, for you anyway," she said, tilting her head at him as she tried to ignore the flash of jealousy at the idea of just who might have owned that jumper originally.

He smiled, an echo of the wide grin from earlier and once again her stomach clenched of its own accord. "It used to be bigger," he admitted. "When I was first left to my own devices, I didn't realize you couldn't wash wool the same way you do other things."

"You can't?" she repeated. "I suppose I never thought of it."

"Why would you?" he asked, and then handed over the sweater.

"It ought to fit you fine, though. Keep you warm in the rain anyway. And for your head…"

He trailed off and caught up a wide, floppy-brimmed hat from the coat rack. He popped it onto her head and laughed as it drooped over her eyes, blocking her vision for a moment. She felt him step closer in the dimness and then his fingers brushed the brim back, stroking across her forehead as he did so.

She looked up at him. They were very close now. So close that she forgot everything but him for a brief, dangerous moment. Then she swallowed.

"You—you aren't casting me out to sea, are you?" she asked, hoping the quip would lighten the mood. "For crimes against timepieces?"

"I wouldn't do that while you were wearing my favorite hat," he promised, and then stepped into the misting rain outside. "Come on."

She followed him, pushing the hat back as they went so she could see the trail he cut across the island. He took her toward his workshop, the one she hadn't yet asked him about, and she caught her breath. But they didn't go in. He moved her past the place, into a small circle of trees. One of them had a target painted on it, worn and full of holes.

"Archery?" she asked.

He scoffed. "Archery is for children. Better than that. I'll be right back."

She watched as he moved into the workshop and returned a moment later with a folded rectangle of leather in his hands. When he reached her, he opened it and revealed a set of six knives, gleaming even in the rainy, filtered light. The blades weren't like a cutting or carving knife, but pointed to a sharp edge with perfectly symmetrical sides. The handles were ivory, intricately carved with the faces of men or the sultry naked bodies of women.

She blushed and glanced up at him. "Knives?" she asked. "What am I to do with them? Stab out my rage?"

"Something like it." He set the leather holder into her hands and then withdrew one of the knives. The handle had a smiling face on it, long and drawn out and a combination of silly and sinister.

Without speaking, he pivoted and flicked his wrist, releasing the knife to go circling through the air where it stuck into the middle of the target with a satisfying chunk of sound around them.

Her lips parted and she stared from him to the target in awe. "I—how did you do that?"

"Years of practice, darlin', just like anything you want to do right."

She dipped her head at the suddenly flirtatious tone of his voice. That rough quality of it, the way he called her by an endearment, it sank into her skin and made her hate herself all the more. Made her hate whatever thing was inside of her that caused her to feel this wicked way.

And also made her want more of it. More of the tingle that worked through her body. More of that dizziness that made her hands shake.

He cleared his throat and his voice was normal again as he said, "It's the best way to get out some aggression, at least for me. You throw now."

She stared up at him, shock erasing the other feelings in an instant. "Throw the knives? I couldn't. It's not—it's not ladylike."

His brow wrinkled. "And hurtling innocent clocks across a room is?"

She pursed her lips. "The clock wasn't so very innocent."

He flashed a smile at her quip. "So the clock had it coming. If you say that's true, then I accept that. But you aren't in a ballroom, Anne. You're on my island, alone with me. I don't give a tinker's damn if you're ladylike."

"I won't be any good at it," she tried, staring at the knives with a longing she didn't understand. "And they're beautiful pieces. I-I wouldn't want to ruin them."

He shrugged. "That's why I brought the cheap ones for you."

He reached inside his coat pocket and drew out a flimsy fabric rectangle of the same size as the leather one she still held. The knives within it were certainly not so fine. And judging from the nicks along the handles and scratches on the blades, they had been well used.

"Try it," he insisted. "Unless you're afraid."

She straightened her spine at his taunt, hating that he'd probably done it to force her hand and she'd fallen for it. "Fine," she ground out. "But I can't do it while I'm holding these."

He bowed his head and took the finer set back. He found a stump and set the cheaper set on it, the blades flecked with water droplets from the rain. "Just look at them a moment. Don't throw anything yet."

She nodded and watched him rather than the blades as he went to the tree and pulled the knife from its trunk in a smooth motion. He wiped it clean on his coat, then wrapped the carved blades up in the leather and placed them in his inside pocket.

"How do you do it?" she asked.

He drew two knives from the holster and handed one over as he stepped up beside her. She was very aware of his size, of his warmth as he positioned the knife in his hand. His long index finger rested on the top of the handle almost all the way to where the metal blade began.

"Keep a loose grip while still holding it," he said, watching as she curved her fingers in a similar way. "Then you arch back and release right about here."

He flicked his wrist as he had the first time, and the knife flew from his hand and chunked into the target again.

She nodded, though she'd been more mesmerized by the movement of the knife than the position he'd been trying to show her. Still, she flicked her wrist in some facsimile of what he'd done and the knife flew and ricocheted off the tree to land on the ground before it.

She shook her head. "I told you I'd be rubbish at it."

"It's the first time you've thrown a knife, I'd wager," he said with a shrug of his shoulders. "The fact that you hit the tree at all is an accomplishment in itself. Here, let me help you."

He snatched up another blade and handed it to her, then slid behind her. His fingers closed on her hip and her breath hitched at the pressure of every digit against her body. No matter how much she tried to tell herself it was no different than a man holding her like this while they were dancing, it felt different.

"Shift your weight forward on that foot," he said, his voice close to her ear.

She swallowed hard and tried to focus on his words and not his presence as she did as he asked. His hand slid upward slightly and he pressed against her body gently.

"And now pivot a little so you're in a more angled position. Yes." He nodded and his hand left her side, leaving her both relieved and bereft. He moved it to her fingers, though. She wore no gloves, nor did he, and she stared at his big hand engulfing her own. "Move your finger, loosen the grip just a touch."

He stepped away at last and off to the side so he wasn't directly behind her anymore. "When you're ready, take a deep breath and throw again."

She bit her tongue. Take a deep breath? She couldn't even find a shallow one thanks to this frustrating, interesting, mysterious man. But she did her best, focused on the target and threw a second time.

The knife hit the trunk again, but bounced off a second time. This time it made a different sound, though, and he let out a whoop. "Excellent! That one almost stuck. Here, let's adjust a bit more."

She held her breath as he urged her forward half a step and went about some movements around her body to put her into a better position. Every time he touched her, she could feel each nerve ending of her body. And it seemed to do nothing for him. He didn't even seem to notice that air was thick and she couldn't speak.

Was she doomed to want men who didn't want her back? What was wrong with her?

"Anne?"

She shook away the thoughts and let the knife loose again. This time it stuck, just for a moment, and then it fell downward.

"Good!" he shouted. "Here's another. This time throw it harder. Throw it angry. Throw it like you threw the clock."

She glanced at him. "Rook—"

"If you're going to tell me it isn't ladylike to rage against that tree, I swear to you I will scream the house down," he grunted. "Think about my cousin, for God's sake. Think about whatever made you run away with him. Think about whatever isn't fair in this world that makes you lay awake at night staring at the ceiling. Feel the damned anger, Anne. Feel it and then let it go on the blade of that knife."

Her lips parted at that surprisingly passionate order. And at the way her stomach clenched in response. Then she flicked the knife with a guttural cry that came all the way from her soul.

It chunked into the wood and stuck there. Six inches below the target, but it stuck.

She whooped just as she had when she found her first clam and he joined her. She jumped up and down before she launched herself at him without thinking. He caught her, spinning her in a circle as he held her tight against his chest. She clenched her fists against his back, turning her cheek against his shoulder.

He set her down but didn't release her from his embrace. When she dared to look up at him, she found him looking back at her, his pupils dilated and his stare intent on her lips. He cleared his throat and stepped away.

"Good show, Anne," he muttered, his voice gruff. He turned his back on her and went to collect all the knives. "Very well done."

She smoothed her skirt with both hands, trying to force her heart rate back to normal. It was almost impossible to do when she could still feel his remarkably strong arms around her.

He handed over one knife, then sat down on the stump and put the rest in his lap. She positioned herself as he'd shown her and threw again. The knife stuck, higher than the target this time, but she still felt the thrill of accomplishment that was unlike any other she'd ever experienced.

He was quiet as he handed over another knife and let her throw again. This one didn't stick, and she grunted her disappointment as she adjusted herself slightly and took a third knife from him.

"So," he said as she prepared to throw again. "Do you want to tell me what happened?"

She froze, her hand angled back. She knew what he was asking, but she shrugged. "I didn't release at the right time."

She threw again and missed again, distracted by his questions. He let her take another knife, his dark gaze following her as she did so. He didn't press until she'd thrown again and this time the knife stuck in the outer edges of the target.

"Good shot," he encouraged. "But you know I wasn't asking about the knives."

She sighed as she took another knife and avoided his gaze. She positioned herself carefully. "You mean what happened between me and Ellis?"

She threw and hit next to the other knife in the outer circle of the target. She shook out her arm, flexing her fingers before she turned. He was holding the last knife of the set out to her by the blade, his dark gaze focused on her own. She took the handle carefully and only then did he nod.

"If you want to tell me about it."

She pivoted away, heat suffusing her cheeks. *Did* she want to tell him? There was part of her that didn't. Didn't want to reveal what a fool she'd been. Didn't want to say out loud, especially to this man, what she'd done and allowed and fallen for like a fool.

And yet there was also part of her that desperately needed to confide in someone. Since meeting Ellis, she'd kept everything close to her chest. She hadn't told her sisters about her feelings, about her plans. She hadn't told her maid. She'd locked everything away and now it all boiled inside of her, ready to explode with the pressure silence had created.

She cleared her throat and tried to line up her shot to hit on the more inner circles of the target. If she started talking, she knew what would happen. She would spill everything to this man. This stranger who didn't feel like one anymore. This confusion personified who made her so much more aware of her apparent weaknesses when it came to her heart and her body.

But then, perhaps that was what was meant to be. She threw the knife and watched it bounce off the tree. Then she turned to look at him as he rose from the stump in a smooth unfolding of muscle.

"I was supposed to marry someone else," she said. "That was how it all began."

CHAPTER 7

R ook tried to keep his reaction from his face as he walked past
Anne and gathered the knives. He certainly didn't want her
to see what those words engendered in him. The jealousy he never
should have felt that was now multiplied by two. Jealousy of Ellis.
Jealousy of this nameless man who'd been her intended.

He drew a breath as he picked up the knives on the ground and
pulled the three she'd stuck in the tree. She was a natural. Watching
her perform made the need that rose in him all the more powerful.
But he pushed that aside as he returned to her to hand over a knife.
Her face was drawn down, she refused to look at him and he hated
that. He had to act naturally so she would do the same.

"Adjust your weight on your left foot a bit more. Release when
your hand is just starting to come down. It's like you're just letting
go, not trying too hard," he said.

She nodded and put herself back in position. As she lined up her
shot, he drew in a deep breath and said, "Who was he? The man you
were supposed to marry?"

She released the knife and it bounced off the tree with a ding of
metal on wood. She huffed out her breath in frustration and
remained with her back to him. "Just an earl like a dozen other earls.

My father wanted the connection. It's all he's ever cared about, furthering himself through us. Me and my sisters."

Rook nodded. So she had sisters. "How many?"

"Sisters?" she asked, turning back. Now she had a faint smile on her face. "Two. We're…we're a bit of an anomaly, I suppose. We're triplets."

Rook lifted both brows. That was a rarity—most multiple births didn't result in happy endings for mother or children. "Truly?"

She nodded. "The exertion nearly killed our mother." She frowned. "And later did, when my father insisted she try again for a son. His damned son. She didn't survive the pregnancy and neither did the baby."

Rook dipped his head, thinking of his own mother, lost through an illness that had taken her when he was just six. A moment that had changed his life forever. A moment that had put him in the path of his cousin, who was already living a wild, unchaperoned life on the street at the ripe old age of ten.

"My father wanted his prize and the earl needed my dowry," she continued, bringing Rook back from the dark memories that clouded his mind. "So the marriage was arranged. I had never met the man. I wasn't particularly impressed once I did."

Rook frowned. This was the way of the world, of course, especially the way of the rich, but it had always troubled him that women could be so easily forced into situations they did not desire. "You couldn't convince your father to reconsider?"

She snorted a rather unladylike laugh and threw the knife. It hit the dead center of the target and stuck there for a brief moment before it fell. She pivoted to face him, eyes wide with shock and accomplishment.

He pushed to his feet and grinned. "Perfect shot, Anne!"

She lifted her hands to her flushed cheeks. "I can see why you do this to purge your ill feelings. It is thrilling. May I continue?"

He held out the next knife. "If you'd like. Throw until your arms are tired, if it helps."

She took the knife and smiled. "It does."

She turned away and he remained on his feet, watching her, waiting to see if she would return to the more uncomfortable conversation about her arranged marriage and how that had brought her to Ellis. She threw the next knife, hitting the target on the second ring.

"You asked about my father," she said, taking the next blade without meeting his gaze. "There could never be a way to turn him from what he thought would benefit him. My sisters and I are tools to him, nothing more."

"So how did Ellis come into the picture?" he asked.

The next knife hurtled from her fingers and she shook her head as it landed far short of the tree. She flexed her arms and stretched her fingers, but didn't return to take the next blade. She stood there, staring out at the tree even though he doubted she saw it now. Memory seemed to take her over, unpleasant or pleasant.

"It was a ball to celebrate our union in my future husband's country seat," she said softly. "I stepped outside on the terrace, and there Ellis was. Like he was waiting for me. Or like I'd been waiting for him. I thought that at the time, that it was some kind of destiny that had brought us together. I suppose that was how I justified it to myself. He was…charming."

Rook pursed his lips, tamping down the jealousy again. "He can be that."

"He was what I'd pictured a man *should* be."

"Handsome," Rook provided, thinking of his cousin's nickname and how he'd learned to use his looks to his advantage when it came to women and grifting.

She shrugged. "Yes, that. But it was more that he saw me, if that makes sense. He seemed to like me for myself. He laughed at my quips—my fiancé never did that. And he offered this idea of adventure and romance and freedom that…well, it was all very attractive to me. It also felt like my only escape hatch."

She snatched another blade and threw it, wincing as it pinged off the tree and bounced into the sandy grass at their feet.

"I doubted it," she whispered. "Doubted him in my darkest moments when I was alone. But I still thought he was the better choice. The—the only choice."

Rook hesitated. He had never betrayed his cousin, not in all the years they had run together. Not even when he'd been against Ellis's decisions. But now, looking at the young woman beside him, he wanted so much to help her. To make her understand that this wasn't her fault.

He wanted to comfort her. And the truth was the only way to do that.

He cleared his throat. "You cannot be blamed. He made himself look that way, by design, I would assume."

She looked at him in confusion and, he thought, a little defensiveness. "By design? That would imply he had an ulterior motive. What do you think it was?"

"He approached you, didn't he? On that terrace you talked about. He came to you, probably from the shadows. He was mysterious. He asked about you, focused on you."

Her lips parted and her eyes went wide as saucers. "I-it is like you were there."

"Because I was there many times, when he did it before, even though I wasn't that night." He moved toward her a long step. "Anne, you must understand something and I don't say it to hurt you. My cousin is a trickster, a liar. What he did to you...he's done it a dozen times or more before. It's his trade."

She stepped back, staring at him both as if she didn't comprehend what he meant and as if she very much did and wanted to unhear the bell he'd rung in her head. "I don't understand."

He nodded. "I know. I'm sorry. Ellis grew up very...rough. We weren't part of your world, but one far beneath yours. We had to learn to survive on the streets by any means necessary. For Ellis... for me...that meant crime."

She gasped and the color left her cheeks. "Crime?"

"Petty things, mostly. Pickpocketing, stealing." He shook his head as he thought of Ellis teaching him that trade, telling him his six-year-old hands were smaller so he could do it better. "Worse as we grew older. Ellis realized in his teens that his handsome face could get him more if he played at seduction. Games of love, he called them, meant to divorce a lady or her family from their purse."

Now she went from pale to green and she staggered slightly. He caught her elbow, supporting her so she didn't collapse. She stared up at him, her eyes wide and filled with unshed tears. Her lower lip trembling. She was so very lovely. And now she was broken. Because of Ellis. Because of him.

This was why he'd left that life. This and a great deal more. And yet here he was.

She bent her head. "I am such a fool," she whispered.

He caught his breath and slid his fingers beneath her chin. Slowly, he tilted her face up and drew her a little closer, until her skirts tangled against his boots. Until he could feel her breath stirring his chin.

"Anne," he said, his voice rough. "*You* are not the fool. He is."

Her tears cleared with those words, replaced by something else in her stare that he didn't want to focus on. Shouldn't focus on. But couldn't look away from. Her hand lifted and shook as she rested it on his chest.

She licked her lips and he was lost. Need poured through him, rough and dirty and dangerous as any weapon he'd ever held. He wanted her to distraction and he knew that once he touched her, he would burn her to the ground, first with pleasure...but inevitably with pain.

And yet he still wanted to kiss her. Just a taste. Just a moment they could both pretend to forget later. He found his mouth lowering toward hers, felt her shift as she arched up to meet him.

But just before their lips met, the misting rain that had been falling off and on around them all morning turned to something heavier. It doused them both in a sheet of frigidity and he gasped as he stepped away, reminded by nature that this woman was not his.

She stared up at him, eyes wide, unblinking, still heavy with desire and perhaps some disappointment that they hadn't finished what he started.

He stepped away so he wouldn't dare to do it despite the rain.

"You may keep throwing the knives or go inside out of the cold," he muttered. "I ought to…to check on some things in case the storm grows worse."

He inclined his head and paced away without a backward glance. He didn't need one. The image of her was burned on his mind now and he feared it would never go away. Nor would the regrets that he hadn't done exactly what his worst impulses demanded.

Anne stirred the fire she had been tending for the past few hours and tried not to look at the door behind her for the tenth time in the last thirty minutes. Staring at it since sundown hadn't brought Rook in from the cold. It wasn't going to make him return any faster.

Not that she was certain how to proceed once he did come back. How did one manage a man who had looked like he wanted to kiss her? Devour her? Then he'd just walked away. How did one manage the only person on this earth who knew how badly she had been used and discarded…and yet told her that her foolishness wasn't her own fault?

The door behind her creaked as it opened, and she spun from the fire to watch Rook step inside, removing his soaking wet hat and hanging it up before he followed with his coat. He ran a hand through his messy hair and cast his glance over to her. He looked disinterested. Like the man who'd nearly kissed her in the woods had never existed.

Probably better for her and she ignored the sting his disregard caused.

"Would you like something to eat?" she asked. "I warmed up the remainder of that broth from earlier today, and there's bread."

His brows lifted in what seemed like surprise. He nodded once. "Yes. Let me dry off a bit, though."

He moved toward her at the fire and she skittered back, giving him space. Giving herself the same because she wasn't certain if she would launch herself at him or not if he got too close. Rejection was something she'd become very familiar with lately. She didn't want more of it from him.

She cleared her throat as she paced across the little sitting room, worrying the blanket draped on the back of the settee. "I've been thinking," she began, wishing that her voice were more certain.

He didn't answer but continued to rub his hands together before the fire. So the grunting hulk had returned. Well, that was probably better.

"I-I need to go home," she continued.

His hands stopped moving and he slowly faced her. "To England?" he said.

She nodded. "Yes."

He shrugged. "I suppose that is for the best considering that we've determined my lout of a cousin doesn't have true intentions toward you."

She flinched. "But I-I can't go alone. I've learned how useless I am by coming here, so I realize I wouldn't even know how to go about it safely. It's only a day or two, isn't it? Such a small period out of your life? Please, won't you help me?"

His eyes went wide and he stared at her for what seemed like forever. "Anne—" he began at last.

She rushed forward. "Please, I know you've been dragged into this enough as it is. I know it isn't fair to ask you when you never wanted me here in the first place. But there will be money for you if you do this."

She hesitated, for she didn't know if that was the truth. Her father could have cut her off for all she knew, or would the moment he saw her. Running away with a man, that was ruin, whether Ellis had ever touched her or not. It was a consequence that would destroy her as punishment for her recklessness.

Still, she had to hope she could convince her father to pay for her return. If only to reduce the scandal by some portion.

He shook his head. "It isn't about the money, Anne. But you said it's only a day or two, and that's not true."

She wrinkled her brow. "The boat ride across the sea only took five or six hours. And the ride back to the earl's estate a few more. It cannot be more than two days to get from here to where I need to go. Or even just to Beckfoot. I might be able to reach my father from there and you could return to your life here."

He pursed his lips. "We cannot take the boat."

She blinked. "What?"

He motioned toward the rain that lashed the windows outside. "It has been raining off and on for days, sometimes heavily. The passage would be much more dangerous now, something even the larger, more steady boat couldn't do. And even if we could contact that captain and convince him to brave the weather, he wouldn't take us. We stiffed him on payment when we came in to the island. I'm certain he's told every seafarer on the closest mainland cities not to give me passage anywhere."

Her lips parted. "Why did you not pay him when he…" She trailed off as the answer to the question became clear. "Ellis?"

He nodded. "My cousin lied to me and said he paid for both ways of passage in order to protect you, but—"

"But he never truly cared if I was protected," she finished with a shake of her head. "And you were left with all the worst consequences of that."

He shrugged. "Not all worst, I promise you."

She glanced at him. He was trying to comfort her, she thought. But knowing he hadn't hated having her here didn't make things better. It only made her think of things she knew she couldn't have.

"What about your boat?" she pressed. "I saw it on the dock."

"It's tiny," he said softly. "Only meant to ferry me back and forth to the mainland for supplies every so often. Not to make a longer trip across a wild sea."

She scrubbed a hand across her face. "So if we were to do this, we'd have to go to the mainland with your smaller boat. And travel to England by land," she said softly.

"Yes. It would be a long trip, a long time on the road together. There would be…" He turned his face and his voice grew rougher. "There would be consequences."

"Like—like what?"

He drew a long breath. "We'd have to stay at inns at night. For your safety, we'd have to pose as a married couple."

She stared at him as what he was suggesting became clear. "You mean we'd be expected to share a room."

His gaze found hers, held there, heat and regret all at once again. "Once we did that, whatever is left of your reputation would be gone."

"Oh," she whispered, blinking at the tears that filled her eyes. Tears because she knew he was correct. Only her reputation had been *gone* since the moment she stepped into Ellis's phaeton what felt like a lifetime ago. And being alone with Rook didn't seem like the worst thing, despite being a terrible temptation she shouldn't want so much to face.

He watched her face closely, as if he were trying to read her thoughts. At last he folded his arms. "I wouldn't pursue you, Anne. I hope I've proven you aren't in danger from me during the last week." He shook his head. "I just need you to understand what you would be facing if we make our way toward your family together."

"What would the alternative be?" she asked.

"Trying to get a message to your father or your former fiancé, I suppose," he said. "Which could take just as long to reach them from here. And then hope they would come here or to the village on the Scotland side of the mainland and fetch you."

She shivered at the idea of waiting so long without any guarantee she would be found or fetched.

"Think about it," he said softly. "Now, why don't we have that supper you warmed?"

She flinched. "Just the idea of eating a bite makes my stomach turn right now. I think I'll just go to my room and do exactly what you suggested. Think."

He nodded. "Very well. Good night."

She repeated the same and slipped to the bedchamber. There she paused and watched him go toward the kitchen with that certain, long stride she had come to know so well from watching him since her arrival.

She stepped into the bedchamber and shut the door, leaning against it as she closed her eyes with a heavy, shaky sigh. The problem she faced about traveling with Rook wasn't that she feared he would take advantage of her. It was that she thrilled at the idea of being alone with him in a small room at an inn every night. She thrilled at the idea of being confined in a carriage at his side.

She thrilled at the idea of pretending they were married.

And the kind of person those feelings made her was…well, she had to face that as much as the consequences of her actions if she said yes. If she wanted to go home, she had to face what she desired and figure out if she could control it as easily as the man in the other room seemed to be able to do.

CHAPTER 8

R ook bent to tug his boot up over his calf. The fire had burned low during the night and there was a chill to the air in the main room. He was about to get up and add a few logs to make the room brighter when the door to the bedchamber opened.

Anne stood there for a moment, watching him with those green eyes that were like emeralds he wanted to steal. She reached behind her and drew out her small bag, and his heart somehow soared and sank at the same time.

"I know there will be many difficulties," she said softly. "But I also know I need to get back to my family. And since I put myself in this mess with my own bad decisions, I must try to make it right somehow. If you're willing to help me, I'd like to take the mainland route together. At least to Gretna Green, where I can probably find a way home on my own."

Rook took in her face in the dim light of the early morning that filtered through the windows. Her shoulders were thrust back, her hands clutching the bag at her side. Her gaze might be a little uncer-tain, but it was also strong. And in that moment he knew how much trouble he was in. He could try to pretend it away all he liked, but he wanted this woman. He wanted to strip her naked and teach her to beg for his tongue. He wanted to bury himself deep inside of her and feel her fingers dig into his back. He wanted to taste her release, watch it flow across her features, feel it ripple around his cock.

He wanted all those things and more, and it was going to be harder than ever to ignore those desires when they were in the close quarters travel required.

"Give me a moment to gather some things," he said, breaking the hold of their gaze with difficulty. "We can leave straight away."

She stepped aside and allowed him to pass by her into the bedchamber. He gathered a few items for the road in a small bag, including a stash of blunt he had hidden in the floorboards. He sighed as he counted it. There was enough here to get them where they needed to go, but little extra. It was too late to dig out more of his hidden reserves off the island. It would be a lean trip.

When he exited the room, she was no longer in the main living space, though her bag was by the door. He left his beside it and went into the kitchen. He found her standing at the table there, gathering apples, bread and cheese, which she wrapped up.

He lifted his brows as she looked at him with a weak smile. "I thought we might need food on the road."

He nodded, though he was shocked she would think of such a thing. In the week she'd been on his island, she had certainly taken on more than she'd likely ever considered in her life in Society.

He took the food and placed the packet carefully into his inside pocket, then motioned her to the door. They exited the cottage into the cold morning air, made darker by the clouds rolling in toward them. He frowned in the direction of the coming storm. Still, there was no choice, this was the path now. She followed him not to the dock where they had come in from England a week before, but to the opposite side of the island, where he had another boat tied to a stake buried deep in the sand.

He loaded it before he glanced back at the approaching clouds. "If we go now, we may get ahead of that storm. Though I warn you, it might not be steady sailing."

She nodded, but he could see the green enter her pallor even before he took her hand and helped her into the tiny craft. She situated herself in the back of the boat to create stability and he took his place at the oars. With a quick push they were off, and he angled them in the right direction, toward the shores of Scotland, which they could already see on the faint horizon.

"Luckily there's a current and a wind at our back that will help our journey," he said with as much enthusiasm as he could muster.

She forced a small smile, but he could still see concern in the expression on her pale face. She clenched her hands in her lap and stared off toward their destination, and they were quiet for a while as the waves rocked them none too gently.

The green increased in her cheeks and she gasped for fresh air after half an hour had passed. She shook her head. "I think talking might help."

He almost laughed. He'd spent a year talking to no one, and here came this woman who expected his chatter. And he didn't hate it, truth be told. He *liked* talking to her, even if they were from vastly different worlds and should have had little to say to each other.

"What is the plan?" she asked, making a sick, garbled sound in her throat.

He rowed harder, hoping speed might reduce her discomfort. "We'll reach the mainland in twenty minutes at this pace. There's a small village there, and if we're lucky we'll catch the stagecoach coming through."

"If we're lucky?" she asked, drawing deep breaths between each word and turning her face into the breeze so it stirred her dark blonde hair.

He nodded. "Out in the wilds, there's no telling the schedule from one day to the next."

"How long will our journey take then?" she asked.

He hesitated. In some ways he'd hoped she wouldn't ask this question. The answer was going to crush her. "It might be as long as a couple of weeks," he admitted at last. "With the weather, the state of the roads and schedules put into place that are out of our control."

Tears filled her eyes. He saw them before she blinked them away. Then she looked at him from the corner of her green gaze. "I-I hate to ask, as it seems very rude, but how will we pay for our fare on the coach? Or rooms at the inns at night?"

He pursed his lips. "I don't have a great deal of ready money, but there is some. Enough to pay for cheap rooms and cheaper fare on our route."

She bent her head. "I have all but destroyed your life, I think."

He wrinkled his brow before he leaned forward. He wanted to cup her chin. To force her to look up at him. He couldn't because of the oars. But his movement made her dart her gaze toward him anyway.

"It's not your fault," he said. The words seemed to ease her a little, for her tense shoulders relaxed at last.

"I'll pay you back," she promised softly. "Keep a daily tally of your expenses and I'll be certain you receive back your costs for the trip along with any reward I can squeeze out of my father."

He opened his mouth to argue that, but she held up a hand as if she could read his mind. Or at least his expression. "*Please*," she said before he could speak. "Don't make me your charity. I couldn't bear that kind of pity. Let me pay you back in some way for your kindness."

He turned his face as he rowed harder, so she wouldn't see that the kind of payment he wanted wasn't blunt. It was something else, something far more inappropriate and wrong, given the circumstances.

He shrugged at last. "Fine. We'll come to terms when we reach your father."

She seemed satisfied with that answer and was distracted from further conversation as the small town of Tayport, which was ten miles west up the coast from Southerness, rose up in the distance. She sat up straighter as they rowed into the small port, which was more sheltered than the open sea, so the boat didn't rock quite so hard. She smiled at him as she looked at the brightly colored houses and busy shops which dotted the shore.

At last they reached a low dock, where a man rushed up to take the rope and secure them. Her expression was almost conspiratorial as she waited for the boat to be steady. Like they were in this together, even though Rook knew that was an illusion. She needed him to get home. That was all there was between them.

It was all there could ever be. So he didn't return her smile. He just got up and got out of the boat, helping her do the same before he released her and motioned to the bustle around them.

"Welcome to Tayport," he grunted. "Come on."

Her smile fell as she followed him into the town proper. He felt her confusion at his sudden shift in attitude, and he hated himself for it. But it was better for them both. He just had to remember that.

Anne's stomach had stopping rolling the moment she stepped off the boat onto dry land, but now it tightened and turned again at Rook's sharp tone and dismissive glance in her direction. She knew she was putting him out, of course. How could she not be? He didn't want to haul her all the way to Gretna Green just because she was too foolish not to see the lie in his cousin's eyes.

And now he resented her, despite any promise of money as a reward for her return. That bothered her more than it should, since she barely knew the man. It only felt like she did, an illusion she'd clung to and now realized she had to let go.

Whatever she thought was between them, it was clear it didn't exist. She had to stop making a cake of herself and focus on getting home.

Like Rook seemed to be at present. He was currently standing with the driver of the stagecoach, which had pulled up almost immediately after their arrival on the boat. He handed over coins to the man—she couldn't see how many—and tossed over their bags to be loaded at the top of the rig before he waved her toward him.

She followed the crook of his finger and tried to smile as she reached him.

"We're in luck. There was a couple getting off here in Tayport, so he has a spot in the stage for us."

Relief flooded her. "You see, it's a good sign for the journey. How long until we depart?"

His lips pressed together, though she didn't understand the reason for his apparent annoyance. The sooner they got going, the sooner he would be rid of her. It made sense he would want that. Didn't it?

"They'll stay here a while longer to change the horses and let the others eat and stretch their legs, and we'll be off."

"It will be afternoon by the time we head out, then?" she asked.

He nodded. "Yes."

She frowned. "And how far do you think we'll go before we stop again?"

He arched a brow, and she couldn't tell if he was further irritated by her question or not. "It won't be far, I admit. The stage is the slowest route—they stop often for passengers to rest or eat and get off. But it's cheapest and safer than the mail coach."

"Safer?" she repeated in confusion.

He gazed off in the distance up the road. "Bandits," he said simply. "They know the mail coach carries valuable cargo."

Anne shivered at the thought. She'd always ridden in her father's private carriage or barouche if they were in town. The driver could make his own schedule as to their family needs and the ability to trade horses. She'd never taken public transit before with its restrictions and limits and money involved.

She felt so sheltered, so spoiled whenever she talked to Rook about the reality of those around her. As if she'd been completely blind to the world until she met him. In truth, she had been. Now she looked around the little port town, with its brightly painted shops and people of all sizes and shapes and colors entering and exiting the buildings, talking on the street in rich accents and different languages.

Her world felt very small in comparison.

"Come, we'll eat your lunch supplies at that table by the dock there. It's not raining, so we should take advantage of the fresh air while we can get it."

She followed him to a worn wooden table that faced out to the sea. He drew out the bundle of food she'd packed that morning and laid it out before them. Then he smiled. "We can afford one more thing. I'll be back."

He rushed off, leaving her alone for a moment. She stared out to sea, toward where she knew her family waited. Or at least, she hoped they waited. What if they had left Harcourt once her plan had been revealed? What if Harcourt had sent them away? It was possible she would reach her destination and not have anyplace to go. She'd have to find her own way to London then.

A dangerous prospect, indeed.

"You look as though you're waiting for the coach. Are you new passengers?"

Anne glanced up to see a man dressed in a bright waistcoat with a pretty lady on his arm. She was wearing a rather low-cut gown, but she had a nice smile as she looked down at Anne and her picnic.

"Er, yes," Anne said, thinking of the ruse Rook had suggested they'd follow on the road before she continued, "My—my husband and I just bought passage."

"The tall, handsome one who passed us a moment ago?" the lady purred as the two plopped down at their table without asking Anne's leave. "What a lucky lady."

Anne shifted, pulling her food from the middle as her new "friends" began to unpack their own meal and spread it out across from her. "I'm Herman Talon, at your service. This is my wife Imogen."

"Pleased to meet you," Anne said with a smile for the lady. "Anne Sh—Maitland."

"Shmaitland? That's an odd name," Mr. Talon said with a laugh and an elbow for his wife.

Anne shook her head and was about to correct him when Rook flopped into the seat next to her. "That's because Anne is still getting accustomed to being Mrs. Maitland," he explained with a chuckle as he slung an arm around her shoulders. The weight of it sank into her body and the heat of him seemed to warm her from head to toe. "She's always trying to use her maiden name."

She blushed and it wasn't forced. "Yes, silly me."

"It's very good, my love," he said softly. "Our new friends forgive you, I'm sure, as do I. Constantine Maitland, at your service," he said, holding a hand out to Mr. Talon.

She jerked at the given name he used. *Constantine* Maitland. Was that his real name? The one he'd avoided giving her all this time? She let it roll around in her head. It was such a big name. So formal and regal. She'd not expected it.

"What do you think, Anne?"

She jerked at Rook's question, spoken close to her ear. She blinked as she realized Mr. and Mrs. Talon had introduced themselves and Rook had been talking to them while she lost herself in thought about his name.

"I'm sorry, I'm afraid I was woolgathering," she admitted with a blush.

Rook pointed at the bottle of wine she hadn't realized he'd set on the table at some point during the conversation. "I said I thought you'd be happy to share our wine with our new friends."

She nodded. "Of course."

He made quick with opening the bottle and pouring into two glasses as Mrs. Talon rushed into the shop and came back with two more.

"To new friends," Mr. Talon toasted as he lifted his now-full glass. They clinked and as she drank, Anne felt the man's eyes sweep over her. Rook's fingers tightened on her shoulder as if he saw it too. She inched a little closer to his side.

"What business are you in, Talon?" Rook asked.

She watched him as the two men talked. He was different here with these strangers. His accent was heavier, harder, and he was more gregarious. It was like he was playing a game, and she wondered what part of Ellis's schemes he'd performed in the past. Not just a powerful brute, it seemed.

They talked for a while. Although the Talons were nice enough, she found herself nervous around them. She didn't look forward to a long ride in the carriage with them. It would be so close and warm and Mr. Talon never seemed to stop speaking.

Soon enough they finished their meal and wine and everyone got up to stretch their legs.

"They'll be loading up soon," Talon said, shifting his head toward the coach. "You coming?"

"We'll be sitting long enough soon," Rook said, sliding Anne's hand into the crook of his elbow. "I think my wife and I will take a short walk before we join you."

"Very good." The other couple walked away.

As soon as they were gone, Rook's smile fell and he watched them closely. "Stay away from them," he said softly. "Don't be alone with them."

She tilted her head as he guided her away from the coach and toward the path of the dock. "Why? They seem harmless enough, don't they? Just noisy."

He faced her, his dark eyes serious and intense on hers. "I know how to spot harmless. This isn't."

Her eyes felt wide as saucers as she glanced over her shoulder at the retreating backs of their former companions. "What could be the danger?"

Rook shifted like he was uncomfortable and then he ground out, "I'm fairly certain Talon collects women for entertainment. That's certainly not his wife. I swear I recognize her from certain kinds of shows in London. She might have been brought up to Scotland as a private entertainment for some rich man, with Talon as her escort... and 'protector.'"

Her mouth dropped open. "Oh."

"Yes. You'll be safe with me, but just...don't tell them too much about yourself. I wish we'd given another name than my own, honestly. He might know my cousin. Ellis involved himself with men like that...men worse than that...at one time."

She was nervous now about the ride with these potentially dangerous strangers and trying to stifle that response. "Did you give your real name? Constantine?"

He stopped walking and looked off into the distance. "My name is Rook, I told you that."

"That isn't the name you were given at birth," she said softly. "But the other is, isn't it?"

"I go by Rook," he said once more, and turned her toward the coach. "And they're loading the carriage, so we'd best go back."

She didn't press and allowed him to guide her back to the carriage and their supposed new friends. But she realized she'd seen two things that afternoon: a glimpse of the real Rook Maitland, and a glimpse of the man he'd pretended to be. And she wanted to know more about them both.

Rook walked up the narrow, smoky staircase in a cheap inn hours later, a frown on his face. It had been a very long afternoon in the coach. It stopped too often, it carried too many and it smelled vaguely of fish. Not to mention their friendly companions.

Talon and his "wife" had hardly drawn breath the entire ride. The man had dropped enough hints that Rook was more convinced than ever that they were a couple who ran a bawdy house in one of the cities and were out collecting ladies who would be open to such a place as an escape from whatever hell they were currently living in. It was a trick he'd seen before, performed by a different man. A very dangerous one. One who'd been the reason Rook had walked away from his cousin.

He hated how interested Talon was in Anne.

He hated *everything* about the day for Anne, honestly. She'd been quiet, she'd never complained, but he could tell she was over-whelmed by exposure to a rougher, louder life she'd never probably imagined, let alone lived.

She'd gone up to their room a while earlier. He'd arranged for a bath to be drawn for her and had stayed behind to give her privacy. Now he followed and tried very hard not to think about what he would find there in what was certainly going to be a tiny chamber that he would share with a beautiful, alluring lady he shouldn't touch.

The one he wanted to touch so much that his fingertips itched every time he got near her.

He sighed as he paused at the chamber door and tried to pull himself together. After a few breaths, he knocked.

There was rustling on the other side of the door, and then she opened it a crack. He caught his breath as she pulled the door wider to allow him entry.

Her hair was down. Wild, dark blonde waves bounced around her shoulders and covered up the demure nightrail she had changed into after she left him downstairs. Her hair looked soft and he could already smell it—roses, he thought, probably infused in the soap at the edge of the tub that had been placed behind the screen in the corner of the very tiny room.

Too tiny for two unless they were intimate, indeed. A narrow bed was pushed against the wall on one side of the room. Against the other were a settee and a table for tea. The tub and screen took up the corner beside the fire, and that was all there was.

A room meant for one person or a romantic couple. There would be no escape for him. No respite from being so close to her.

"Thank you for the bath," she said. "I hope it won't be too cold for you."

He shuddered as he thought of sinking beneath the waves of the water where she had washed herself a short time before. Perhaps a cold bath was best, after all.

"I'm certain it will be fine," he said, his voice rough with the desire he was having a hard time hiding now. If she looked down, she'd see evidence of it pushing out his trousers and making it hard to think because all the blood in his body was bent on reminding him that she was so damned close.

She took a step closer to him, worrying her hands in front of her. Her chest rose and fell on short breaths, her pupils were dilated and her cheeks flushed as she whispered, "Thank you for coming with me."

He tilted his head. "What is there to thank me for?"

"I-I couldn't have managed on my own," she said with a shake of her head. "I needed you." She worried her lip with her teeth and he was lost. "I *need* you."

It was too much. Even a monk couldn't have survived it. He reached his hand out, watching in what felt like slow motion as his fingers grazed her jawline, her cheek. She let out a shuddering sigh and leaned into his palm, lifting her face toward him in mute offering of the thing he'd wanted for days.

Probably since the first moment he saw her.

And he no longer had the strength to resist. He edged closer, his arm circling her waist as he tugged her flush to his body. She made a tiny sound of surprise and relief, but it was lost as he lowered his lips and finally claimed hers.

He hadn't planned for the kiss, but when he knew it would happen he had thought he would be gentle. A brief brush of lips and then release her. But that didn't happen. The moment their mouths met, it was chaos. Every hunger he'd ever felt, every need he'd ever suppressed came rushing to the surface and turned him into an animal who had finally conquered his prey.

He glided his tongue along the crease of her lips. She opened with another soft sound of pleasure, pulling him closer as her arms came around his neck.

There was nothing gentle about the way he claimed her, nothing sweet or careful. He devoured her, taking everything she offered, taking more and more as he tried to find the limit.

But she didn't request a limit. She met him stroke for stroke, timid at first, but then passionate as she tangled her tongue with his, as she lifted into him with a natural movement that spoke of passions she had been told never to feel. But of course Anne would feel them anyway. She was too independent to listen to anything but her own heart and mind.

Right now those things were steering her toward him. They were deepening the kiss. They were mewling out cries into his mouth that he swallowed as if they could sustain him like food or water. The fact that she had the same lack of control as he did only made things worse. He pushed at her, backing her toward the wall behind her, pressing her there as he dragged his mouth down her jaw, to her throat. He sucked and she slammed her hips against him with a shuddering cry that seemed to flutter through her body.

She tugged at him, and then she whispered, "Rook."

He froze. Rook. His name from the street. He was from the street, and he didn't belong in her chamber or her mouth or her bed or her body. He didn't belong. She only welcomed him in out of fear and upheaval and a need to find something solid to cling to.

She was compromised by the trauma of the past few weeks. He couldn't be so low as to take advantage of that any more than he had.

He pushed back, running a hand through his hair as he turned away. "Fuck."

She was silent for what felt like an eternity, and then she said it again. "Rook?"

He faced her slowly, trying to regain control. Trying not to let that animal take over again. The one that would lift her nightgown and make her come until she was weak and then put her in that bed and rut with her for as long as she would allow him that pleasure.

He would not listen to the worst part of him, the one that didn't care if he became her greatest regret.

"I'm going to take my cold bath," he panted. "And then I'm going to sleep on the settee."

Her lips parted. "Wh-why?"

He closed his eyes at the question. At the need laced in that simple word. "Because if I don't, I will do more than just kiss you, Anne. And that is a terrible idea. Please go to bed."

She stared at him a beat, and he thought she might refuse his request. He thought she might take what he wouldn't offer and he knew he wouldn't be strong enough to refuse that a second time.

But then she nodded. "Very well."

She turned away and got into the bed, sliding beneath the covers and turning her back to him. He shook his head and went behind the screen to undress and bathe.

And his hard cock and regrets were his only company as he did so.

CHAPTER 9

After lying awake half the night, painfully aware of Rook on the settee so close beside her, Anne had been certain she would never sleep. But she must have, for she woke the next morning to the sound of heavy rain pelting the glass windows. She stared up at the cracked ceiling above her, girding her strength before she lifted her head and peeked toward the settee.

Rook was gone.

She supposed she should have been relieved. After all, what had happened last night...The Kiss—she had to refer to it as *The* Kiss because it wasn't just *a* kiss—had haunted her mind ever since. It had been a foolish thing to allow. A wrong thing. A thing that proved she was somehow unfit, somehow broken when it came to her desires...

But God, she wanted more. The moment his mouth had claimed hers, all she'd wanted to do was find a way to get closer to him. All she'd wanted to do was explore those wicked things she'd read in the book she'd found in her father's study months ago.

She'd wanted his hands on her and his tongue on her and his body joined with hers, wherever and however she could get it. Caution and reason and prudence had fled whatever tiny corner they occupied in her mind, and she'd been left with throbbing, pounding, wicked need pulsing through her blood.

And then he'd rejected her.

She frowned as she got up and shook out the dress she'd laid out for herself last night. Slowly, she put herself together, gown and hair, and pinched her cheeks as she looked at her pale, drawn face in the cracked mirror.

She'd felt the passion of his touch last night. But he'd been fully able to break away from her. He was capable where she was not.

She shook her head as she took another look around the room. His things were still stacked neatly on the settee by the low fire. It looked uncomfortable, and she supposed she could take some small, cold comfort in that. At least he probably hadn't slept well either. She sighed as she left her small bag next to his things and made her way downstairs to look for him.

As she exited the chamber, she caught a whiff of delicious breakfast scents. She followed the bacon-and-bread aura down into the dining hall at the bottom of the stairs. When she entered the room, she stopped.

Rook was there, seated by the window where rain streaked down. He was reading the paper, a plate of food half-eaten before him.

She drew a deep breath, trying to control the rapid increase of her heart, and approached with a wavering smile. "Good morning."

He glanced up at her and for a moment, his stare was only possessive heat that curled its way into her belly and made her legs shake and clench. Then he darted his gaze away and nodded. "Good morning."

She sat without waiting for his leave and smiled as the barmaid across the room waved to indicate she'd seen her enter. Rook carefully folded the paper and she noted that the date on the item was over a week old.

"Like to read the old news?" she asked with what she hoped was a light smile.

He didn't return it, but sipped what appeared to be black coffee. "This paper only arrived today. It always takes these things a while to get out here, but with the weather and the state of the roads…"

He trailed off and she winced. "I assume that means our own journey will also be slowed."

He nodded once, his mouth tightening. "I asked about the stage this morning and it sounds as if it may hold back today and not go until tomorrow, if even then. They fear the wheels being stuck in the muddy roads."

She caught her breath. That meant at least one more day on the road once they got started at all. One more day away from her family and the forgiveness she'd be forced to seek when she saw them again.

One more night in this inn and the room that felt so small whenever Rook was in it.

It felt like an eternity. But he showed no reaction and smiled up at the barmaid who set a plate in front of Anne and poured her tea before bobbing away, whistling a little tune like the world wasn't falling apart around her.

He truly wasn't affected by the kiss. That was evident. Yet he had driven it, claiming her lips with abandon and then stepping away just when she was ready to surrender. Why? Why, if he didn't even want her?

"Why did you kiss me?" she asked, then clapped a hand over her mouth. She hadn't actually meant to voice the question out loud, the answer might be too humiliating.

He choked on his coffee, coughing into his napkin as he stared at her with watering eyes. She shook her head. At least she had moved him to some kind of reaction.

When he'd regained his breath, he glanced around the room, as if someone might have heard her.

She shrugged. "They all think we're married anyway, Rook. But we're…we're not."

He drew a long breath and fiddled with the lip of his cup with the tip of his finger. It was an oddly mesmerizing motion. Then he said, "I kissed you because you're stunning. And I've spent almost every moment since the first one I saw you wishing to do just that. Any pot left on the fire long enough will boil."

She gaped at him. Every moment since the first he'd seen her? She'd had no idea. She'd honestly thought he didn't feel much of anything for her, especially in the early days of her arrival on his island when she'd hidden. He'd done nothing to press his case.

Even when she'd seen the fleeting desire in his eyes, even when she'd caught him...pleasuring himself...she'd believed that was general need, not specifically about her. And yet Rook claimed, quietly and calmly, that he desired her. That he had been unable to resist when he took what he'd denied himself.

Her blood quickened with the unexpected confession.

"Oh," she managed to squeak out.

He lifted his brows. "Oh?"

She shook her head and dropped her gaze. She couldn't look at him when she said, "I-I just thought the desire was only on my side. A deficit of my character and mine alone."

"A deficit of character? What does that mean?" he asked.

She still didn't look at him, she couldn't bear to, but stared at her clenched fingers that trembled in her lap. "I was engaged to one man, I convinced myself to run off with another, and now here I am with a third man and wanting...wanting what I do not even know how to describe, let alone ask for. You *must* think ill of me, you do not have to hide it. Anyone would."

He was silent for what felt like a very long time. Then he cleared his throat. "There may be many things I feel which I hide from you, Anne," he said softly. "But none of them are ill, I assure you."

She did glance at him then and saw that he had leaned forward and was staring at her intently. His gaze held hers for a moment, a long, charged moment. Then he shook his head and pushed back from the table.

"But we can only want, not act," he said. "That's all we can do."

He stood. "I'll check again on our options. I think carrying on the road would be our best option if there is any way to do it."

She watched him stride away, longing for the very thing she chastised herself for, that he denied her. Then she shook her head as the air left her body in a shuddering sigh.

"You're a lucky one."

Anne looked up as the barmaid took Rook's plate with a smile for her. "Lucky?" she repeated weakly.

"To be married to a man who looks at you like that one does," the girl explained. "I see a lot of folk come through these doors. Not many as handsome as him. Or as besotted."

She walked away, leaving Anne to rest her elbows on the table edge and her head in her hands. Besotted Rook was definitely *not*. It was *she* who had the complicated, unstoppable feelings. And the longer they stayed together, the harder she knew it would become to deny them.

R ook walked down the muddy street, tugging his hat brim low across his forehead and hunching his shoulders against the unrelenting rain. He was cold and miserable and only half of that had to do with the weather.

The other half? Well, that was all about the lack of options he had when it came to getting Anne home, or at least to Gretna Green where he could assure her safe passage more easily. The coach was held up and the driver was talking about staying a third night to let the roads dry up even if the rain stopped soon.

The mail coach wasn't expected for another two days either, and Rook couldn't afford its higher fee. Perhaps if he sent Anne on alone, but after watching her be ogled by Talon the previous day, he wasn't about to set her free into a world of danger.

There were no other options, not with the amount of blunt in his pocket, which had to be budgeted for rooms and board, as well.

He was stuck. They'd spend another night in the bed at the inn together. And tonight he might not be able to stop himself when temptation stepped around the screen in her thin nightrail.

If he touched her again…

But no, he couldn't think of that. He couldn't *stop* thinking about it, but it wasn't right. Wasn't right to picture her up in that tiny room even now. Wasn't right to fantasize about joining her.

He shook his head as he rounded the last corner toward the inn. The stable for the carriages and horses was full thanks to the weather, and as he moved to pass it, the sound of a familiar feminine voice caught his attention. He pivoted and found Anne standing beneath the awning, speaking to the horsemaster, an earnest expression on her face.

He moved toward her in time to hear her declare, "Thank you for your help, sir. You do not know what it means."

"A pleasure doing business with you, Mrs. Maitland."

A flutter of emotion came over her face at the name, but she merely nodded and shook the man's hand before she turned and nearly ran headlong into Rook. Her face lit up as she stared up at him, and his heart stuttered against his will.

"What are you doing here?" he asked.

She smiled. "Come inside, it's too dreadful to discuss in the rain. You can warm up and I can explain everything."

He thought to argue, but she was right about the weather, so he followed her back into the inn, divesting himself of his dripping greatcoat and hat. The steamy main room was buzzing with activity as the trapped guests had their afternoon tea and gossiped with each other in a merry cacophony of sound and smells and sights.

She caught his hand unexpectedly and drew him toward the stairs. "Why don't we talk in our chamber?"

She had gone up two steps when she said it and he stopped, bringing her up short, as well. She turned back, her eyes bright as she stared down at him. They were almost equal height now, she only an inch higher thanks to the stairs. He stared into green eyes and felt the test of her suggestion in every inch of his aching body.

"I don't know if that's a good idea," he murmured.

There was an emotion that flashed over her face. Pain. Rejection. Then she smiled. "It would be better to have privacy for what we need to talk over. Please."

It was the please that did him in. He nodded and followed her the rest of the way to the room. The bed had been made and the place tidied, he thought probably by Anne since the coverlet was slightly cockeyed. He smiled despite the pressure of being alone with her and shut the door behind himself before he moved to the fire to warm up.

"What did you need privacy to discuss, Anne?" he asked. "And what were you doing at the stable?"

She clapped her hands together. "I have found a solution to our problem."

He cocked his head. "A solution to our traveling problem?" He doubted it, but he shrugged. "What is that?"

"I bought two horses."

He had been angled away from her at the fire, but now he pivoted in shock. "What?"

She smiled. "I couldn't stop thinking about it, Rook. Any carriage we could hire, whether the stage or the mail coach or even if we could afford something private, the problem will remain the same. Muddy roads, ruts that break axels…and company like the very unpleasant Mr. Talon. It's too slow and too dependent on others. And it occurred to me that we could buy horses, and then we would be dependent only on their needs and our own for rest and recovery. They'll handle the mud better. And once the roads become dry, they could make the trip fast as a dream."

He had stared at her in silence as she declared the utter truth of the situation without explaining herself in the slightest. He stepped toward her. "Horses are expensive," he said. "And I wonder how in the world you paid for them."

She swallowed and the brightness left her expression as she shifted away from him. "It doesn't matter."

He flinched. He knew several ways to trade for what she had arranged. God, was she so desperate she would give away the thing he had sought last night in this very room?

"Tell me," he said, lower, firmer as he caught her arm and turned her back into him. Touching her was torture, as was the way she lifted her face toward his. He saw the tremble of her lower lip, the dewy glaze of tears in those startling green eyes.

"I simply traded something I didn't need."

"Anne!" he burst out. "I cannot let you do something like that. To trade your body is of no little consequence. And you cannot imagine—"

She jolted back from him and ripped her arm away. "Trade my body? No!" She shook her head as she stared at him in shock. "I-I wouldn't even know how to go about doing such a thing. Certainly I can imagine the circumstances where a lady might be ready to give that little thing that is so valued by society, but *I* didn't make that kind of arrangement, I assure you."

Relief flowed through him like a raging river and he sank into the settee to stare up at her. "Then what *did* you trade?"

Her finger moved up to her neck and he watched her fingers flutter around the bare spot there. He wrinkled his brow. She'd had a necklace before, a little cross with emeralds that matched her eyes.

"Anne," he breathed as he rose to his feet. "You didn't."

She shrugged and tried to make her expression bright, as it had been earlier. "The necklace was given to me by my father. My sisters have a matching one."

"It was likely worth more than the two nags we'll end up with from that stable," he said. "Certainly, it is worth more in sentimental value."

She struggled for a moment, her hands clenching at her sides, her chin lifting and trembling. Then she cleared her throat, fighting for the strength he so admired in her from the beginning. "My *family* is worth more. So what is the better thing, Rook? The sentimental attachment to a *thing* which represents them? Or returning as early as possible to beg forgiveness for the pain and fear I no doubt caused my sweet sisters?"

He tried to think of an argument against that, but he couldn't. And she was right that having horses would make the trip back much faster and easier for them both, though not as sheltered as the carriage would have.

And yet he saw the drive on her expression. The dedication to making amends to the sisters she truly loved. How could he deny that, if nothing else?

He moved toward her a step, closing the distance that separated them in the tiny room. She caught her breath as she looked up at him and the chamber shrank all the more. He realized he had to touch her again. He realized what that would do.

But he did it anyway. Slowly he caught her elbow, his fingers folding across the soft fabric of her gown as he met her gaze and held there with difficulty.

"If you are set on this course, I won't argue," he said. "I hear the rain letting up and we can likely make at least a small portion of travel today if we leave within the hour on your horses. But if you question this decision to leave some part of yourself behind here in this village, I'll go down and do everything in my power to get that necklace back for you."

Her lips parted and then she shook her head. "I've left a part of me behind everywhere I've been since the moment I ran from my fiancé's home, Rook. At least this is my choice. And it will help me get home. I think of it as atonement."

"Very well," he said softly. "I'll go down and get everything set for our departure. Meet me in front of the inn in half an hour and I should be ready to depart."

She nodded. "I'll arrange a bit of food for the road."

He turned to go, but she reached out, resting her hand on his chest, right above his heart. The warmth of her touch immediately permeated all the layers of wool and linen, like her skin was against his even though it wasn't.

"Rook," she whispered. "Thank you. I know I've said it before, but I must keep saying it, I think, for your kindness seems to know no bounds. And your support for what I know is a foolish plan is much appreciated."

He frowned, for what he wanted to do was sweep her into his arms and carry her to that bed and take away the pain for a few moments. Quiet the desperation even a fraction with his mouth and his cock.

But he couldn't do that. Not for her sake, not for his own. So he merely tipped his head and stepped away from her touch. But as he exited into the hallway and away from her, he couldn't help but ponder her desperation further. It endangered her. It already had. And so did he, when he came to the truth of it.

He had to be careful from now on. And remember that Anne Shelley wasn't his to kiss. Or comfort. Or anything else.

CHAPTER 10

As punishments for foolish decisions went, having to ride a horse in the misery of Scottish rain was fairly high on Anne's list. The storm had ultimately eased about an hour into their ride. There were even pockets of time when the rain ceased entirely and there was gray, filtered sun that hit the muddy road before them.

But as the afternoon faded and the evening grew near, the cold was not put off by the layers of cheap but serviceable wool Rook had purchased for her at the village before they left.

"About half an hour and we'll make it to our stop," he said, as if he could read her mind. Or perhaps just the shiver she hadn't been able to control when it wracked her body.

"Good. I suppose we haven't made much progress on the road, have we?" she asked, already guessing the answer from the slow gait they'd had to utilize in the horrid weather. "*Dreich* is truly the word for it."

He laughed at her quip and the sound of it warmed her briefly. "No, but better than staying behind and waiting two to three days to get on the road," he reassured her and then he grew serious again. "I will do everything in my power to make the sacrifice you made for the horses be worthwhile in the end."

She smiled at the vow. But it made her wonder about this man who seemed to have some honor, a great deal of it, actually.

"You and your cousin are so different," she mused. "It seems so odd to me that you would work together at criminal endeavors."

He tensed on the horse, a subtle movement that she noticed but doubted anyone not so focused on him would. He was very good at hiding his heart, his emotions. "I told you, it was a rough life," he said, obviously through clenched teeth. "We did what we had to do to survive it."

"But you left," she said softly.

"How do you know I left?" he asked, tossing her a wink and using that same tone he'd used with Mr. Talon in the carriage the day before. False and bright and not like the Rook she knew at all.

He was hiding from her with that gregarious attitude. Playing at being someone and something he wasn't. Which meant he wasn't comfortable with the truth. But did she respect that boundary he had erected or push it?

"I think you must have left," she said, unable to do anything but push, just as she'd done all her life. "Why else would you sequester yourself on an island in the middle of nowhere, whittling beautiful things with your knives instead of throwing them, and reluctant to aid Ellis when he asked?"

"Not so reluctant," he muttered. "I did it, didn't I?"

"I suppose. But you seemed to take no pleasure in the action, at least at first."

"Some pleasure," he corrected with a quick glance. "More than perhaps I should have taken."

He meant their kiss. Her body tightened at the reminder of his mouth on hers. His hands on her. That tingling, fluid feeling he created in every muscle and bone and nerve in her body with just a brush of his fingertips.

And yet that reminder was another wall, not an open door. She pursed her lips. "You certainly don't have to tell me anything. I owe you far more than you owe me."

He was silent for a moment, his gaze focused straight ahead on the road. Then he sighed. "I'm not sure that's true. Look, Anne…"

He trailed off and she felt him gathering himself, fighting for words. She leaned forward as she waited for them and they came at last, halting and pained.

"Ellis is four years older than I am. He was on the street before I was. He was already in the life before he dragged me in to…" His voice hitched. "…to save me."

"Save you?" she repeated, leaning to look at him better, frustrated when he turned his face so she couldn't.

He shook his head. "He needed a tool. I was that tool."

"His rook," she said softly, the truth of him and that nickname coming clear.

"Yes," he said. "Ellis was raised by the street and so was I, but he knew strategy and the game and a lot of other things that people of your lofty class don't give mine credit for. He taught himself to read with my help. He studied and beat the street accent out of us both. He forced us to find a way to fit into worlds where we didn't belong so we could strip them of their valuables. But his favorite thing was chess. People recognize the importance of the queen in the game, but some underestimate the rook. Underestimate a man like me. *He* counted on it."

"You were the piece he used to protect the king," she mused. "To protect himself."

"Yes." There was something to the hesitation in his voice that told her that there was yet more to this tale that he still held back.

"Did you like that?" she asked.

"No," he admitted. "Not always. Not toward the end. You said I left, and I…did."

"Why?"

He was silent for what felt like an eternity, and she fought every instinct inside of her to allow him to be silent. To remind herself that she wasn't owed this story. She wasn't owed anything.

At last he said, "He went too far." She was going to press for more detail when Rook pointed toward the horizon. "There is the town we'll stop at. They're already lighting the lamps for dusk. Come, let's ride harder to get there before whatever little sun we have left vanishes."

He didn't leave room for her to argue, but dug his heels into the horse to urge it forward. She followed with a nicker to her mount as they trotted toward the village and the future, leaving the past he had revealed behind in the mud.

But she couldn't forget he'd shared that past with her. Or that by knowing him better she only wanted what he had to give all the more. No matter how dangerous the prospect. No matter how terrifying. Because she was running out of anything to lose with surrender, and if she didn't, she would always wonder what if.

Once again, Rook and Anne had shared a meal together at a small roadside inn that was part of a tiny village along their road. She had talked about books she liked, music, about the weather and the roads.

He had felt her desire to put him at ease after his confession. The one he'd never intended to make. And yet with Anne, the words had spilled from his lips, the memories burning his brain. Thoughts of the life he'd led on the street. Thoughts of the reasons he'd abandoned his cousin at last.

Things this woman could never know without coming to hate him, fear him.

He didn't want that, not when their affiliation was meant to be so brief. He wanted it to remain sweet. And so he pulled away before he said or did too much.

She'd gone up to ready herself before him, just as the night before. There would be no hot bath waiting for him tonight, as there had been in the last inn. But the innkeeper had offered one tomorrow if they decided to delay their ceaseless march toward the inevitable parting.

He sighed as he mounted the stairs. He could only imagine the room tonight would be even smaller than the one before, for the inn was smaller. It might not even have a settee, and that would be a challenge.

He knocked, she told him to enter and he did so, his heart racing like an out of control phaeton. She stood before the mantel in her nightgown, her hair down around her shoulders. The light from the fire outlined the silhouette of her naked body beneath, and everything in him clenched as he shut the door behind himself and stared at her.

She smiled, faint and nervous, but also welcoming. And he couldn't help himself or stop himself or check himself. He moved across the room toward her and gathered her into his arms before he dropped his mouth to hers for the kiss he'd been longing for the last twenty-four hours.

Anne had known Rook would kiss her from the moment he stepped into the room. His expression had burned too hot and fierce for it not to happen. But when his mouth met hers, it was still a surprise at how sensation ricocheted through every part of her being. He was fire and danger and monsters under the bed, only she wanted all those things despite everything she'd been told all her life.

Perhaps *because* of what she'd been told and how she'd bucked against rules from the moment she could stand on her own two feet. She was the wicked triplet, and she wanted wicked things tonight.

She wrapped her arms around his neck and lifted to get closer, rubbing her cotton-clad breasts across the linen of his shirt, hissing out pleasure as his hands settled, one on her lower back and one on her hip, where his fingers dug into her flesh and left a tattoo of his desire in their wake.

She wanted the mark there. She wanted to have a reminder that she was his, even for a fleeting moment.

She'd thought of nothing else since he first kissed her, and those thoughts had gotten louder all through the day today. She wanted him. She needed him.

So when he pulled away at last, his breath short, his trousers straining against what she knew was called his cock, her heart sank. He would deny her a second time. Too much honor, despite being a thief, for her to convince him with her lips.

"I can't," he said.

She shook her head, stinging from the rejection. "Why? Is it for lack of wanting me?"

He bit back a bark of laughter that had no humor to it. "Look at me, Anne." He motioned to his trouser front with a scowl. "If it was just about wanting, you would be on your back right now."

She shivered at the crass, direct words and the way they made her nipples tighten even if they were meant to frighten her back in line. "Then is it a lack of respect for me? That you think I'm a wanton?"

He rolled his eyes. "You are not a wanton, no matter what you tell yourself about the last six months of your life. Even if you were, wanting is natural. Needing to be touched and pleasured is natural. You *should* want and find a man who revels in providing your pleasure. But it isn't that."

She threw up her hands, as frustrated as she was drawn to his acceptance and withdrawal balled up in one. "Then what? If you want and you think I should want as I do, what keeps you from putting me on my back, as you put it?"

He rubbed a hand through his hair and then down his face with a loud exhalation of breath that sounded very much like a muffled curse of the highest order. "You know what I told you today, even if

I shouldn't have," he snapped. "*That* is why I shouldn't touch you. Won't."

She caught her breath. He kept away from her to protect her, not to protect himself or because she had something lacking in her. But she didn't want to be protected. Not from him. Not from the heat that gathered between her legs or the tight need that coiled in her stomach.

She knew what she wanted. And it had always been her nature to take it.

She stepped toward him, shaking from head to toe as she tried to find some confidence. Normally it didn't take this much effort, but months of self-doubt had crushed it. Still, she stopped in front of him, watching how his eyes widened and his hands trembled at his sides.

Then she took a deep breath and slid the straps of her nightgown down her arms. The entire garment pooled at her feet with the barest shimmy of her hips and she was naked in front of him.

"Fuck," he muttered beneath his breath as she struggled not to cover herself in embarrassment.

She'd heard that word before. Rook had said it after he kissed her. She'd read it in that book of her father's. She knew what it meant.

"Yes," she said with a shaky smile. "That's the idea."

His pupils dilated until his gaze was almost entirely black, and he reached out and caught her wrist. When he dragged her forward, it was rough, and she collided with his chest as she lost her balance. His mouth covered hers again, but this time there was nothing gentle to it. Nothing he held back.

He lifted her against him, grinding their bodies together as he carried her toward the bed along the back wall of the room. He tossed her there and then stepped back to unbutton his shirt and tug it over his head. He toed off his boots and shoved at his trousers, and then he was as naked as she was.

Her breath caught. Once again, books did not do truth justice, even the most scandalously illustrated ones. This man's body was... well, it was unlike anything she'd ever seen or imagined. He was built of stone. His broad, defined shoulders were crossed with scars, but they were also firm with muscle and sinew. There was a beauty to the rippled, toned stomach that put her to mind of sketches of the David. And then there were the trim hips and strong thighs, between which his cock rested.

Only it wasn't exactly resting. It was erect, hard and proud as he stared down at her.

"You look frightened," he drawled, a hint of a smile in the corner of his lips. "Do you want me to stop?"

There was a brief moment when every inch of propriety that had ever been screamed into her by members of her family and exasperated governesses came back to haunt her. Their words echoed and her fear at what would happen next bloomed, and she thought of saying no.

But then she looked at that smirk and realized he was challenging her. Trying to turn her back by being rough and passionate and too big and too...too everything.

She scooted back on the bed to give him room and crooked her finger.

"I'm not afraid of anything," she whispered.

There was a flash of sadness in his stare. "Perhaps you should be. But not this."

He dropped to his knees on the bed, bowing the thin mattress with his weight and sliding her toward him an inch. He grinned and then he caught her legs, his fingers closing on flesh that no man had ever seen, let alone taken in hand. He dragged her toward him before he caged her with his arms and dropped his mouth again.

She opened to him, drowning in his taste and the feel of his tongue swiping over hers over and over. She arched up against his bare chest, her hard nipples rasping against the sprinkling of chest hair there.

He pulled back and smiled down at her, still wicked, still something between her quiet, serious protector and the false game he played in the carriage. Then his mouth dropped, but not to her lips. He pressed kisses along her jawline, her throat, her collarbone.

She gripped at the coverlet with shock at the sensations he caused with those kisses. How could her whole body feel alive like this? How could the brush of his stubble or the stroke of his tongue over her shoulder make her body shake with anticipation?

He licked lower still, settling his head between her breasts. He kept eye contact with her as he lifted them, squeezing them together gently, stroking his thumbs over the peaks until she gasped out a cry in the quiet room.

His grin broadened and became more possessive as he sucked one nipple between his lips. His tongue rolled around the nub and then he sucked, not gently but not too hard. Her head lolled back as sensation unlike anything she'd ever felt before rolled through her. Her legs clenched helplessly, her body felt loose and liquid, and she dug her fingernails into his bare shoulders as she clung for purchase on this rolling sea of desire.

Just when she thought she couldn't take it anymore, he moved to the opposite breast and repeated the action, drawing her to the heights of pleasure and need, then moving his mouth away as she groaned in disappointment and pleasure mixed.

She expected him to return his mouth to hers, to open her legs like she'd seen in those drawings and take her. But he didn't. To her surprise, his mouth glided down her stomach, his teeth nipping gently as his fingers massaged her hips. She shut her eyes as his hands settled on her thighs, fingertips grazing sensitive skin and making her hiss and jolt with sensation.

He did push her open then, making a wide space between her legs for his shoulders. Her eyes flew open and she stared down her body at his dark head between her legs. The stolen book hadn't shown this. Hadn't allowed her to expect that a man would be eye level with her most private of places. She felt exposed, more so when he brushed a finger along her length and looked up at her to gauge her response.

"You're still certain?" he asked. Challenged.

She set her jaw and nodded. "The only one hesitating is you."

His mouth quirked, though there was a dark storm in his eyes. He stroked her again with his fingertip. She arched up, heels digging in around his hips as he touched her so intimately. How could something that set her on fire be something she craved so deeply and powerfully?

He pressed his thumbs against her outer lips and gently massaged her until they parted, revealing the entrance to her core. She sat up, her hand coming to settle against his thick hair. "Rook," she whispered.

His eyes lifted and he was no longer teasing her when he whispered, "I'll stop if you want me to, Anne."

She shook her head and caught her breath at his dark gaze staring up at her from such an intimate position. "Don't stop. I just...I'm...I am..."

"You don't have to say it," he reassured her as he lowered his head again. "Just feel it."

His tongue touched her, and she cried out. The feel of him against her tender flesh was a shock both emotionally and physically. He was licking her, over and over, gentle at first, allowing her body to grow accustomed to this intimate invasion. But as the crackle of electric heat whizzed through her veins, he increased the pressure of his tongue, flattening it against her entrance, pushing it inside of her, stroking his nose along the bundle of nerves at the top of her sex. She jolted and cried out again, and he darted his tongue up to circle her in a smooth, steady rhythm that pushed pleasure through her entire body.

"Rook!" she cried out again, clinging to the coverlet, pushing against his mouth.

He glanced up, breaking contact for a moment so he could look at her. "Constantine," he panted.

Her eyes went wide as they stared at each other. So the name he gave the day before *had* been his true one. And now he was asking her to say it, to moan it, to cry it out as he returned his mouth to her sex and sucked her clitoris.

She obliged, repeating his name as she lifted her body and ground against him. They moved together, one body, her cries increasing, his tongue doing the same, and at last the pleasure he built burst like a dam with too much behind it. She trembled, her body spasming against his mouth as wave after wave of unbelievable pleasure slammed into her body. He licked her through it all, offering no respite until she went weak against the pillows, sweat on her brow and legs shaking with release.

He crawled up the length of her body, nuzzling her stomach, caressing her breast with his rough cheek until he was face to face with her. He leaned in and kissed her, letting her taste the sweet and salty flavor of her own orgasm.

Then he pulled away, his face still close to hers. "I want you, Anne. More than I have ever wanted anything in my life. But I am not worthy."

She opened her mouth to argue, but he dropped his finger on her lips gently. "I'm a villain, even if I walked away from my past. I'm not good. I don't deserve your body, I didn't deserve your pleasure. I won't deserve your innocence."

"Constantine," she whispered, hating how broken his expression was. Hating that he believed all these things to be true. Hating that they might be, for she didn't know the lengths he'd gone to, even if she couldn't picture him as a true villain.

He flinched at the use of his name, as if he didn't want to grant her that intimacy now that he was no longer between her legs. He shook his head. "I *will* take you if you offer yourself to me again."

"Then take me," she murmured.

He laughed, but it was pained. "No, you need to think a little harder about the consequences of what you want. Truly think about it, Anne. Think about the kind of man you want to share that gift with. And I'll ask you tomorrow night what your thoughts are."

He kissed her again, this time more gently, and rolled away from her. He pulled the covers up, put his back to her and that was the end of the discussion.

She stared at that muscular back, eyes wide and utterly confused about what had just happened. She'd seen the irrefutable evidence of his desire and he'd given her pleasure she never could have imagined even in her wildest, hottest dreams. And now he was...snoring?

Was he *snoring*? As if it meant nothing. As if his declaration that he would have her if she asked him just one more time didn't hang in the air all around her. She flopped a hand over her eyes and let out her breath in a long, frustrated stream.

He had shattered her into a thousand beautiful pieces and she knew she'd never be fully the same again. She didn't want to be the same. She wanted him. Only it was more than wanting now, wasn't it? It had gone beyond wanting what felt like a long time ago, not just days.

She was beginning to feel connected to Rook...Constantine. And that was what she had to ponder. Because if he took her, there would always be a part of her that belonged to him. And that was more terrifying a prospect than anything else.

CHAPTER 11

R ook had had many women. Sex was something he enjoyed—
it was something he sought when his body needed it, and it
was something he knew he was good at. He couldn't be satisfied if
his partner wasn't equally or more so, and he'd developed every
talent he could to ensure a woman who left his bed left flushed with
pleasure.

But he'd never felt anything in his thirty years that compared to
the need that burned within him for Anne Shelley. He'd pretended
to be asleep last night after he brought her to explosive completion
in that bed, but he hadn't slept. He'd stared at the wall, his throbbing
cock punishment for going too far, and he'd just...*thought* about her.

Not about taking her, though those fantasies were in full force, it
seemed, at every moment. But of being with her. Of making her
laugh, of hearing her whoop of accomplishment when she found a
clam in the sand or hit a target with a knife. He thought of her
strength of character and her good heart and her focused drive to
pursue what she wanted.

He thought of all the things that would make it so easy to do
more than merely want her. And he thought of all the ugly reasons
he would never earn the right to do so.

He frowned as they picked up their pace on the road. They'd risen early, gathered their things and been riding ever since. The morning had been difficult, with spattering rain and muddy, rutty roads to manage. But after their brief stop for a cold lunch, the weather and the roads had improved. They wouldn't reach Gretna Green tonight, but they would only be a day's ride from it.

A day's ride from a potential separation he didn't want to think about.

She shifted, seemingly as anxious as he was if her expression was any indication. She had grown quieter as the day grew long, and he had to wonder if she was pondering his statement that he would ask her again tonight if she wanted to give herself to him.

That he would not resist if the answer was yes.

"Why Constantine?" she finally blurted out with a quick side glance for him.

He jolted at the question and the way she'd said his name yet again. He'd asked her to do it while he pleasured her because he didn't want to be the man who had done those things that made her an impossible dream. Now when she said it, the sound of each vowel and consonant in her husky voice put him on edge.

"Why…what?" he asked, trying to focus.

"Your name," she clarified with a small laugh at his misunderstanding. "It's so…it's such a big name. Why did she pick it?"

"You have a lot of interest in my names," he said, trying to keep his voice light, maintain distance by being playful.

She arched a brow at him. "How could I not be when—"

She trailed off and he stared straight ahead. "When I ravished you?"

"Er, no. Well, *yes*, I suppose that should make a person interested in a name, but I meant more that we've become…friends. Haven't we, Rook…Constantine…Rook?"

He smiled despite himself at her stammering confusion about what name should be his. He rather liked both coming from her lips, even though he hated each name for various reasons.

"If you are offering to be my friend, I certainly recognize that is a gift," he said with a slight incline of his head. He pondered the question again for a moment. Ran through every reason he had not to answer it. Then he did it anyway. "My mother earned her living on her back and was often dismissed for being nothing because of it."

He saw her glance at him, but couldn't tell her reaction to the statement that his mother had been a lightskirt. So he continued on, "She had a *brilliant* mind. She loved to read, which is where I learned. History, especially, fascinated her. And she loved Scotland —she grew up here. Not far from my island, actually. Constantine was the name of two kings of Scotland. I suppose she had loftier goals for me than I had for myself."

"It's a fine name," she said softly.

"Finer than I deserve, considering what she would think of the path I took." He stared straight ahead at the road, trying to picture the mother he'd lost so long ago that he could hardly remember the color of her hair or the sound of her voice.

"It sounds like you picked a path which allowed you to survive, and I'm sure that's what she would want for you," Anne said slowly. "You said she died when you were quite young."

He drew a shaky breath. He never spoke about this, not with anyone. Not even Ellis, though his cousin knew the particulars. But now he found himself wanting to tell Anne about his mother. For himself, but also to help her better understand the decision she was making by giving herself to someone from such a different world.

"She had a protector, or he called himself that."

"Like Mr. Talon," Anne whispered with a shiver.

He flinched. "Yes, I admit Talon put me to mind of the bastard who affiliated himself with my mother. Perhaps that was part of why I reacted so strongly. My mother's man managed who she spent her time with. He controlled her money, though that just meant stealing it and drinking and gambling it away." He shook his head. "He beat her when he thought she deserved it. He beat me because he hated that I existed and proved the bitterest consequences of what she did. And perhaps because she loved me and didn't love him."

Anne's sharp catch of breath drew his attention back to her. She was watching him as she rode, her face pink and her eyes filled with unshed tears at his story.

"She got sick," he said softly. "And that meant she couldn't work. And that meant she was of no value to him anymore. He tried to get me to work for him instead. He didn't care how he got his money, he just wanted it."

"You were a child!" she burst out. "You mean he wanted you to—"

He turned his face and tried not to think about the truth even as he explained it to this woman who was so far removed from that bitter world.

"There are men with…appetites—" He cut himself off because it was too much for her. Too much for him. "It never happened because of my cousin. Ellis was older, ten to my six years. He somehow heard about the bastard's plan and suddenly he was there. He told me to run away with him, that I had smaller hands so I could get into tight spaces to steal better. I ran. I never saw my mother again." He cleared his throat, wishing he could clear the emotion that burned in him. "She died a few weeks later."

"Constantine," Anne whispered, pulling her horse to the right off the road and into a field that ran alongside it. She got off, patting the animal absently before she paced into the field without care for the water that clung to the vegetation and dampened her skirts.

He followed, for what choice did he have, and got off his own mount. He watched her as he stretched his back and waited for her disgust or her judgment about the terrible story he'd told. When she faced him, though, it was none of those things he saw.

She moved toward him in three long steps and reached up to cup his cheeks. "What you went through is something I cannot even imagine, having been raised in my ivory tower in a place so far from where you began."

So she knew. So she understood. He supposed he should be happy for that. It was better for her.

She lifted on her tiptoes and brushed her lips against his, then wrapped her arms around him and just...held him. He stiffened, for he couldn't recall the last time he'd been hugged. It felt so good he thought might melt into her and never be free of this.

He'd never want to be free.

She rubbed her face against his collar. "You are so remarkable. Your strength is so admirable."

He drew back and stared down into her upturned face. She wasn't playing him for a fool, she wasn't placating or pitying him for his past. She looked at him and saw him and it was...terrifying.

He took a long step back and nodded. "Very good. We should move on, though. We're close to the next village where we'll stop for the night."

Her lips thinned at his rejection of her support, but she didn't confront him about it. She simply walked to where her horse was grazing in the field and patted her flank again gently.

"How far to Gretna Green after tonight?" she asked.

He focused on retying the knot on his saddlebag that was perfectly fine. Anything not to look at her and let her see into his soul again. "Ten miles or so. With these improved roads, we should have no trouble reaching the town by tomorrow afternoon."

She nodded, but it was slow in his peripheral vision. "There will be more choices for transportation there, I think."

He hesitated. "Yes. Post carriages, private ones. It's a big enough city, you may even bump into acquaintances who could carry you to wherever you'd like to go."

She looked at him long enough that he was forced to return the gaze. Her face was expressionless. Utterly flat as she whispered, "I suppose you could go home after that. Back to your life if you did not wish to carry me the rest of the way."

He shrugged like that thought didn't matter. "I suppose I could. We'll have to see how things go tomorrow when we arrive."

She winced ever so slightly. Then she swung herself up on the horse and adjusted her seat carefully. "Best be off, then."

He followed suit and led the way back to the road. "Best be off," he agreed.

They were quiet as they rode along, and he should have been pleased by that. But he couldn't help but feel he'd lost an opportunity she'd been offering him. One that might not come again, except in regretful dreams when she was out of his life for good.

Anne watched Rook eat his supper from the corner of her eye, marking every movement and every expression. The rest of their journey that afternoon had gone without incident. He'd talked to her about nothing of importance, as if the conversation about his mother, about his terrible, traumatic past, had never happened.

And now she couldn't read him. As if they didn't know each other at all. Her heart ached for what had been lost between them. Ached for the walls he'd erected between them, ached for the fact that he'd been forced to build them at all by terrible abuse and neglect and fear.

"Tell me more about being a triplet," he said.

She jerked her gaze up to find he had leaned back in his seat and was swirling the last sip of ale in the tankard in his hand. She shifted. "I'm not sure what you want to know. It's just being sisters, only we are the same age and have a similar face." She sighed. "Some would say the same face."

He tilted his head. "That troubles you, looking like them?"

"No. I *love* looking like them. It's the only life I've known, so it's comforting to me to look over and see Juliana or Thomasina with an expression I recognize immediately because I've felt it on my own face. And it allows us to trade places, for the purpose of games or…" She shook her head as she thought of what she'd convinced Thomasina to do for her weeks ago. "Or in the case of mistakes."

He was quiet a moment. "And what is your least favorite part of it?"

She stared at him. No one had ever asked her that before. She and her sisters were considered an anomaly by most. Multiple births of even surviving twins were so rare. Triplets were almost impossible, a miracle upon miracles. Few people wanted to know more about them. The subject seemed to make most uncomfortable, even as they leered.

"We are seen as one person," she said softly. "One personality. Aside from my mother, very long ago, no one outside of ourselves has ever been able to tell us apart from each other. So I've never been Anne Shelley. I've always been a Shelley Triplet. First and forever."

"Even the man you would have married couldn't tell you apart?" Rook asked with an incredulous expression.

"No," she said with a sigh. "The earl didn't care enough to try, I suppose."

"If he didn't make an effort to get to know you, he was a fool." Rook leaned forward and took her hand, folding it between his before he lifted it to kiss her knuckles gently.

And suddenly everything in the room shifted with the heat of his mouth on her skin, even in this benign way. She shifted in her chair as tingles started between her legs, running through her stomach, tightening her chest.

"You must think my troubles very small and foolish," she choked out. "Compared to yours."

He arched a brow as he turned her hand palm up and pressed another kiss on the skin below her thumb. His tongue darted out gently and she heard a garbled sound come from her throat.

He smiled up at her. "Why compare it? I had a hard life, that is a factual truth. But I always knew who I was. And I made sure everyone else did, too. Not being separated out as an individual must have been trying. No wonder you ran. No wonder you looked for someone who saw you."

"Pretended to see me," she whispered. "Ellis only pretended to see me."

His brow furrowed and he threaded his fingers between hers, stroking the length of them with his own, gliding his thumb across her palm and inside her wrist as her body screamed with fire and anticipation.

His gaze found hers again. "I see you."

Those three words hit her so hard in the stomach that it felt like the air went out of her. This man she had never expected gave her the gift she'd always wanted. Easily. Genuinely. And so many other gifts too. It made the feelings that rose up whenever she looked at him so much harder to tamp down.

"I know you do." She cleared her throat, needing distance from those feelings even more. "You said you would ask me a question tonight. And you are driving me mad doing that."

He laughed. "Doing what?"

"You know what," she gasped as he let the nail of his thumb abrade the sensitive skin of her palm again. "Doing that with my hand."

He lifted that same hand again, pressing another kiss to the palm and then the wrist. She caught her breath. How could he do something so simple and have it feel so powerful?

He kissed her wrist again and said, "I'm not sure you'd want me to ask the question. We're so close to Gretna Green now. You might want to go home and forget you ever kissed me. Or that I kissed you. There..." He motioned to her mouth. "Or anywhere else."

She swallowed hard at the reminder of his dark head between her trembling legs. Of the magnificent pleasure that was echoed now as he just barely touched her hand.

"If you might go away, if I might never see you again," she whispered. "It makes me want you to ask the question even more. I have few chances left to answer it."

There was a moment when pain came over his expression. As if touching her and wanting her were the same torture for him as they were for her. Then he nodded.

"You told me you wanted me to ruin you," he whispered, focusing so fully on her that the rest of the room seemed to disappear. "To take your innocence and let you feel the kind of pleasure you've never dared dream about."

"I did." Her voice cracked.

"Have you thought about the consequences, Anne, of giving such a gift to a man like me? A man you know isn't meant for you. A man with a dark past that a woman like yourself should never even know exists. Do you want to open your legs to a man like me?"

She couldn't breathe as he spoke all those words, asked all those questions, tried to warn her off and instead drew her further and further in. She lifted the hand he wasn't holding and guided it toward him. She stroked her fingers along his jawline, letting her thumb glide along his full lower lip.

And then she whispered, "I want that so much, Constantine. I want *you* so very much."

He didn't move for a moment, didn't react at all. She wasn't certain if it was because he didn't like the answer. Or because she'd used his real name again. Or because he didn't want her despite the show he was making.

But then he pushed his chair back with a screech that brought the attention of the room to them for a brief moment. He tugged her to her feet and nodded.

"Then let's go upstairs," he growled. "Now."

He held her hand as they weaved through the crowded dining hall toward the narrow, smoky stairwell in the back corner of the room. Up one flight of steps, two, and they were at the top of the small building, in the row of cheaper rooms where their chamber for the night was located.

The hall was empty and he shifted her in front of him, wrapping his arms around her waist and pulling her back flush against him as they moved together awkwardly. She could see the room ahead of them, just ten paces, though it felt like a lifetime when he'd begun kissing the side of her neck gently.

She groaned as they both reached for the door handle, fumbling to get the key in the lock, turning it together, their fingers interlacing as they staggered into the tiny room that just had a narrow bed wide enough for two and a fire that warmed and brightened the space.

He turned her as he pushed the door shut, wedging her there as his mouth came down to claim hers.

He'd last kissed her just twenty-four hours earlier and yet Anne felt starved for it. She glided her fingers into his short hair, pulling him closer, urging the moment to go on and on as he tasted every inch of her mouth. His hands began to rove over her. He cupped her breast and she gasped as she thought of his mouth on her like it had been last night. He let his fingers continue down her sides and to her hips, tugging her close enough that she could feel the hard ridge of his erection against her belly.

She arched against it, rubbing until he broke the kiss with a moan. "You are a minx," he growled as he spun her around and backed her across the room toward the low bed. She bumped it with her calves in a few steps and smiled up at him.

"You like a minx, I think," she said softly. "You'd be bored if I didn't challenge you."

"That's probably true," he said as he reached around her back and flicked her buttons open without any effort. Her dress gaped forward, and he tugged it down and off in a smooth motion. "But no one could get bored with you."

Tears stung her eyes at that statement. She knew she could be difficult. But he liked her anyway. Maybe even *because* she wasn't easy. That was the gift as much as the bedding tonight.

She cupped his cheeks and kissed him, pouring all her need into him, all her heart, all the things she felt for him and had tried to deny until this moment when it washed over her in a wave. She was too afraid to name those emotions but she gave them all to him with her lips and vowed to give them all to him with her body.

He pulled away and looked down at her with concern in his dark eyes. "No desperation," he whispered, and hooked his fingers beneath her chemise straps. He dropped them down, tugging the silky fabric around her hips, pooling it at her feet with her gown. And she was naked, save for her boots and her stockings. He stepped back, eyeing her from head to toe, like he was memorizing the moment as he stared.

"Take the rest off," he growled, his voice rough. "Please."

CHAPTER 12

Anne sat on the edge of the bed and did exactly as she'd been told, stripping her boots off in a few smooth motions and rolling her stockings down. She didn't care that she snagged one as she did it, didn't care that she didn't exactly know where she threw them. She needed this man and this was the path, so she took it as fast as she could.

When she glanced up, he had stripped himself naked from the waist up, removed his own boots and was working diligently on his trousers. She laughed at the focus on his handsome face as he nearly popped buttons free in his haste.

"How can you be so quick?" she giggled.

He glanced up at her with a fleeting grin. "I am inspired." The trousers dropped and he kicked them free to stand naked before her.

She stared as she had the night before, but this time she was even more fascinated by the hard thrust of him that curled toward his stomach. He would put that in her. She wanted it very badly. She also feared it, especially considering the rumors she'd heard about pain and duty and everything else.

"May I touch it?" she asked.

"So polite and genteel." He edged forward so she could reach him. "Aye, my lady. Touch away."

She glared up at his playfully proper tone but was quickly distracted by the sight of him so much closer. She reached out and traced her finger down the length of him. His skin was satin soft, the muscle beneath hard as stone. Such a dichotomy.

She caught him in her fist next and stroked him from head to base.

"Fuck. Shit," he growled, surging against her fingers.

"What happened to propriety, good sir?" she asked as she glanced up at him with a smile despite his bawdy language. "You shall burn my innocent ears."

"I'll do something to your innocent something," he laughed. "Stroke it again."

She did so, amazed at how the tension was still there, hot as his cock when she stroked him, but there remained an ease between them. He teased her and she was comfortable enough to do the same. The mood was playful and hot, and she wasn't afraid of what he would do.

He would take care of her. She knew that.

"You licked me," she whispered, meeting his eyes as she stroked a third time. "Would it feel good for you?"

He let out a low sound from his throat as his eyes came closed. "You are trying to kill me. That's the only explanation. You were sent on a mission to kill me and *this* is your method. A devastating assassin."

She ignored his ramblings and leaned forward. She darted out her tongue and stroked it across the mushroom head of him. His fingers drove down into her hair and he sent the pins scattering. "Anne!" he burst out.

She smiled up at him as she licked him again. "Is that wrong?"

"No, it's not wrong, but I swear if I teach you how to take me into your mouth, I will not last the night. I won't last the minute, and that's not how your first time at this should be. So…"

He caught her armpits and drew her up to her feet. He crushed his mouth to hers, driving his tongue into her with hard and heavy intention. She tilted her face for better access, drowning in his kiss. Drowning in him. So focused that she only realized he was moving her when he laid her head onto the pillows and took a place beside her.

His kiss dipped lower, just as it had the night before. This time she was ready and sighed in surrender as he stroked his rough chin against her throat, licking a trail to her breasts. She arched to him, offering herself. He feasted, licking and plucking her nipples, setting her on fire as he brought her to life. The pleasure ricocheted through her, but it always returned to the pulsing need between her legs. She found herself opening them as he kissed down her stomach, across her hip, against her thigh.

His mouth touched her sex like it had the night before, and she keened with relief and pleasure. He opened her, stroking his tongue across her over and over, leaving her wet and trembling as he edged her gently, carefully toward the orgasm she had dreamed of since the night before.

She felt it coming, that desperate sensation of being on the edge of a cliff she very much wanted to fly from. But he held back, softening his licks. She lifted her head to look at him, to question, and he held her stare as he inserted one finger into her sheath.

She caught her breath at the strange sensation of being invaded, and he stilled so she could grow accustomed to the feeling. He stroked then, once, and she gasped again at how that touch increased her pleasure.

He didn't speak as he went back to licking her clitoris, now adding the stroke of his fingers to the act. She found herself grinding against his mouth and his finger, reaching for that release even more. When he added the second finger, stretching her even farther, she thrust her head back against the thin pillow with a gasp.

She couldn't respond further, though. In an instant his mouth was gone, his fingers gone and she felt his mouth returning on the lazy path up her body.

"You are so close," he murmured as he pushed her legs a little wider. "I want to feel you come around me."

She reached for him, anxiety mixing with anticipation, for it was clear the moment had come. He would take her. That would be the end of one life and the beginning of another.

But he didn't. He just looked down into her eyes, examining her face, and whispered, "I want you to say my name while I take you. Say my name, my real name."

She nodded and gasped as he reached between them to stroke his cock back and forth against her wet entrance. And then he was pushing, pressing into her inch by inch.

"Constantine," she murmured against his neck, burying her head there. "Constantine," she repeated as he stretched her and the pain whipped through her in a heated sizzle. "Constantine!" she cried out as he filled her to the hilt and then rested there, letting her adjust to this new sensation.

"Does it still hurt?" he whispered, pressing kisses to her neck and her shoulder.

She shook her head. "No," she said, her voice barely carrying in the quiet dark. "It just feels full. So this is it."

He laughed against her skin. "Not exactly." He ground against her, and her body jolted to life like it had with his mouth. "That is it." He ground again, thrusting gently so she felt every inch of him move inside of her. "That is it."

He kept saying it, kept moving, and she found herself lifting into him, grinding when their bodies touched, gasping when he pulled his length through her and back inside, over and over and over again. He reached between them, smoothing his thumb against her sensitive clitoris. With a few swipes of his finger and thrusts of his hips, she was on the edge again, gasping and clawing as he took her.

He met her eyes, holding her gaze steady, and just when she

thought she might lose her mind, he whispered, "Now. I want to feel you now."

It was all too much, and the dam of pleasure burst in that moment. He captured her cries as she spasmed, gripping him with her body as he continued to stroke inside of her. His pace increased, she felt the strain as he panted against her mouth.

Then he growled out her name, sucking her tongue hard as he pulled from her body and pumped himself between them. The kiss gentled, his free hand digging into her curls as he rolled to his side and pulled her against his heaving chest. She rested her head in the crook of his shoulder and traced patterns on his chest as their breathing slowed, her heart rate returned to normal and a sleepy contentedness washed over her.

She had done it. Ruined herself in truth as well as rumor. And she didn't regret it. Now that it was done, it didn't even feel like ruin. It felt right. And she would always have a night with this man to remember when he was gone and she was alone.

That was worth it all. That was worth everything.

"Sleep," he whispered as he pressed a kiss to her temple and drew her against him closer. "Sleep now."

So she closed her eyes and let sleep come.

R ook hadn't slept. How could he? This was very likely his one and only night with Anne, and he knew that fact painfully clearly. He wanted to lie there, savoring the way her body felt in his arms. Savoring the soft sound of her breathing, feeling it on his chest. He wanted to experience every moment he held her.

Because he loved her.

He didn't want to love her. But that wasn't how the heart worked and he knew it. The heart set fire when it set fire, and Anne Shelley had been striking flint against the icy barriers he'd erected for a long while now. The facts were clear and they told him that he loved her.

It didn't change a damned thing, except how miserable he would be once they were parted.

The filtered light of dawn edged around the dark curtains at the window and he cursed its appearance. In a few hours, they would be off. They'd reach Gretna Green, and the bigger town with all its visitors would offer Anne opportunities to speed her way home. Away from him.

She moved against his chest, her fingers clenching against his skin gently as she murmured in her sleep.

When she moved against him, his body woke of its own accord. But then again, he'd been on edge from the moment he came. He wanted more. He wanted all of her until they both forgot everything they had to lose.

He let his fingers travel the length of her bare back, memorizing the feel of her smooth skin. She wiggled against him again, this time with a soft sigh of pleasure.

Her eyes came open and she gazed up at him sleepily. He waited for her to start or stare at him with some kind of betrayal or a hint of regret for what she'd given to him.

She didn't. She wound her hand up around his neck and lowered his mouth to hers. They kissed, gentle and lazy in the quiet morning and the warmth of the bed.

He felt her pulse quicken and it matched his own. Slowly he cupped her hips, kneading the flesh there as he shifted her over him. Her legs opened as she straddled him and her hair came down around him as she continued to probe his mouth with her tongue.

She shifted, rubbing her wet sex against his hard cock. Saying nothing, she reached between them and positioned it, taking him inside of her with a shuddering sigh.

"Does it still hurt?" he asked, trying to keep his senses when she flexed tight heat around him that was as close to heaven as he'd ever be allowed to go.

She shook her head. "It never hurt much at all," she said before she began to move. "Not as much as it felt good, at any rate."

She was a natural despite her lack of experience. She rolled over him like waves against the shore of his island, reaching for her pleasure and naturally giving his in the process. As she straightened up a little to change the angle of their bodies, he leaned up and caught her breasts, licking from one to the other, sucking her nipples as she mewled out growing pleasure with every grind of her hips.

When she came, he hesitated, watching her face contract with wordless pleasure, feeling her body pulse around him, milk him as she rose harder and faster. She collapsed down against him with a panting groan. He took the lead then, lifting into her from beneath, holding her steady as he stroked and stroked. His balls grew heavy, tight against his body as his seed began to move.

How he wanted to come inside of her. Mark her in a new way. Maybe create a life that would never let her forget this moment. But to do so would be cruel. She would hate him for keeping her from any kind of good future. He would hate himself for hurting her and the child they could create in this heated moment.

So he slid her forward, off his cock, and came in intense spurts as she continued to rock over him. He kissed her, drinking in every inch of her before she adjusted herself to lie across his body, their legs tangled, her head resting against his chest as she looked up at him with a smile.

"I could wake up that way every morning."

He returned the smile even though it pained him. How he would love to wake up with her every day. Make love to her every day.

"What time do you think it is?" she asked as she ran her hands up and down his sides absently, not aware of what a fire she stoked with just that innocent touch.

He shrugged as he lifted his head to look at the window. "Not sure. Dawn, though, judging from the light around the edge of the curtains. The beginnings of the day."

She yawned. "I have not slept so well in weeks. Months. Not since my engagement was announced."

He frowned at the reminder of the man she had vowed to marry. She'd mentioned him many times, though never named him. But Rook knew he was titled. Powerful. A match on paper, at any rate.

"Was he cruel to you?" he asked softly.

She lifted her face in surprise. "No," she said, quickly enough that he could tell it was true. "No, he was...he was just *nothing*. I was a business arrangement. Nothing more."

He frowned. The thought that a man could have this woman in his life and not want more and more and more of her was so odd to him. If she could be his, he would show her every day just how much he cared.

But she couldn't be his. He wasn't worthy to shine her boot. That hadn't mattered until it did. But now it did.

"It hasn't rained all night," he said, changing the subject before he could make a fool out of himself by perhaps confessing his heart. He could only imagine how she would react. She had to feel he was nothing more than a mere affair to her. "We'll surely make it to Gretna Green today."

She let out her breath slowly. "Yes. Well, I look forward to seeing our options for getting home, I suppose. You must be ready to return to your island, too. I know we spoke of a reward. I could have it forwarded to you in that village where we started if you give me its name before we part ways."

He stiffened. She was already aching to be rid of him, it seemed. Perhaps this was her kind way of managing it. Reminding him that she didn't need him once she was in a place where she had access to more options.

It was better for her, of course. Better for him to let her go before these feelings in his chest bloomed even further. But it stung, nonetheless. Everything about this stung like a lash across his back.

He rolled from under her, getting to his feet. She shifted and lifted the sheets to cover her breasts as she watched him dress as quickly as he'd divested himself of his clothing hours before.

"I should ready the horses then, since we're both anxious to be off," he said, hearing the clipped nature of his tone. "Take your time getting dressed and we can be on the road as soon as you are able."

"Rook—" she began.

He winced at her use of his nickname. He didn't even know why, for he'd told her that was what she should call him. Constantine was the man who pleasured her. He only existed when he perched between her legs.

"It's best if we carry on," he grunted as he moved to the door. There he paused and turned back to look at her one last time. In his bed, mussed by him. His.

But it was an illusion. A mirage he'd believed in for a moment.

"I'll see you downstairs," he added. He turned on his heel and left her, trying to ignore the pain that action caused. Trying to ignore the voice inside of him that screamed at him to go back to her instead of walking away.

CHAPTER 13

Before she and her sisters came out to Society, Anne's maiden aunt had pulled them aside to talk to them about men. It had been a very unenlightening conversation on the whole. The woman had no experience herself and a hard look on the opposite sex. But she had said one thing that now rang in Anne's ears as they trotted along the road in the warming sunlight of the afternoon.

If you give a man what he wants, he'll leave.

It was meant as a strategy, of course. Play the hard-to-get diamond and men would chase. But it had also been an admonishment not to kiss behind flowerpots or give up one's innocence too easily. Anne had done just that. The innocence, not the flowerpots.

And now she felt Rook pulling away from her. Oh, he was polite as they rode. He was amiable as a travel companion could be. But he no longer looked at her with smoldering intent. He no longer teased with her. He no longer asked her about her past or her family and surrendered no information about his own.

They were like faintly acquainted travel companions now. Not friends, as she'd once felt they were. Not lovers.

Her heart broke for the loss of both roles, even though she knew it might be for the best. She'd come to care for him, to want him to distraction, but he didn't feel the same way about her. Pushing her away now was a kindness. It allowed her to start to plan for the frightening future she would face once she returned to Harcourt and the family and fiancé she had abandoned there weeks before.

They reached the top of a rise and Rook trotted his mount off the road and to an overlook. "There," he said, pointing in the distance. "The infamous Gretna Green."

She looked down at the little hamlet. It was a busy, pretty little village just like a hundred others that dotted the countryside in Scotland and England.

"Hmm," she said. "I thought somehow it would be grander or glitter in the light. The way it is spoken of, it almost feels like fairyland."

He smiled. "Folks like the romantic notion of it, I suppose. But the blacksmith shop is exactly that, you know, a blacksmith shop. A bit dark and drafty for my taste."

She jerked her head toward him. "Does that mean you've come here before?" she asked. She couldn't help the smile that quirked her lips. "Tell me you are not secretly married."

He shook his head and a faint echo of his usual grin crossed his face. "I am not. Just a curious tourist, as are most who stop there."

"Then you'll have to take me around the town when we reach it," she said, and nickered to her horse to go back to the road. "Come, we'll be there before supper."

She urged her horse forward and heard Rook follow after a moment. She was in no hurry to reach the town, of course. To see this time together end as it might when they reached the bigger town. But she had to put on a good face. Not let him see that it mattered to her when it meant so little to him.

That was the only way to survive this with a fragment of her dignity intact.

They entered the gates of the town in less than an hour and pulled their horses up before an inn that was easily three times as big as any that had housed them along their route. As Rook helped her from her mount, she forced another smile. "Oh, I cannot wait for a bath to wash the travel from my bones."

She thought there was a flicker of desire that darkened his stare at that statement, but he blinked it away.

"Inquire about a room within," he said. "And have them send up the water. I'll take care of our horses and ask around about safe transport for you from here. If it seems likely you could get home faster any other way, I'll also ask about a price for the horses."

She bit her lip at his efficient explanation about how he would rid himself of her and nodded. "Very good. Thank you."

He turned away, leading the horses up the busy lane toward the stable. She entered the inn, greeted by scents of baking bread and the sounds of travelers, drinking their ale and telling their tales of the road. It seemed a good-natured group, and she felt no fear as she approached a woman behind a desk.

"Good afternoon," she said. "I'm inquiring about a room for the night. My—my husband is out tending to the horses and making some other arrangements."

The woman made quick with finding a room and handed over a key to Anne. "It's the third on the left on the second floor," she said. "Supper will be in an hour, though you might want to come down early. Our inn is buzzing with the better weather, as you can see. A large group of travelers arrived from Harcourt just today."

Anne jerked her head up from where she was signing the ledger for the hotel and turned to look at the loud group of men by the fire. Her heart almost stopped. They were the Earl of Harcourt's cronies, men from his shire. She hadn't recognized them when she entered, but now she saw a few familiar faces in their crowd.

She turned away swiftly, hoping they hadn't seen her. Of course she didn't look half so fine as she had when she ran away into the night.

"Harcourt, you say," she said softly, glancing over her shoulder.

"That's a pretty shire. I know it a little. They seem a rowdy lot. What has them in such a dither?"

The innkeeper's wife leaned in, her gaze brightening with pleasure. "Well, I'm not one to gossip, of course. Everyone says I'm silent as the grave. Can keep a secret like no other. That's what they say."

Anne pursed her lips. If that wasn't the beginning of every gossip's big confession, she didn't know what was. "I'm sure you're very discreet. As am I."

The woman nodded. "That lot keep talking about a terrible scandal back where they come from. Something about their lordship and a broken engagement."

Anne's blood roared so loudly through her ears that she could hardly hear anything else. She swallowed, trying to calm herself. "That's a terrible thing. But I suppose a thwarted wedding is only a scandal until the next one comes around."

"'Tweren't thwarted, though." The woman all but clapped her hands together. "They say the man's fiancée ran away...so he married her *sister*."

Now the blood *was* all Anne could hear. Certainly she couldn't have heard those words right.

She tried to breathe, but spots were beginning to appear before her eyes. "Lord Harcourt married one of his intended's sisters instead?" she asked, her hands shaking, her knees shaking.

"That's the news from that group there," the woman said. She blinked. "You've gone pale, miss. Do you know the couple?"

"I-I do." Anne pressed both hands into the desk, trying to find purchase when the room was tipping. "It cannot be true. It cannot be true that Harcourt married one of the remaining sisters. Which one? Do you know which one?"

She knew the answer even though she asked. Thomasina had been the one she'd forced into her games. Thomasina was the one who would agree to such a thing out of penance if she were caught. Sweet, innocent, good Thomasina, married to Jasper Kincaid, the Earl of Harcourt. A man with no heart.

"I'm sorry, miss, I don't. You could ask the men the particulars. Miss? Oh, miss!"

But Anne hardly heard her as she began to suck air in and out of her lungs. Her knees gave and she barely caught herself. Then hands were touching her, coming around her waist. She turned toward them and saw Rook's face swimming in her vision. His dark eyes were wide, filled with pure terror as he swept her up and carried her up the stairs, the innkeeper's wife not far behind. The woman was talking, speaking about something, she didn't know what. Her fainting, perhaps.

She didn't hear it at all. All she could think of, all she could understand, all she could focus on was what she had done. What she had forced upon her sisters. Her selfishness had compelled one of them, probably Thomasina, into marriage. A loveless marriage meant for Anne that had closed around one of her sisters like a trap.

And as she let out a long, pained cry, everything around her went dark at last.

Rook cradled Anne in his arms on the bed, slapping her cheeks gently. At least the rambling innkeeper's wife had left, off to search out smelling salts and water for the basin.

"Anne," he said, slapping just a touch harder to shock her awake. "Anne, wake up."

It had been terrifying to walk into the inn just in time to see the woman he loved buckle and nearly deposit herself on the floor. People had run to help, there had been shouting and good will...he hadn't cared about anything but her. Her pale, stricken face as she stared up at him and wailed, "It's my fault!"

Then she was gone, fainted dead away from a shock he couldn't understand because the innkeeper's wife was going on and on about earls and marriages and something about a group of men across the room who hadn't even seemed to notice the hubbub because they were so deep in their cups.

He didn't know what the hell was happening, all he knew was that Anne stirred at last. Relief flooded his entire being as he smoothed the hair from her face. "It's all right now. I'm here." She lurched as if to rise, but he held firm. "Shh, don't get up, you fainted."

She stared up at him, her face still as stricken as it had been the first moment he found her. She shook her head. "Tell me it's a dream. A nightmare. It cannot be true."

The door opened then and the innkeeper's wife scurried back in. She had a tray with smelling salts and water, and she almost looked disappointed when she saw Anne awake.

"Oh, there she is," the older woman cooed. "Poor lamb, the road can take it out of you and that's a fact. You rest now and let your man tend to you. Shall I bring up food?"

Rook's appetite had fled the moment he saw Anne fall and he could see how green her skin was as she turned her face, so he shook his head. "If it's not too much trouble, perhaps you could bring it up in an hour or so. Let my wife rest and let me ascertain that she doesn't need a doctor."

"Aye, for certain," the woman said. "A good man, then. Yes, I'll leave you be. Please fetch me if you need a thing. I'll set two plates aside for you."

She left them, shutting the door behind her. Only then did Anne sit up a fraction. "I don't need a doctor."

"Perhaps not, but it made her happy and it made her leave," Rook said. "Now tell me what happened. Was she right that it was all brought about by mere exhaustion of the road?"

She rocked forward and tucked her knees up, putting her head against her hands. "No," she whispered, pain in every sound. "Oh God, no."

"What is it?" he repeated, this time sharper. "You need to tell me now."

His tone seemed to shock her out of some of her panic, and she took a few long breaths before she forced herself to meet his stare. The tears that sparkled in those bright green eyes broke his heart and he took her hand, smoothing his fingers over her skin in the hopes it would comfort her.

"When I ran away from my arranged marriage, I used my sister to do it. I told you that we used to trade places—" She let out a hiccupping sob, but managed to continue. "Well, I convinced my sister Thomasina to do this one more time. I lied to her and she believed me and put on my dress and went into a lion's den."

He shook his head, both at the idea that Anne had concocted such a plan and that now she was so upset by it. "I know you think your sisters will be furious at you for your escape," he soothed her. "And perhaps that weighs more heavily on your mind because you are so close to reaching them, but—"

She lifted a hand to stay his words. "You don't understand. Rook, that group of men downstairs…they just came from Harcourt."

He flinched at that name. "Harcourt?" he repeated, his voice sounding tinny and far away as shock flowed through him.

"Yes, my fiancé was the Earl of Harcourt." She tilted her head. "Have I never told you his name?"

Slowly Rook got to his feet and backed away from her a long step. His heart had begun to pound. "No," he whispered. "You never said his name."

"Well, that is it." She bent her head. "The men downstairs told the innkeeper that—that…that Harcourt had married one of the remaining sisters. The wedding went forward and one of them was forced to take his hand. And it's my fault! To escape a loveless marriage, I doomed one of the people I hold most dear to the same."

She collapsed again on the bed, wracked with sobs. He couldn't stay away, and perched on the edge of the bed, smoothing his hand across her shaking back even as his own mind reeled.

He knew the name Harcourt, but not from gossip. He knew the man because his cousin Ellis had been involved with his brother.

JESS MICHAELS

The previous Earl of Harcourt had been a gambler and a drinker and a rabble-rouser.

He was also dead. And Ellis had a hand in that. It was part of why he and Rook had parted ways. And now this woman Rook loved, this woman Ellis had destroyed with his desperation, said she was tied to Harcourt, as well. He didn't believe in coincidence, but even if he did, this couldn't be one.

He shook off his reaction, his horror, and focused on Anne. She was still weeping, utterly gutted by her grief and guilt. God knew he was familiar with those concepts.

"Anne," he soothed. "You mustn't do this to yourself. We have no idea what has truly happened. Those men might be telling tales, they might have misunderstood a rumor within a rumor."

She shook her head and when she lifted her head, her cheeks were streaked with tears. "I *saw* them. I *recognized* them. There are three men from Harcourt down there. Three who would have been invited to my wedding. Why would they tell such a tale?"

He straightened up. He wondered the same thing, as well as a great many other things. And there was only one way to answer those questions.

"We'll ask them," he said, rising.

She jerked her red-eyed gaze to him. "I cannot. They would know who I was the moment they saw me. They all met me as Harcourt's intended bride weeks ago."

He frowned. Of course she wouldn't want to be seen as she was now, with the company she kept now. "I'll go," he said. "I'll find out all the information we need without revealing you are here or that we've traveled together."

Her lips parted. "You would do that for me?"

He wrinkled his brow at her apparent shock. "Of course. We need to know the truth, don't we? To understand all the facts before we make our next plan. Strategy alone dictates I understand the situation. And you need to know for your own peace of mind."

144

He smoothed his jacket as he walked to the door of the chamber. When he reached it, he heard Anne's voice, weak and shaky. "Rook?"

He turned back. She had sat up and looked so forlorn it nearly broke his heart. Her face was puffy with tears, her hair was cock-eyed and half fallen from the bun at her nape, and her tone was so sad. She was still the most beautiful thing he'd ever had the privilege to lay eyes on.

"Yes?" He made his own voice as gentle as he could.

"Thomasina is the sister who took my place. Juliana is my other sister. I need to know which one married Harcourt, if the rumor is true. I *need* to know."

"I'll find out," he promised as he left the room.

He hurried back into the main room downstairs and as he rounded the corner, he was met with the bustling innkeeper's wife, Mrs. Sanders.

"Oh, Mr. Maitland, how is your dear wife? Do we need to send for a doctor?" she asked, leaning up to look toward the stairs behind him, as if Anne would materialize.

"She is fine, Mrs. Sanders," he assured her. "I think a bit tired from our long travels is all, just as you surmised. She was over-whelmed and now she just needs to rest."

The older woman nodded slowly. "Of course, sir. Your plates will be sent up later for you and if there is any other way I can oblige, you'll let me know." He moved to go around her to the men who were still gathered in the corner, but she caught his arm. "Have you considered she might be in a family way, sir?"

He froze and stared first at the fingers that held his arm and then at the hopeful, upturned face of gossip who owned them. The very question curled down into his bones. Anne, pregnant with his child. Something that bound them together forever.

He had been careful when they made love. It didn't mean acci-dents couldn't still happen.

"No," he said softly. "I don't think that's it. We certainly appre-ciate your kindness, though."

He pulled away with a forced smile and weaved through the boisterous crowd of travelers to the men in the corner. They were talking and as he approached they glanced over toward him with smiles of greeting.

"Ah, another traveler, here to take his rest," said a half-drunk, red-faced man with a wide and friendly smile. "Do you need a seat, young lad? We have several."

The rest of their group laughed heartily, though Rook wasn't exactly certain why the statement was so funny. He smiled none-theless. "I appreciate the warm welcome," he said as he took a chair at the outer edge of their group. There were introductions all around and then they talked amiably about the weather and the bad roads. After a while, Rook leaned back and casually asked, "I have heard told you men are traveling from Harcourt?"

"Aye!" said one of the men, very tall and almost gauntly thin. "Mr. Smithins, Squire Golding and I are all from Harcourt, on our way to Edinburgh for a wedding."

Squire Golding, who had been the first to greet Rook, laughed. "Hoping it won't be so eventful as the one we just left."

Rook nodded, for he had been handed a gift of the open door for the information he sought. Now he struggled to maintain the years of training he'd had in extracting that kind of information. It was much harder when he knew Anne waited upstairs, broken hearted.

"An eventful wedding," he mused. "That could mean a great many things."

Mr. Smithins nodded. "In this case, it is quite the scandal. I think it could reach the gossip sheets far and wide."

"My interest is raised even further," Rook said. "And I've always loved knowing the gossip before anyone else. What is the tale?"

Squire Golding clucked his tongue. "Well, the Earl of Harcourt was meant to marry a lady. One of three sisters, all who look alike... triplets, I think they call that. Very unsettling. At any rate, when the wedding occurred, it wasn't his original intended who walked the long aisle to his side. It was one of her sisters."

Rook bent his head. He had hoped the words he said to Anne upstairs might be true. That these men were just telling tales to entertain themselves. But it was clear that wasn't it. They were good-natured drunks, but they didn't seem to be exaggerating the circumstance.

Still, he feigned great surprise and tried to keep a grin on his face. "Great God, that *is* a scandal. Did he simply prefer the other sister, faces alike or no?"

"Seems the original intended ran away," Mr. Smithins said. "Though it was only whispered about, never confirmed."

"Which sister did the man ultimately marry?" Rook asked.

The men all blinked at each other, then stared at him as if they didn't understand the question.

"Er," Squire Golding said. "Who's to say, eh? All the same face, it might as well have been the same woman. I think it started with a T. Anyway, they're married now, easy as that, and we wish them happy."

The men all raised their glasses with a boisterous, "To the earl!"

"And his poor wife," Squire Golding added with a laugh.

Rook raised his glass with the rest and drank, but the ale was sour to him now. He leaned in. "You know, I once knew a man who did business in Harcourt," he said. "Perhaps you know of him. Tall, broad shouldered, dark hair a bit too long. Handsome fellow, goes by Maitland?"

The men looked at each other and shook their heads slowly. "Bit of a vague description," Mr. Smithins said. "And I don't know the name."

Rook forced his disappointment from his face and got to his feet. "Well, I thank you gentlemen for the sharing of your tales and your ales." They laughed at the rhyme like it was the funniest thing they'd ever heard and Rook shook his head slightly. "But my own lovely wife awaits upstairs, and I ought to be sure she doesn't need anything."

"Just be certain it isn't her sister!" one of the men said, and the rest laughed boisterously and slapped their hands against their thighs.

Rook waved as he headed back across the room and up the stairs. The men were simply silly with liquor, but they had no idea how close to the mark they'd come. Or what a burden they'd laid on Rook's shoulders when it came to breaking Anne's heart.

CHAPTER 14

Anne had already known the truth. She knew one of her sisters had been thrown to the wolves because of her. But the moment Rook opened the door and stared at her, she couldn't pretend he might tell her anything different. She pushed to unsteady feet and clenched her hands so tightly in front of her, it hurt.

"He married one of them," she whispered.

Rook nodded as he closed and locked the door behind himself. He looked tired as he exhaled a long, unsteady breath. As if having to be the one to tell her this truth was not something he wished to take on. It was too big, too awful. Too crushing.

"Yes," he said softly after what felt like an eternity had passed. "Harcourt married one of your sisters. You were right—it was probably Thomasina. The men below thought the name started with a T."

The room spun around Anne, and she gripped at the back of a chair to steady herself, warding off Rook's advance to help her with a raised hand. "You sat with those men, you saw their expressions and heard their voices. Was it merely casual gossip, tall tales? Or do you believe it to be true?"

He nodded slowly. "I'm sorry, Anne. I had no reason not to believe them."

She sank into the chair and covered her face with her hands as her mind spun with horrible images. She heard Rook move and glanced up at him. He had dragged the other chair in the room closer and took it, letting his knees brush hers as he searched her face. "Tell me about Harcourt," he said.

She shook her head. Harcourt. Oh, Harcourt, who she despised more than anyone at that moment, even more than Ellis. Harcourt, who had taken the freedom and future of one of her beloved sisters. Who didn't care, didn't love, didn't give over even a fraction.

"I've told you everything already, even if I somehow didn't say his name to you," she said on a sigh. She tried to sort through the jumble of her thoughts. "He was cool, distant. The marriage was arranged by my father. Harcourt had inherited the title and a mountain of debt when his brother was killed in that scandalous duel."

Rook flinched. "Yes, even those of my class heard about that."

She nodded. "He needed my dowry to save himself and rebuild his legacy. My father wanted to buy a connection to a title. Once the house of Harcourt was a fine one—I suppose my father thought he was buying low in the hopes to one day trade high."

"But you have two sisters," Rook said. "Why did he choose you for the duty?"

She bent her head, thinking of her attitude and actions over the past twenty-two years of her life. How many times had her father said she was running wild, that he would have to find a way to bring her to heel, that she would spoil things for her sisters if she didn't settle herself down?

It turned out he was right after all. And that stung down to her very soul.

"Although he would claim otherwise, I think he wanted to rid himself of me because I was most likely to make trouble."

"You?" Rook teased gently.

She couldn't make herself smile at the effort. "I have always been the one to do so. I certainly did this time."

"So you were given to Harcourt so you would be his problem instead of your father's. And a wedding date was set. You said the man wasn't cruel, just cold," Rook said softly, and now he took her hands and held them between his warm ones. That touch brought her the smallest peace. One she sank into with a ragged sigh.

"Yes."

"Then your sister *isn't* in danger," he said. "At worst, she took your place in an arranged marriage no different than many in the titled class. A marriage that could have easily been arranged for her instead of you in the first place, had your father taken a different mind."

"You don't know Thomasina," Anne said, and the tears returned to her eyes. "She is so gentle a soul, so good a person and so dear a sister. To think of her married to a man who could not love, could not *feel*...it is gut wrenching. What she must think of me as she endures..." She trailed off and yanked her hands from his as she paced the small room. "I can't think of what she has endured. And our other sister, Juliana, she must despise me to my core."

Rook hadn't moved, but she felt his stare burning into her back. "Why would you think that?"

"She is the one to fix the messes we all make," she said, facing him. "And this is the worst one of all. She could *never* forgive me for putting Thomasina in a position where she could be so...so...so..." She sank down on the bed a second time, and the tears she'd been fighting returned. "Hurt," she finished on a sob.

He moved then, jumping from his chair and crossing to the bed. He lifted her limp body into his arms, cradling her against him as he smoothed her hair and rocked her as she wept. Wept for the life she had destroyed with her selfish decisions. Her sister's life.

And she cried for her own. Because it was now painfully clear to her how much she had lost by running away with Ellis Maitland. And what little she had to go home to.

R ook smoothed Anne's hair as she stirred with nightmares for the third time since she had collapsed in exhausted sleep hours before. She hadn't woken to eat, she hadn't woken at all. It was as if she'd collapsed in on herself, and seeing her in such pain broke his heart in ways he never could have imagined possible.

That was the risk, he supposed, in loving someone. He'd not had many people in his life he had allowed into his heart that way. His mother. His cousin. He'd always hurt for their pains, too.

He cradled Anne closer as she stopped muttering in her sleep and sighed.

His mind returned to his cousin. Ellis had created such a mess by pursuing Anne, and now Rook's blood ran cold at the deeper ramifications of it all. He'd known Ellis had involved himself with the previous Earl of Harcourt, Solomon Kincaid. The man had been a lout, a drunk, a cad of the highest order. He and Ellis had been well matched in some ways.

But where Rook had always tried to temper Ellis's worst impulses, Solomon had only seemed to encourage them. Ellis had taken worse risks, gone into situations without consulting Rook. Involved himself with dangerous people. One very dangerous one especially. A man named Winston Leonard.

And Solomon Kincaid was dead because of that. He would never forget Ellis's face that awful night when his friend had been cut down. A duel, gossip said. But it hadn't been a duel.

It was a murder, plain and simple.

They had a code, or so Rook had thought. There were certain things he and his cousin had vowed they would not do. And so he'd walked away, leaving Ellis to clean up his own mess.

And *this* was how he'd done it. Pursuing the new earl's fiancée for…well, Ellis couldn't think of what purpose his cousin might have. But it couldn't have been a good one.

Ellis had been so desperate when he came to him weeks ago,

demanding Rook's help. Begging for it. Now Rook looked down at the woman asleep in his arms, the one Ellis had used for his own ends. He'd put Anne in danger. She was still in danger, because a desperate Ellis had never been a safe Ellis. Recklessness was his downfall, every fucking time.

"Rook?" Her voice was muffled against his shoulder, this time not as heavy with sleep.

He leaned back to give her more space, and she looked up at him. She said nothing, but her hand slid up his stomach, bunching his shirt as she dragged her fingers along his abdomen. She arched against him gently, her lips parting on a sigh. His body reacted, even if he didn't want it to do so.

"Anne," he whispered. "You've had a hard day and I don't think—"

"I just want to forget," she whispered, lifting closer to brush her lips against his jawline. "Please. Please help me forget for just a moment."

He shut his eyes. He was no match for her when it came to this. No match for her touch or her voice or her need or for his own. And perhaps, in the end, they *both* needed to forget.

He rolled her onto her back as he kissed her, probing her lips with his tongue, deepening the kiss when she opened to him with a sigh. She dug her fingers into his hair, angling even closer as they fell into the deep abyss of pleasure.

He let one hand move over her, over the wrinkled dress she'd fallen asleep in, across her shoulders, down her sides, over her hip as it surged against his. He dragged his fingers back up her center, cupping her breast as they broke the kiss and stared, panting at each other in the dim darkness.

"More," she demanded. "I want more."

His eyes narrowed. Now it was *she* who sounded desperate, and he didn't like that any more than he had when it was Ellis. Desperation led to dark thoughts and even worse decisions and he didn't want—

His thought was cut off as she dragged him in for another deep kiss. His brain emptied, because when she swirled her tongue around his, when she ground up against him, he couldn't remember coherence or concerns. He had so little time with her now, he didn't want to waste it.

Not when every time he touched her might be the last.

So he thrust away his regrets and instead pushed to his knees between her legs, bunching her skirt so he wouldn't kneel on it. He tugged her to a seated position and stripped the buttons along the back of her gown open with a flick of his wrist. The dress gaped and she pushed it to her waist along with her chemise beneath.

He let his fingers play along the bare, warm skin along her spine, stroking fine circles there until she shivered and his name exited her lips: "Constantine."

He glanced down at her with a smile. So that was how they'd play. Constantine when he was pleasuring her, Rook the rest of the time. He had never liked either of his names more than when she said them. Moaned them. Whispered them.

He leaned down and captured a nipple with his lips, swirling the tip of his tongue around the hard peak, spelling *I love you* on her skin. She jerked against him, her soft cry like music in the quiet room. He sucked harder, harder, cupping her hips as they surged against his, arching her back as he pleasured her ceaselessly.

This was what she needed. He intended to provide. When she was mewling sounds of pleasure, he released her and got to his feet. She stared up at him, foggy gazed and almost confused. "Don't go," she begged.

He shook his head. "I would never. Just want to remove some clothes."

She blinked as if she hadn't realized they were still dressed. She lay back on the pillows and kicked out of her dress and underthings, then rolled her stockings away. He tried to focus on his own clothes, but that was almost an impossibility when she was now laying there naked on the bed they'd share, her legs open, her gaze devouring him as he tugged his shirt over his head. He removed his boots and then got back in the bed with her.

He grabbed her hips, tugging her closer and flattening her on her back as she giggled. He loved the sound of her laughter, for it meant he had actually done what she requested. Made her forget, if only for a moment.

He bent his head, stroking her thigh with his cheek. Then he took a deep whiff of her sex. The musky sweetness was so uniquely her, so beautifully her, and he wanted to remember it forever. To bathe in it so he would always be able to recall every part later. He darted his tongue out and swept it over her, once, twice, until she balled the coverlet into her fist and twisted, until she murmured an incoherent moan of pleasure. His cock hardened at giving her pleasure, more even than it did at the idea of receiving it. There was just something so bewitching about stealing her control and making her quake beneath his tongue or his fingers or his cock.

He never wanted to lose that, even though it was inevitable.

He sucked on her clitoris, hardening it with his ministrations. Scenting her arousal increase, feeling the trembles of pleasure begin deep within her as she ground against him while he licked. He added a finger to her sheath, loving the slick welcome of her flexing body, loving the catch of her breath as she was invaded. He added a second finger, adjusting until he found that rough patch deep within her and curling his fingers against it until she pled for more and less and everything.

She came in a hurried burst of trembling, clenching flesh, a wet gush of arousal and a moan that certainly would leave no question to the neighbors as to what they were doing. He continued to lick and stroke her through the crisis, dragging her pleasure further and further until the earthquakes became tremors became tiny spasms, and she panted as she flopped an arm over her face.

His cock felt like steel as he freed it from his trousers and kicked them aside. He crawled his way over her body, licking a trail back up that followed the one he'd taken down earlier. She didn't open her eyes, but caught his cheeks, bringing him in for a deep kiss as she shifted to make room for him between her legs.

There was no resistance when he entered her, that same clenching sex that had welcomed his fingers squeezing around his exquisitely sensitive cock. Already he felt his balls tightening, his seed moving as he took the first long thrust through her heat. He dropped his head into her neck, sucking her throat as he took and took and took in slow, rolling waves. She met him on each one, shaking as he ground his pelvis to hers.

When she came a second time, digging her nails into his bare back, groaning his name against his mouth and his shoulder, it was too much for him to bear. He thrust harder, faster, driving toward the powerful, life-changing pleasure that was just there out of his reach. The pleasure he didn't deserve but would take regardless because he needed it, he needed her. He needed tonight as much as she did.

He caught it in a long burst, pulling from her body just as he came. He was panting as he collapsed over her, kissing her, soothing her, loving her with his body the way he'd never be able to do with the rest of his life.

And hoping it would be enough to give her a little extra strength in the difficult days he knew were coming.

CHAPTER 15

When Anne woke the next day she stayed in the bed, staring up at the ceiling and hoping she would discover that everything from yesterday was a terrible nightmare. Thomasina was safe, Rook was hers...nothing had changed.

Only everything had. What had happened wasn't a nightmare, it was a consequence. Thomasina was the Countess of Harcourt, trapped at Jasper Kincaid's side forever. And Rook was gone from their bed, the only evidence of his existence the dent in the pillow beside hers and the scent of him in the air. She tugged the sheets up to farther cover her naked body and let out a long sigh.

Somewhere out there, Thomasina was waking up too. Beside Harcourt. She'd probably been doing the same things Anne had been doing. Anne's eyes flooded with tears at the thought of her sweet, innocent sister experiencing such a thing. How could it be endured when it didn't come with love?

She jerked to a sitting position at that thought. Love? That wasn't what she felt, was it? She had great gratitude toward Rook for helping her when he hadn't been under any obligation to do so. She felt a physical connection to him, thanks to the amazing pleasures they'd shared over the days they traveled.

And she *liked* him. She liked his quick quips and his quicker laughter at her own. She liked his quiet strength and his calm voice when she panicked. She liked his self-sufficiency and the faith he had in what he knew about himself and the world.

She *admired* him, but that wasn't love. It couldn't be love.

The door to the chamber opened and Rook stepped inside, carrying a tray laden heavily with food and drink. He smiled as he saw her sitting up and pushed the door shut with his hip.

"The princess awakens at last. I was beginning to fear your slumber was enchanted and I would have to wake you with a kiss."

She forced a smile at that. "You may wake me with a kiss anytime, fair prince."

He tensed as he set the items in his arms down on the table one by one. "I'll remember that," he said softly.

She worried the edge of the sheet. "Thank you for bringing me food. How late is it?"

"Very late. After luncheon, actually," he said.

Her eyes went wide. "Is it? I'm sorry to have kept to my bed so late. No wonder you called me a princess. I am as spoiled as one."

He arched a brow. "In the past few weeks you have endured a great deal, Anne. I think if anyone has earned a morning to catch up on their sleep, it is you." He sat down on the edge of the bed and reached out to drag his fingers along her jawline. "And I called you *princess* because you are beautiful. Even with your hair sticking up in five different directions."

She lifted a hand to her locks and found he was correct—it was wild. She smiled. "Get me my brush, then. That, at least, I can fix."

He did so, and as she combed her hair and tried to get it back into some semblance of normalcy, he loaded a plate with delicacies for her. "We could take a few hours on the road, despite the late hour. Make it into England at the very least."

Her eyes went wide as she stared at him. "On the road?"

He nodded as he handed over the plate. She set it aside on the coverlet. She couldn't think of eating, no matter how lovely all the food was. "I know you are anxious to get back to your family."

She ran the brush through her hair again and refused to meet his stare. "I thought you were looking into alternatives for my travel. You must want to go home to your island more than ever."

His jaw tightened. "Trying to get rid of me, are you?"

She bent her head. "No," she said after a moment. "I just know I am creating chaos for you. I can—I can find my own way, you know. I must learn to do it at any rate."

His face jerked toward hers and he took a step closer. "Anne… what does that mean?"

She cleared her throat. Well, the time had come to tell him what had been on her mind. "I am…I'm not going back to Harcourt or my family, Rook. I can't, not anymore."

"Why would you think you couldn't return home to them?" he asked. She could tell he was trying to sound calm even though he was upset. She saw it in the faint twitch of his jaw, the tightening of his fist at his side.

She shook her head and put her brush on the table next to the bed as she tried to gather her thoughts. "My sisters *must* hate me for creating the consequences of what I did. How could they not? I cannot imagine facing them again and seeing their anger and heartbreak."

"Anne," he said softly.

She held up a hand. "I know you are going to try to convince me of a dozen reasons why I'm wrong. You're going to tell me they don't hate me."

He shrugged. "I won't tell you that because I don't know them, and I don't know what their reaction is. But neither do you, in truth. You have no idea the chain of events that led one of them to marry Harcourt. Nor what has happened to either of them in the time you've been gone."

He was right, of course, but it gave her no solace. "But I know the result, don't I? My actions have led to Thomasina's suffering. You cannot know what that means."

His jaw tensed again. "I know *exactly* what that means," he said. "And how the guilt can rot a person from the inside."

She stared at him when he said those words with such passion. Even now she saw guilt in his eyes and wondered what exactly he had done or thought he'd done to put it there. She longed for a world where they could just...comfort each other.

But that had been a fantasy, hadn't it? Now she had to put herself back into reality, a world where she would likely have to make it on her own here in Scotland. She would find work, that was all there was to it. She didn't know how to do anything, but surely she could learn.

Her heart sank at the thought, but she ignored it.

"I can't face them," she said, more firmly than the first time. "I will stay here. I'll change my name. And I will take the punishment I deserve for my bad acts."

His lips parted at her certainty, and the frustration he felt was evident in the lines of his face. But then he bent his head, she thought in surrender. "Fine," he ground out. "*We* will stay here."

"Rook," she said, inching forward on the bed. "You don't have to stay to—"

He cut her off with a snort. "I won't abandon you without knowing you're safe. *We* will stay and I'll let you come to grips with this shocking knowledge about your family. And you *will* change your mind."

She shook her head. "I won't."

His expression softened, almost with pity. Then he sat down on the bed beside her. He gathered her closer in his arms and pressed a kiss to her forehead as she wrapped her arms around his waist and took the comfort he offered even if she didn't deserve it.

"Whatever you need," he whispered.

And she nodded against his chest, because she knew he would give her just that. And more. Even if she didn't deserve it or him.

Rook had thought he'd known exactly how the past two days would play out. When Anne refused to return home, when she insisted on staying in Scotland and taking on some life she couldn't begin to understand, he'd thought she'd turn from that concept by supper.

She hadn't. For two long days, she had stuck to her course. She'd asked around about work available in Gretna Green and other small towns close by. He'd observed her watching the barmaids and peek into the kitchen as she tried to learn the things she'd been sheltered from her entire life.

He would have admired her tenacity even more if her spark had not been extinguished, as well. Oh, she still talked to him, she still went for the occasional walk when the weather permitted, and she even made love to him. But she rarely smiled and never teased or joked with him anymore.

He hated it. He hated all of it and he wanted to fix it, but he couldn't. He knew better than most that sometimes when a person stopped running, all the pain caught up with them. And he could see that happening to the woman he loved.

Now he glanced up the staircase where she had gone a short time before to lie down after lunch in the inn's dining hall. He needed to talk to her again about going home.

And it was time to explain to her just why it was so important, even if it destroyed the tenuous bonds they'd built between them.

He swallowed hard and climbed the stairs. He entered the chamber at the end of the hall with a long sigh, one that ceased when he saw her. She was sitting by the fire, her slippers on the floor in front of her, reading a book she'd nicked from the sitting room downstairs earlier that day. She was bent over the book, fully engrossed as her eyes darted back and forth.

"It must be quite an adventure," he said as he shut the door behind himself.

She let out a gasp and nearly tossed the book in the air. "You frightened the life out of me," she gasped with a playful glare in his direction. "Has no one ever taught you to alert a person to your presence in a room?"

"Talking to you was how I alerted you to my presence," he said with a shrug.

She smiled, one of the few smiles she had gifted him with in the past forty-eight hours, and for a moment the world stopped. He could see a future with her in those green eyes. They could go back to his island and hide there together. He could make love to her day and night. He could laugh with her and make a life with her where no one could intrude or interrupt. No one could make them think about the past or the wrongs they had each committed.

Then the smile faded and so did his fantasies. She deserved more than that life in the end. He knew too well what hiding away did to a person's soul. He wouldn't do that to her, or allow her to do it to herself.

"Anne," he said, taking her hand as he sat in the chair beside hers. "I want to take you home."

Her eyes went wide. "To—to your island?" she whispered.

He barely held back a pained groan. She had said it, voiced the fantasy as if she craved it just as deeply. And now it came to life in color in his mind and he had to fight to push it away a second time.

"No," he said with great difficulty. "To your family."

"No," she said, pushing to her feet and shaking his hand away. "We already discussed this days ago, Rook. I'm *not* going home."

"Instead you plan to stay here, abandoning your identity and living a life atoning for your sins?" he pressed.

She turned her face. "It's what you did."

He flinched. "Yes, I did. I lived alone on an island for a year, and it was cold and dark and desolate. Your presence brought back some of the joy that I'd told myself I didn't need or deserve."

Her lips parted at that admission and his stomach twisted. What would her expression be like if he admitted he loved her? What would it be like when he told her *why* he'd run away from the world?

"But what if I really *don't* deserve that happiness?" she asked softly.

"You made a mistake," he said softly, and caught her hands in his. "I won't pretend that you didn't. There have clearly been consequences for that mistake, both for you and for your family. But one mistake, committed in desperation, doesn't deserve the life sentence you're pondering."

She bent her head, and he could see her contemplating his words, rolling them around in that wonderful, complicated mind of hers.

He squeezed her hands a little tighter and let out his breath in an unsteady burst. "If there were danger for your sisters and your return could protect them, would you do it?"

"Of course," she said without hesitation. "I would face anything to protect them." She shook her head. "What danger do you mean?"

He sucked in his breath. Now was the time to confess all and see her faith in him shatter.

He leaned forward, closer and closer, trying to find the words. Trying to find the confession he'd never wanted to make. "Ellis," he managed to croak out. "Don't you think it's too coincidental that a man like him, one who has made a living from trickery and lies, would have chosen *you* to pursue when he knew you were engaged to someone important like the Earl of Harcourt?"

She tilted her head as this new information penetrated and she thought it through. "You mean his ulterior motive might have had to do with my fiancé, not myself." She gritted her teeth. "But then why not come back for me? If I were leverage, wouldn't he have collected me to cash in?"

"He might have meant to," Rook said, stomach turning at the thought. "Except Harcourt married your sister instead."

She pushed to her feet as the color left her cheeks and understanding dawned in her eyes. "And I had no value anymore. Harcourt wouldn't need me. He had his price another way."

"But my cousin might still be pursuing whatever it was he thought he could take," Rook said. "And that could be dangerous. I know it all too well."

He meant to say more than that. To talk about Harcourt's late brother, to explain the details of the danger at hand and his own role in it, but before he could, she wrapped her arms around his waist and stared up at him with those emerald eyes he never wanted to lose or look away from. The eyes that held his heart and his soul and, in that moment, his tongue.

"Do you really fear Ellis would harm my family?"

"I *hope* he wouldn't," Rook whispered as he ignored the vice tightening around his heart. "The man I knew, the one who saved me, the one who taught me to survive, the man who treated me like a brother…" He trailed off as his voice caught. "I *hope* he wouldn't harm anyone."

She took his hand, and their fingers threaded together. For a moment they simply breathed together, in unison, their eyes locked.

Then she nodded. "If you think going home will protect my sisters, I'll do it. Even if I'm not welcomed. Even if I can't stay. I'd face their wrath."

"Of course you would," he said. "You are too brave not to do so."

She moved to the table and picked up a few sheets of paper that had been resting there and a quill he hadn't noticed earlier. She must have been writing before she started to read.

"I'll compose a letter to my sisters to tell them we're coming," she said. "It will surely arrive there before we do. And did you say we could leave today?"

He hesitated, for a sound had begun outside. One that thrilled him even if it shouldn't. "It's raining," he said. "Probably best wait until the morning."

She peeked around the corner of the curtain and shook her head. "Our only luck is bad," she murmured.

He caught her hand and lifted it to his lips. "Write your letter and I'll take it down to be off with the mail coach when it passes through shortly. And then I would like to find something to occupy our time."

Her gaze glinted with desire that replaced the worry, just as he'd hoped it would. She drew him down for a kiss that went on just a moment too long. Then she sighed.

"I know you will crow about this, but you're right, of course. The only way for me to know my path forward is to resolve what I did. And I know you don't want to go, but I appreciate you being willing to accompany me."

He said nothing, but took her abandoned seat before the fire and picked up the book she had set aside. He couldn't say what he wanted to say. He couldn't admit that he would be willing to accompany her to hell if it meant a moment more in her company.

He couldn't say it to her, because it could never be. He couldn't say it because she still didn't know the whole truth about him, about Ellis and about exactly *why* his cousin would do such dastardly things to the earl Anne's sister had married.

CHAPTER 16

Anne sat up straight on her horse and looked down into the valley where Harcourt Heights was nestled. It was a fine prospect, with a lake to one side and the sea just in the distance to the west. Whatever the Earl of Harcourt's financial difficulties, he hadn't yet allowed them to put the estate in disrepair. Probably why he had been in such a rush to marry a Shelley Sister and receive a fine dowry.

Once upon a time she had resigned herself to being mistress of the estate, though she had never found any love for the place in her heart. And now that same heart throbbed in terror as she gazed down at its stone façade in the distance.

"You'll need to breathe for any of this to work," Rook said softly, tearing her from her tangled thoughts, just as he had been doing for the past week as they rode through terrible weather and road conditions to make it here at last.

She nodded without taking her eyes from the estate. "Mmmhmmm."

He caught her hand and lifted it to his lips. Though she wore riding gloves, she felt the pressure of his mouth against her hand, the warmth of his fingers on her palm, and for a blissful moment calm settled through her. She glanced toward him with a grateful smile.

"Thank you," she said softly.

He cocked his head and his gaze held hers with dark intensity. "I'm here for you, Anne. For as long as you want me."

Her heart stuttered as he released her. She feared she'd never stop wanting Rook Maitland. Even when he left her, at last, as she knew he would do.

She drew a ragged breath. "I suppose we should go rather than sit on this hill all day. Face the consequences."

He nodded and nickered for his horse to start down the hill toward the house. They were both silent for a short while, then he looked at her from the corner of his eye. "Whatever happens next, I will never regret what was between us."

Her lips parted at that admission. At the sweetness of his tone when he said it. She smiled at him, trying to keep the tears from her eyes. "And I will never forget it."

They entered the gate at the end of the long drive and came around a slow curve where the manor house was revealed. Anne could hardly breathe as they crossed the last quarter mile to the stone staircase that led to the home she had abandoned just weeks before.

Servants came from the stables, but it was Rook who slung down from his horse and helped her from her own. As she squeezed his hand and released him to turn toward the house, the door flew open and Anne's heart all but stopped.

Her sisters were practically shoving each other through the narrow space and then racing down the stairs toward her, tears streaming down both their faces, just as she felt her own on her cheeks. Juliana and Thomasina hit her at the same time, and then it was just arms around her and sobbing, completely garbled words as the Shelley Sisters were reunited at last.

"That's enough now."

Anne stiffened at the sound of her father's voice. Slowly the sisters parted, with Juliana taking one side of Anne and Thomasina the other. As if they were guarding her, just as they'd always done. Judging from her father's angry expression, perhaps she needed it.

"Do you know how much damned trouble you've created for everyone?" he snapped as a greeting.

Before he could say anything else, Jasper Kincaid, the Earl of Harcourt, came out onto the step. His gaze was first on Thomasina, but then it settled on Anne, and all the rage she had felt in his forcing her sister to wed burst up in her, out of control. She rushed forward, her fists raised in anger.

"You bastard!" she shouted as she lunged at him. "How could you? How could you destroy my sister's life?"

Rook caught her before she could swing at the earl, yanking her back toward his chest by both elbows. Thomasina jumped between them, her hands up to ward Anne away.

"No!" Thomasina said as she backed toward Jasper and touched his arm. "Don't, Anne! I love him. Do you understand me? We love each other."

The words crackled through the air like a whip lash, and Rook clung tighter to Anne as she stared at the Earl and Countess of Harcourt, who were now standing beside each other, Thomasina's hand in the crook of his arm, him gazing down at her with what was clearly adoration.

Then Anne looked at her still-angry father and the unreadable Juliana. She made a tiny sound in the back of her throat and sagged against Rook, like the past few weeks were catching up with her. Like she could no longer support herself.

Thomasina and Juliana gasped as she folded, but Rook shook his head gently to ward them off as he balanced her. "It's all right," he said into her ear softly. "I'm here."

The Earl of Harcourt was staring at him now. His eyes

narrowed. The ones that looked so much like his dead brother's eyes. Christ, all the damned chickens were about to come to roost today.

"Why don't we go inside?" Harcourt suggested. "We obviously have a great deal to discuss, and it looks as though you two could use some tea after your long trip home."

Rook wrinkled his brow. He never would have guessed their host would be so solicitous, but here they were. As for Anne, she flinched at his use of the word home, but she seemed to have gathered herself, for she straightened, no longer leaning on Rook, and nodded. "Yes. That is very wise, Harcourt."

Harcourt inclined his head toward her and then guided his wife into the house. Juliana shot her sister one last look. Their eyes held a moment and Rook gaped at the unspoken bond between them. At the communication that flowed like a river.

Juliana pursed her lips and gave a brief nod before she grabbed for her father's arm. "Come, Father, you can bluster while you drink some tea."

"I think I need scotch for this," their father said, loudly and with another glare over his shoulder.

"Well, Harcourt has that, too," Juliana said with a heavy sigh. "I'll partake, as well."

That left Anne and Rook together. She glanced up at him with a weak half-smile. "They're only part the way to the stable with the horses. What do you say we just run away?"

She was voicing his own desires once again, and it felt like she'd put her hand around his heart and squeezed each time she did it. But he patted her hand and guided her into the house as if she didn't tempt him at all. "I think we'd not get to the gate before Harcourt would have us followed, put in bindings and returned."

"Best just go in for tea then, eh?" she asked with a dry laugh.

"Best, I think," he agreed.

They had reached the parlor where the others had entered and they moved inside together. As soon as they crossed the threshold,

Anne released his arm and crossed away from him. A reminder that she was entering her world. He didn't belong here. So he moved to the opposite corner, folded his arms and waited for whatever would come next.

"Why don't we start with introductions?" Thomasina said after tea had been brought and the door to the parlor had been closed for some semblance of privacy. She sent a pointed look at Rook.

Anne shifted and moved a little closer to him. "This is Rook."

Rook knew why she didn't say his entire name, but he flinched regardless. Harcourt straightened up and glared. "*Rook?*" he repeated, through what were obviously clenched teeth. "Bloody hell."

"Constantine," she corrected herself.

Harcourt looked as though he was reaching the end of his rope. His cool gaze held on Anne as he growled, "Anne."

With a shake of his head, Rook stepped forward to end this farce. Anne was trying to protect him, but she couldn't. He didn't deserve it. He sighed and said, "Constantine Maitland, my lord. I go by Rook."

"Maitland," Thomasina gasped as it seemed like the entire room recoiled except for Mr. Shelley, who was too busy downing a tall glass of scotch.

"Like Ellis Maitland, I presume," Harcourt growled as he flat-footed his way across the parlor like a bullfighter.

"My cousin," Rook acknowledged. He certainly wasn't going to lie. Not anymore.

Harcourt's face was turning purple. "You bastard."

He shoved Rook with both hands, and Rook rocked back but refused to step away. He understood this man's anger with him perfectly, but if it came to blows, he wasn't going to back down. A brawl might actually feel good in the midst of all the upheaval.

Harcourt shoved him again as Anne and Thomasina raced toward the men.

"Jasper!" Thomasina gasped, catching her husband's elbow before he could swing the fist he so clearly wanted to.

Anne wedged herself between them, as well, first pushing Rook back a few steps. When he was somewhat out of harm's way, she pivoted toward her former fiancé and threw her arms wide, as if she would protect Rook. He stared down at her, smelling the soft fragrance of her hair. Who was the last person who had defended him? His cousin, perhaps, years before? No one in recent memory, that was certain.

"Stop!" Anne ordered. "This man saved my life. He brought me home. He doesn't deserve your censure, no matter whose name he shares."

Harcourt's jaw was still flexed and he jammed his fists down at his sides as he continued to glare at Rook. "Explain."

Anne glanced up at Rook, her gaze softer. She mouthed *I'm sorry.*

He shook his head and motioned her toward the settee. She squeezed his hand one last time and left him again, this time to sit next to Juliana on the couch.

She bent her head. "I know the trouble I caused," she whispered. She sounded bone-weary. "Running off with Ellis Maitland. Breaking our engagement in the worst way. Forcing Thomasina into my foolishness by making her pretend to be me. But I have been punished for it, I assure you."

Juliana took her hand. "What did he do to you?" she whispered.

"Ellis?" Anne glanced at Rook. "Ellis did *nothing*. I was a pawn in a game I hadn't even realized he was playing. He took me to some little village—"

"Beckfoot," Harcourt interrupted with a glare for Rook. "My man and I followed you there and heard you had gotten onto a boat with some crony of Maitland's."

She swallowed. "That was Rook."

"Yes, I know. So you were part of Maitland's scheme?" Harcourt said. Rook could see he was only just reining in his rage. If the whole family hadn't been in the room, the earl wouldn't have stopped with a few shoves.

Not that Rook could blame him.

Rook straightened. "I wasn't, though I don't expect you to believe it, my lord. Handsome...er, *Ellis* and I worked together for a long time. I won't deny that. But I haven't been associated with him for a year. He showed up begging for my help. I had reasons not to turn him away. But I didn't know anything about Anne or your engagement or anything else. I showed up in Beckfoot and had a woman thrown into the boat. One Ellis was saying he would return for in time. I couldn't leave her there. What else was I to do but try to protect her?"

"I believed Ellis when he said he would return and we would marry," Anne continued. "And when it became clear he wouldn't, I then asked Rook to help me get home. We've been on the road since then, working our way back to all of you. Though I did...er... promise payment for his trouble," she said with a quick glance toward her father.

Mr. Shelley had been quiet during the exchange and now he folded his arms. "If you think I'm going to give a farthing to—"

Rook help up a hand. "I don't want a farthing, I assure you." He glanced at Anne. "There's no debt to pay but my own, Anne. You owe me nothing."

Her expression softened a fraction, and he wanted so much to go to her and hold her. He clenched his fists at his sides instead and stayed where he was.

She turned away with a blush.

"Well, we certainly appreciate your bringing Anne home," Harcourt drawled, his tone still confrontational and cold. The two men locked eyes and held for a moment. Then Harcourt turned his face toward his wife. His look changed in a heartbeat, becoming warm and loving the moment he looked at Thomasina. "Perhaps it would be best if Anne goes up to her room. You three can reunite privately, as I know you are aching to do. We can all take a breath and continue this conversation at supper when everyone is in a better mindset."

Thomasina glanced at Anne and then Juliana. Their sisterly connection was so powerful Rook almost thought he should look away from it. It was theirs and private, even from the men they cared for. He hoped with time Anne could reestablish whatever she had lost through her actions. He hoped she would find a future she deserved.

"Perhaps that would be best," Thomasina said. "And I will have Willard prepare a room for our guest, as well."

"Excellent." Harcourt squeezed her hand. "While you all go upstairs, I will have a moment with Mr. Maitland, I think."

Anne rushed to her feet, lips parting as if she would say something, but Thomasina slowly lifted a hand to her husband's cheek. "You promise you shall not do anything you'll have to apologize for later," she said, her tone quiet, but firm. Guiding.

Harcourt smiled, and Rook was surprised at how many years it took from his face. "I will not let you down, love."

Thomasina and Juliana moved toward the door, motioning for Anne for follow. She did slowly, but as she passed Rook, she hesitated. "I'm sorry," she whispered. "Be careful."

"You have nothing to be sorry for," he said. "And I am always careful."

"No, you're not," she said on a rough laugh as she moved away from him and out the door with her sisters.

All that was left in the room were Mr. Shelley and Harcourt. Rook folded his arms as he waited for the onslaught from them both. But to his surprise, Harcourt glared at Shelley. "I said alone," he growled.

Shelley blinked at him. "I thought—"

"You think a great many things, but you didn't protect your daughters before and you shall not have the benefit of doing so now. Get out," Harcourt ordered, all lord of the manor in his disdainful look and tone.

Shelley sputtered, but did as he was told and left, slamming the door behind himself.

And then there were two.

"You don't think much of your father-in-law," Rook drawled.

"There isn't much to think of, that is certain." Harcourt let out a long sigh. "Do you want a drink, assuming that lout hasn't downed all my scotch?"

Rook lifted his brows. He hadn't expected such hospitality. "I think considering the circumstances, I'd best keep my faculties."

"Excellent notion," Harcourt said, then poured himself a drink. He took a swig as he examined Rook over the edge of the glass. "You and Anne have become close, it seems, during your weeks together."

Rook lifted his chin. He wasn't about to defend himself against a man whose cold demeanor had sent Anne off in the first place. "Yes," he said softly. "Close enough that even if they were dressed alike, *I* think I could determine which was Anne and which was Lady Harcourt."

Harcourt glared at him more closely. More of an examination than anything. "Perhaps you could. As could I. I knew my wife the moment I saw her that night Anne disappeared. But it seems my former fiancée has been telling you a great deal."

Rook shrugged. "There's not much else to do on the road but talk."

"There are a few things," Harcourt said, downing the remainder of his drink in one slug.

Rook refused to respond to that. He wasn't going to tell this man about his relationship to Anne. That was too precious to him. He wouldn't sully it by pretending it was something cheap or tawdry.

"I assume you want to speak to me about my cousin," Rook said. "Not your sister-in-law."

"I want to speak to you about both," Harcourt growled. "But the bigger issue at present is Ellis Maitland." He set his empty glass on the sideboard with a hard clink of glass on wood. "Now that Anne isn't here to disappoint, I want the truth. Are you involved in what your cousin has been doing?"

Rook's jaw tightened, both at the accusation and the realization that there were activities of Ellis's that he didn't know about. Judging from Harcourt's demeanor, ones he wished he didn't have to know about. But to protect Anne, he needed more information.

Rook leaned in. "Tell me everything."

CHAPTER 17

Anne sank into the steamy heaven of the bathwater, letting it cover her shoulders, then her neck, then dunked her head in and lay on the smooth bottom, holding her breath. Perhaps she could stay here under the water forever. Then she wouldn't have to face the sisters who moved to stand at the edge of the tub and stare down at her.

"Anne," Juliana said, her voice tinny through the water. "Stop hiding and talk to us."

Anne sat up, smoothing her hair back and wiping the water from her eyes with a sigh. So much for the plan to become a mermaid.

Thomasina handed over a bar of soap and Anne lifted it to her nose, inhaling deeply of lemon essence and lavender before she dipped it beneath the water and began to lather it gently between her hands. She waited, unspeaking, for the barrage of questions to begin.

Instead, Thomasina leaned in and kissed her damp temple. "We were so afraid for you. And felt so empty with just the two of us here."

Juliana nodded. "I couldn't stop thinking about what horrible things you might have been going through. To see you here with us is…" She trailed off and wiped her eyes.

That set off the tears Anne had been trying to hold back. She set her soap aside and covered her face. "I'm so sorry I worried you. And caused such devastation."

Thomasina slid a finger beneath her chin and tilted her face up. "Not devastation. I told you I'm happy and I am."

"Are you?" Anne whispered. "Could you truly be?"

Thomasina gave a tiny laugh. "Yes. But now that it's just the three of us, why don't you explain a little better what happened?"

Anne took up the soap and washed to distract herself as she began her tale. "I never wanted to marry Harcourt," she said. "When Father came into the room with him all those months ago and declared one of us would be his bride, my mind was screaming *please not me.*"

Thomasina smiled softly and bent her head, but didn't interrupt.

"I tried to be better than what I know are my worst impulses," Anne continued. "I tried to accept what couldn't be changed, but as the time to our wedding grew closer, my panic became harder to ignore. I met Ellis Maitland here in Harcourt, at the first ball celebrating my engagement."

"He approached you," Thomasina said with wide eyes.

Anne nodded. "From everything Rook shared with me, I realize now that Maitland only wanted to use me to get to Harcourt. But at the time, it felt like he offered me a lifeline. He was charming and laughed at my jokes. After a short acquaintance, he seemed like the lesser evil when I thought of my future."

Juliana shook her head. "The lesser evil isn't a very romantic notion."

"Neither is marrying someone you don't want at all," Anne said.

Thomasina shifted behind her and said, "Here, let me wash your hair."

Anne glanced at her in surprise. The sisters had taken turns washing each other's hair for as long as she could recall. But with everything that had happened, she wasn't certain she would be accepted back so easily.

But of course she would. Because her sisters were kind and wonderful and as dear to her as her own breath. She had run, but never from them. And the fact that she hadn't broken their precious bond entirely warmed her heart and her soul.

Thomasina began to lather her hair gently and Anne let out a happy sigh.

"So you ran," Juliana said softly.

"I ran," Anne repeated, refocusing on her story. "And as I said in the parlor, he almost immediately dumped me into Rook's boat and life." She half turned and looked at Thomasina. "And *you* were forced to marry Harcourt."

Thomasina shook her head. "And it is the happiest I have ever been in my life. Anne, if you were silently screaming at Father not to pick you as Harcourt's bride, I was screaming the opposite. From the first moment I laid eyes on him, I longed to be his. When he was made your fiancé, my heart broke, but I felt there was nothing to do."

"You—you wanted him from the beginning?" Anne whispered. She was shocked at that response. Utterly shocked down to her very toes.

Juliana laughed. "You see, Thomasina, I told you that if Anne didn't want him, she'd never be able to imagine someone else could. She *never* suspected your feelings."

"I didn't," Anne agreed. "Thomasina, how terrible that must have been for you!"

"It was," Thomasina said with a sigh. "I couldn't disrupt your future and I had no inkling that he might feel the same for me. So I stood by, silent and cowardly, waiting for my heart to be broken when you two married. The night you asked me to take your place, I did it so that I could pretend, just for a moment, that he was mine. Your leaving set me free, it didn't trap me. When Jasper demanded I marry him in your stead, I wasn't upset—I was joyful. And when I realized he loved me as much as I loved him...*that* was the happiest day of my life."

Anne shook her head. "I cannot believe I was so selfishly blind to your suffering. What kind of sister am I?"

"She hid it," Juliana pointed out. "Now rinse your hair before you blind yourself with the soap."

Anne slid down and dunked her head back, but she couldn't stop thinking about all she'd ignored and pretended away. She sat up and squeezed the water from her hair as she twisted in the tub to look at Thomasina. "You *truly* love him. And you are happy."

"They are delirious," Juliana said before Thomasina could respond. "It is both heartening and horrifying to watch, I assure you."

"Will he truly love you all your life, though?" Anne asked.

Thomasina smiled, and there was no doubt in her eyes. "He almost died for me. So I think yes."

"Almost died for you?" Anne gasped.

"Ellis Maitland showed up here a few days ago," Thomasina said with a shudder. "He believes we have something Jasper's brother Solomon stole from him. I came upon him when he was searching and it got...intense. He is very desperate."

Juliana shifted. "The gun did go off accidentally," she offered softly.

"It still nearly killed my husband when it did," Thomasina said, her spine straightening.

Anne got up and took the towel Juliana offered her. She wrapped it around herself with a shake of her head as she thought of Rook. He cared deeply for Ellis, despite how angry he was at his cousin. Ellis had saved his life. He would be devastated to see how far he'd fallen.

"Anne, is it possible *your* Mr. Maitland, this...this *Rook* is involved in Ellis Maitland's schemes?" Juliana asked.

Anne pivoted to face her. "Never!" she burst out. "He left that life. Ellis convinced him to help this last time, but they haven't had any contact for a long time."

She realized how strong her tone had been when her sisters both drew back at it. Thomasina arched a brow. "You love him."

Anne staggered at the words she had been avoiding saying, even just to herself. Now that they had been spoken, they hung in the air, a demon released from Pandora's box. Worse than that, they were a truth she couldn't deny.

She sank down on the closest chair and bent her head. "Yes," she whispered. "I do love him. Even though it is impossible."

Her sisters exchanged a glance. "Because he's a criminal?" Thomasina asked, her eyebrows lifting.

"I told you, he *isn't!*" Anne huffed, frustrated that her sisters couldn't see the goodness that she knew resided in every fiber of Rook's being.

Juliana worried her lip. "Perhaps he isn't. Perhaps you are right about him, but how can we not worry knowing his affiliations? Knowing that he admitted he once involved himself in illicit endeavors?"

"You two spent a great deal of time together while you were missing," Thomasina said, picking up where Juliana had left off before Anne could argue. "Could you be mistaking your feelings? I can imagine the intensity of being trapped together, of traveling together...of...of whatever else you two might have done together. That could make you believe you felt-"

"It isn't a belief," Anne said, running a hand through her wet hair. "It's the truth. But if you fear me linking my future with him, you needn't. It...it cannot be. No matter what I feel, it is...hopeless."

Her shoulders rolled forward as the finality of that truth hit her in her gut. She would have preferred being struck physically in that moment.

"Why?" Thomasina whispered.

"Because we are from such different worlds," Anne said with a sigh. "Although we might have...connected...he was stuck with me, he didn't choose me. He wants to live on an island alone and I don't even know how to clean a cast iron skillet or throw a knife."

Her sisters exchanged a confused glance. Then Thomasina stepped forward and took her hands. "When you say connected, I assume you mean…sex. That you physically connected."

Anne had meant more than that, but she nodded with a deep blush.

"He took you to bed?" Juliana gasped.

Anne and Thomasina pivoted at her loud voice. "Gracious, Juliana, don't bring the house down," Thomasina chuckled.

"To be fair, *I* did the taking," Anne admitted. "He offered me a dozen reasons not to do it and seemingly as many opportunities to remain untouched. But in the end, I wanted him too much to deny what was between us. If I was already to be ruined by scandal in rumor, I thought I could at least enjoy it in truth."

"I am the only one of my sisters to remain a virgin?" Juliana huffed.

Thomasina laughed and Anne managed a rusty one of her own at the quip, even though admitting she loved Rook gave her little pleasure. It only made their inevitable parting all the more painful.

"I don't know about this person," Thomasina said carefully. "Or his ultimate intentions, either on the road with you or here. I do fear them and it will take time for me to change my opinion. But I do have to say that I don't think a man would allow a woman to drag him across Scotland in the rain if he didn't care for her. Nor look at a woman the way he looked at you in the parlor today."

Anne sucked in a breath at the very idea. But she couldn't be foolish. Not when it came to this, not after every other reckless thing she'd done.

"I have no doubt he *cares* for me," she said. "But that doesn't equal love, nor any desire to do anything but deal with the problem with his cousin and go home. I appreciate your support after all I've done to betray your trust, but in this, I know what is true."

Thomasina opened her mouth as if to argue further, but Juliana stepped forward and placed a gentle hand on her forearm. "We will leave the subject closed for the moment," Juliana said with a meaningful look for their sister. "Let us help you dress and ready yourself. Then we'll go downstairs and figure this out. Together."

Anne smiled as she got to her feet and tucked her towel tighter before she stepped into the open arms of her sisters. "I have missed you two so very much. And you are right, together we can work out anything."

But as she reveled in the warmth of her sisters' acceptance and love, she couldn't help but have a sinking feeling. In the end her sisterly love couldn't truly solve her problems.

And Rook was not hers to keep.

R ook stood in the middle of a chamber that was larger than his entire cottage on the island. It was decorated with a sophisticated flair, from the plain but expensive bedclothes to the artwork on its walls. When he stepped to the window, it looked over a magnificent garden and down a long pathway to a lake in the distance.

It was the home of a king. A queen. A place where Anne belonged. He certainly didn't.

His conversation with the Lord Harcourt had been difficult, to say the least. He now knew the full extent of his cousin's desperation. And if Ellis hadn't been satisfied by the encounter on Harcourt's estate a few days prior, he would surely come back.

Which meant Rook had to stay, as well. Perhaps he could help his cousin. Or at least protect those in his path.

He shook his head. Being here was going to be torture. Looking at Anne and never being able to touch her again was going to be torture. But it was better for her. So he had to be better for her too.

There was a knock on his door, and when he acknowledged it, the door opened to reveal a footman in Harcourt's fine livery.

"Excuse me, sir. Your presence has been requested for drinks before supper."

Rook glanced at the fine clock on his mantel and shook his head. Christ, it was late in the day. Between the excitement of their arrival and the extremely long and uncomfortable conversation with Harcourt, he had lost track of time. "I will be right down."

The footman nodded and backed from the room. Rook looked at himself in the mirror. He had changed from the day's clothing, of course, and been offered a hot bath. But his current outfit wasn't exactly befitting the kind of supper where one was invited to drinks beforehand.

But what was there to do? He smoothed the rough fabric of his jacket and exited the chamber. He went downstairs and stopped at the bottom. He'd forgotten to ask the location of these drinks and it was an enormous estate.

So he began to roam, trying to listen for the sounds of talking from any of the rooms.

The walk was even more evidence of how he didn't belong here. There were dozens of parlors along the hallway, each more dazzling than the next. For a man who was suffering financially, Harcourt didn't reveal it. And Rook wondered if Anne would one day regret not marrying as she'd been intended. Obviously, Harcourt and Thomasina were a better match, but certainly if Anne hadn't run away, hadn't ruined herself with him…she could have had someone just as important. More important.

And now she would only have memories of tiny inn bedrooms and him. Those same memories would sustain him, but would they haunt her in the end?

He heard voices at last and shook off the maudlin thoughts as he entered the last parlor on the left down the long hallway. As he stepped into the room, his gaze immediately moved to Anne. She was standing at the fireplace, staring into the flames. She turned as he entered, and his breath caught.

He'd spent weeks with this woman, captivated by her beauty. But today she was more than beautiful. She was exquisite in an evening gown of fine blue-green silk that matched the sea and made her eyes seem lighter. He hair had been done elaborately on the crown of her head, and tendrils teased around her cheeks as if to draw attention to her lovely face all the more.

The gown was elegant, with a brocading across the bodice that lifted her breasts slightly and gave him a mouthwatering vision of the curves he so adored and had worshipped over and over when they were alone. How he wanted to unwrap this gorgeous package before him and forget all the things that would keep them apart now. How he wished he could ride away with her and pretend like this world didn't exist.

Her full lips parted as if she could read his mind, and she took a step toward him before the Earl of Harcourt scowled and cut her off.

"Maitland," he said. "Good of you to join us. Will you have a drink?"

"Yes," Rook managed past a dry throat. He took the drink when it was given to him and nodded to whatever it was Harcourt said. When the earl walked away, Rook felt compelled to move to Anne. Like a sailor to a siren on the rocks.

Only she would be the one destroyed if he did. So he shook his head and instead walked to the window. He tried to control his breathing as he stared into the gathering darkness, tried to get himself together.

But then she was at his elbow and he was lost in lemony-fresh scent and feather-light warmth as she touched his elbow and turned him toward her.

"Good evening," she said, her cheeks going pink like she was shy despite all they'd done together. He supposed that made sense. Here, in this place, with these people, she was a different person to the one who had surrendered to a villain like him. He was seeing her for the first time.

"Miss Shelley," he said, forcing his tone to be cool.

"Rook?" she murmured, her brow furrowing. "What are you doing?"

"Nothing, I'm just greeting you," he said, turning away slightly as he downed half his drink in one swig. "It's a fine night, isn't it?"

Her lips pursed and her fingers folded into fists at her sides. "I suppose. Was Harcourt too hard on you earlier when you were left alone? I was worried."

He flinched at her care. The care he certainly hadn't earned. "You needn't worry yourself about my well-being, I assure you. You should focus on your reunion with your sisters and your father."

Anne glanced back. Her father was slouched on Harcourt's couch with a drink dangling precariously from his fingertips. Not his first drink, it seemed, judging from the fact the man looked half sauced.

"My father doesn't give a damn about me now that I have no bartering value," she said, pain lacing her tone for a moment.

He so longed to take her hand. To hear more about that pain. To soothe it somehow. But he resisted, because it was not his place. It never had been—that was always an illusion.

"I'm sorry to hear you have troubles," he said, forcing the coolness to remain in his tone. "But I'm sure you are looking forward to supper. You must have missed these grand meals."

She leaned closer. "Why are you being so different?" she asked. "Why are you putting up some wall of propriety between us?"

He gritted his teeth. "Because I didn't do it earlier when I should have, and now I must rectify that mistake."

She took a long step back. "Mistake?" she repeated.

He nodded, even though he hadn't meant that word to hit such a solid mark. He saw how it hurt her. He hated himself for it, even if it was for her own good. For his good. They had to start separating now.

It was imperative.

She inclined her head. "Excuse me, Mr. Maitland."

"Miss Shelley," he whispered as she walked away back to her

sister. Juliana, he thought, since Thomasina was with her husband. She said something to Juliana and they looked at him together. Juliana glared daggers, but Anne's eyes shimmered with wants and fears and pains.

This would not do. She was still too connected to him. Still too filled with whatever longing they had surrendered to on the road. He had to sever the contact at last. He had to find a way to make her not want him.

And he knew one way.

He cleared his throat. "I hate to break up the polite emptiness of this gathering," he said, pushing aside the niceties he'd used as a shield with her. "But I think we need to speak about my cousin."

Harcourt wrinkled his brow. "Did we not fully explore that issue earlier today?"

Rook lifted his chin as he met the man's eyes evenly. "We did not. I withheld a key fact. Ellis was involved in the death of your brother, Lord Harcourt."

He let his gaze slip to Anne. She had lost all the color to her cheeks as she stared at him.

"And I knew it from the very beginning."

CHAPTER 18

R ook heard Anne's short scream as Harcourt made his way across the room and swung his fist. He landed it square across Rook's cheekbone, sending a shot of pain through his face and down his neck, momentarily making him see stars. Otherwise, he forced himself not to react, even though he could have flattened the earl with a flick of his wrist.

"I deserved that," he said, and his gaze slipped to Anne. She had two hands over her mouth and her green eyes were wide and filled with tears. "It may be the only thing I have deserved in a long time."

She flinched at that observation, made to remind her that he didn't belong in her world. Not that she needed it.

She lowered her hands and marched toward the men. Thomasina had already reached her husband and pulled him away. Harcourt was still shouting something—it didn't matter what, some slur Rook deserved—as Anne edged her way between them. Only this time she didn't touch Rook. She seemed to do her best not to touch him.

"Tell me the truth," she said, meeting his eyes. "Tell me *all* of it."

The accusation was thick in her tone, the hurt. He hated it even though he had done this for this exact purpose. He needed her to hate him. It would make it easier in the end.

Rook looked at Harcourt, not her. "My cousin and your brother involved themselves with Winston Leonard."

Immediately Harcourt recoiled and staggered back a step.

"Yes," Rook said softly at the strong reaction. "I think you know him."

Thomasina looked from Rook to Harcourt to Anne and back to her husband. "Why does that name make you flinch? Winston Leonard is the third son of the Duke of Coningburgh, is he not? He's a gentleman."

Harcourt cleared his throat and scrubbed a hand over his face. "He masquerades as such," he said as he slipped an arm around Thomasina's waist. In that moment, Rook saw how protective he was of her. How in love. He saw a mirror of his own feelings for Anne and wished he could be so free with them.

"What does that mean?" Juliana pressed, coming to take Anne's hand. He was happy for the support she had. She would need it.

"There are rumors about him," Harcourt said. "That he is involved in very dangerous activities. That he is not a man to cross, to the point that even the duke is afraid of his son. That he has...he's killed."

"They aren't mere rumors," Rook said as he easily conjured an image of the most vile villain he'd ever known. "Everything said about the man is true. He is *worse* than what you know—it is no idle chatter."

"Damn it, Solomon," Harcourt muttered, referring to his late brother.

Rook let out his breath in a long sigh and then said, "When Ellis and your brother got involved with him, they were working for him. I think...Solomon, you said his name was. May I refer to him as such to reduce the confusion caused by calling him Harcourt?"

Harcourt looked sick, but he nodded. "Yes. My brother never wore our title with honor, and hearing this I think he deserved it less. Call him by his Christian name. How did my brother meet you and your cousin?"

Rook shook his head and tried to push aside the jealousy and loss that question inspired in him. Anne's lips parted as if she could read that pain, and her hand stirred at her side like she wanted to touch him.

He stepped back a little, though he wanted that touch so damned much it hurt. "In a gaming hell, Donville Masquerade."

Harcourt flinched again, and from the settee, the forgotten and very drunk Mr. Shelley called out, "Lovely lightskirts there. Very accommodating before they revoked my membership."

He immediately passed out, removing himself from the conversation, but Anne caught her breath and the other two sisters blushed red. They obviously now knew what kind of place Donville Masquerade was.

"Solomon lost a great deal of money to Ellis that night, but they must have gotten on, because next thing I knew he was introducing your brother to me and telling me he was going to help us." Rook set his jaw. "I warned them both it would end in nothing good, mixing our worlds, but they didn't listen."

"You're a bloody hero," Harcourt growled. "What was my brother doing for Ellis?"

"Providing access," Rook explained. "Ellis and I had been robbing and running love ploys for decades. We did fine, but my cousin wanted even more. Bigger fish, he kept saying. Solomon provided introduction to those big fish for a cut."

Harcourt paced away. "How he must have loved playing the villain, my selfish brother."

"Sometimes." Rook hesitated and moved a step closer to Harcourt. "The game appealed to him, I won't say it didn't. But I think you should know that he also spoke often about how he knew he had destroyed the wealth and good name of your family. There was some part of him that wanted to earn enough blunt to buy back some of the good graces. He also often spoke of you, especially at the end. You two had a falling out?"

Harcourt pivoted to face him, his lips parted. All the color had left his face. Thomasina came up beside him and took his hand, watching his expression. And again, their love was on display. "He told you that?"

Rook nodded without speaking.

"We did," Harcourt whispered after a moment had passed. "A year before his death."

"About the time he met my cousin," Rook said, some of his hatred for Solomon Kincaid fading with this information. In the end, it seemed they were all broken. All lost. He couldn't fully despise a man for that. "Which explains a great deal. He wanted to earn your respect, Harcourt. He obviously loved you."

Harcourt stared at Rook for what felt like forever. Then he whispered, "Thank you for that. It means a great deal. I certainly wish he had gone about it a different way."

"Yes." Rook shook his head. "The two of them got very good at their games. And I was edged out more and more. By the time they met Winston Leonard, they no longer asked for my opinion or listened when it was given. He had heard of some of their schemes and asked them to do some work for him. But those two fools didn't like the terms and decided to take something from him."

"What is it exactly?" Thomasina asked. "Ellis came here, demanding, desperate, but my husband and I thought it was a statue Solomon had hidden and Ellis flew into a wild outburst when he saw it. He was very clear that wasn't what he came for."

"A jewel, my lady," Rook said softly. "As big as your fist. An emerald with the finest cut I've ever seen. Immediately the whole thing went wrong. Leonard came at them like a banshee from hell. I have never seen my cousin afraid until that day when they were called to the dueling field to settle the matter. Ellis tried to negotiate. And Leonard cut Solomon down as an example."

Harcourt staggered and sat down hard in the chair. "So it *wasn't* a duel."

"No, it was a cold-blooded murder. I had followed them, but I was too far off to do anything to help them. Leonard gave my cousin a certain amount of time to return the gem. Honestly, I assumed he had done so until all…this."

Anne moved closer to him. "Assumed?"

Rook met her gaze. There were many things he wanted to say to push her away. "We had a code. Murder wasn't part of it. Ellis might not have struck Solomon Kincaid down, but his actions led to his end. I walked away from him. From everything."

"*That* was when you went to your island," Anne breathed.

Harcourt looked between them with a wrinkled brow. "But he came back and you helped him."

"He isn't all bad." Rook heard the crack in his voice, the one he couldn't control. "He saved me in many ways that I can never express." As he said it, Anne took another step toward him and he both prayed she would touch him and that she wouldn't. She didn't, though her green gaze held his gently. "So I agreed, not knowing the rest. But when I heard your name, your title, in Gretna Green, I knew there was no coincidence."

"It isn't," Harcourt mused. "Ellis thinks we have the gem. His desperation for it is evident."

"And that is very out of character," Rook said with a confused shake of his head. "Ellis has always been nonchalant about his acts. Even when he was threatened, you couldn't ruffle his feathers. When he is desperate, it is never good. That he concocted this terrible plan with Anne and can't seem to control himself about this…it makes me wonder what else Leonard is threatening. What else Ellis thinks he has to lose."

"Is that all of it then?" Harcourt asked, rising back to his feet.

Rook nodded slowly.

"I need a moment," Harcourt said softly. He exited the room

without any further comment. Thomasina made a soft sound of distress and rushed after him.

Anne still stared at Rook, her gaze even and unreadable. Then she turned to Juliana. "Will you take Father?"

Juliana glanced at him. "I don't want to leave you alone with him."

Rook refused to react to that, though Anne flinched. She moved toward her sister, taking both her hands. They said nothing, but the conversation flowed between them nonetheless for a moment. Juliana leaned forward and rested her forehead against Anne's at last.

"Anne—" she breathed.

Anne shook her head. "Please."

Juliana pulled away and glanced at him. Held his stare for a beat, two. Then she sighed. "Very well. I suppose there is little harm to it at any rate."

She paced away to their father. It took a moment for her to rouse the drunken lout and get him to stagger from the room with her. Once she had, Anne moved to the door and closed it gently. She leaned against it, watching him. Reading him. Blaming him.

Then she let out a sigh and said, "Now tell me the truth. How long did you *really* know Harcourt was my fiancé?"

Anne watched Rook cringe and knew the answer before he spoke. Still, she needed to hear it and he didn't disappoint.

"I told Harcourt the truth a moment ago. I didn't know of your connection until Gretna Green. The same time you found out Thomasina had married him in your stead. I swear to you on my life, on my island, on my peace, I didn't lie about that."

She bent her head and wished that didn't give her so much relief. "But you didn't tell me either. We spent so much time together after you found out, both in town and on the road. You talked to me about so much, but never even a hint about Ellis and Harcourt and all this mess."

He turned and walked away to the window. "I know."

"Why didn't you?" Anger rose up in her and she tamped it down with difficulty. "Why did you keep me in the dark?"

He was silent for a long moment. His hands flexed in and out of fists at his sides as he stared into the darkness gathering outside.

"Constantine," she whispered.

He pivoted at her use of his first name. It was the mark she'd intended to hit. His lips thinned before he choked out, "Because every moment with you has been stolen since the beginning. And I knew that once you found out the truth, you would look at me as you're looking at me now. Like I'm shit on your shoe. And I am, Anne. I am."

She flinched. "I already knew what you were, Rook."

"No, you didn't. You romanticized me into a Robin Hood from the old children's stories. Didn't you?"

She ground her teeth. Damn him for seeing through her. "I suppose I might have pictured you as a noble highwayman, yes."

"But I wasn't," he said softly. "I didn't go out to hurt people. Brutality was never my style. But I did what was right for me and no one else. I was not a hero. And what I told you about Ellis and Solomon Kincaid and Winston Leonard and murder and blood and death…that's the closer truth to what I am."

"What you *were*," she argued, wanting to defend him, even to himself. "For some reason, you want to spin your past in the ugliest light. And perhaps that is fair, because I'm certain you suffered greatly and so did others you left in your wake. But I spent time with a different man these past few weeks, Rook. I spent time with a good man. A gentle man. A decent man. You could have proven yourself a brute many times. You always proved yourself to be far more."

He shook his head, his expression broken like what she said actually hurt him. "Don't."

"Why shouldn't I?" she pressed. "You must know what you've come to mean to me. You must know that I—"

"Don't!" he exclaimed, louder as he jerked across the room and caught her elbows. He drew her up sharp against his chest, and every moment of longing she'd ever felt toward him magnified as she stared up into his eyes and saw everything she needed. Not what she'd convinced herself she wanted.

What she truly needed.

"Don't say something foolish that will only cause more chaos," he grunted. "I will do everything in my power to protect you from my cousin and from the villain he managed to enrage to the point of madness. But you and I...we have nothing, Anne. We will *never* have anything. So you need to let go of that notion. And you need to do it now."

He was still holding her, and despite his cold words, she saw the heat flare in his gaze as he stared down into her face. His fingers shifted against her arms, his lips parted slightly.

Then he pushed her away. Not roughly, but firmly. And he left the room and left her broken.

CHAPTER 19

S upper came, and somehow Rook managed to bring himself into the dining hall and face the woman he was trying so hard to lose. It was impossible to avoid her, as their party was very small.

The Earl of Harcourt sat at the head of the table, his wife on one side, holding his hand and speaking softly to him. He looked ragged. Anne was on his other side. Next to her was Juliana, and across from Juliana was where he had been placed. He recognized the buffers being placed between him and Anne.

They were required, it seemed. Certainly they were earned.

As for Mr. Shelley, after his drunken display earlier, he hadn't joined the group. For that Rook was pleased, as the man seemed entirely disinterested in protecting his children. Anne deserved better, that was certain.

It was a mostly quiet affair. No one seemed in much of a mood to discuss the things that had been revealed a short time earlier in the parlor. And yet hardly a person at the table touched their food, either.

At last, as the dessert dishes were placed before them, Harcourt looked evenly at Rook. "I suppose we must discuss what our next move is. Do you believe your cousin will continue to pursue this issue of the stolen gem?"

Rook folded his arms. "I think you know the answer to that question. Of course he will. He believed you had the item. That means he likely searched every other place he thought it might be hidden. He won't stop. Whatever is driving him is too important."

"What do you think it might be?" Juliana asked softly.

Rook shook his head. "I don't know. He has a half-brother who is important to him. Gabriel might be at the heart of this. There is little else Ellis has ever allowed himself to care about. Whatever the reason, the outcome is the same."

"Our return to London is long overdue," Harcourt said with a glance toward his wife. "The estate there is smaller, easier to protect. Public spaces would be safer, I think. And there are places in Town where my brother might have hidden this gem. I could pursue a search and see if I could just find the item and return it to Leonard myself."

Rook stiffened at the idea. "You can handle yourself, that is clear. But Leonard is not to be trifled with. It would be dangerous."

"To protect my family, I would take any risk," Harcourt said, covering Thomasina's trembling hand with his own.

Rook could see there would be no turning him from the idea. Not that he could blame Harcourt. He nodded. "Very good. I think my time would best be spent seeking out Ellis. I have ways of finding him that I haven't utilized in a long time. Shared networks that will know the truth. Perhaps I can curb some of his desperation from my end."

Anne dropped her fork with a clatter that seemed to ring in the air around them all. "You—you would not go with us to London?"

The gaze of every person in the room shifted to him once more. He cleared his throat and refused to meet her gaze. Doing that in the parlor earlier had nearly broken him. "No, Miss Shelley. I don't belong with you in London."

Her gaze narrowed and he saw the spark of her anger along with the devastation of her heartbreak. She pushed her chair back with a screech of wood on wood, threw her napkin across her uneaten cake and left the room without saying anything more.

He shook his head as he set his own fork aside. "She would be better off letting me go."

"I agree," Harcourt said softly. "But as we all know, Anne has her own mind."

"And her own heart," Juliana said with a glance toward Thomasina that spoke volumes. "We'll give her some time to herself and then follow."

Rook got up. "If you love her, do your best to convince her to forget me. Now if you'll excuse me, I have much to ready if I'm to leave tomorrow to find my cousin. Good night."

R ook trudged up the hallway toward his chamber. When he reached a bend in the hall, he hesitated. Turn to the right and he'd find Anne's room. He knew it from servants' talk. He could go there. He could touch her. He could taste her. He could forget, for a moment, that he couldn't be with her.

Except doing that was patently unfair to them both. So he turned left instead and opened his chamber door. He ran a hand through his hair as he moved to the wardrobe. The other outfit he'd brought along on the road had been cleaned and folded neatly inside the drawers, and he tugged it out and looked around for his small bag.

"Going somewhere?"

Rook pivoted, hands raised in fists, at the sound of his cousin's voice.

Ellis stepped from the shadows with a chuckle. "That's twice I've snuck up on you in the last month. You really need to polish those skills."

Rook gritted his teeth. "I left that life, remember? I don't need those skills."

"Everyone needs those skills," his cousin said, and his voice was suddenly weary.

Rook stared at him. Ellis had lost some weight in the past few weeks. He was a little more gaunt than usual and there were circles under his eyes. The casual grin on his face didn't reach those eyes either. His cousin looked tired, he looked grim and he looked...afraid.

The last time he'd seen that light of fear in Ellis's eyes had been the day Winston Leonard struck down Solomon Kincaid in cold blood.

"What have you done?" Rook asked softly.

Ellis's cheek twitched and the smile faded. "Nothing worse than anything else we ever did, eh?"

Rook moved forward a long step. "You've done much worse and you know it. Going after Harcourt's fiancée? Trying to use her as leverage? And what about the damned gem, Handsome? Why the hell didn't you return it months ago?"

"I didn't know where it was!" Ellis said as he paced away to the window. "I have been looking for that fucking thing for almost a damned year. Barely keeping Winston Leonard at bay. Do you know how many beatings I've taken at the hands of his thugs?"

Rook flinched. "Then why didn't you come to me sooner?"

Ellis shrugged and his tone dropped. "You got out, Constantine. No one ever gets out alive. I had to protect you."

Rook's eyes went wide at the use of his given name. Ellis hadn't called him that in two decades at least. Now his cousin's gaze flitted over him from head to toe and there was a slight smile on his face.

"I couldn't drag you through shit again." Ellis sighed, and again it seemed like the weight of the world was on his shoulders.

"I would have gone through that shit of my own volition if you had told me about the danger you were facing," Rook insisted. "At least I would have told you that your plans were foolhardy. I would have kept you from playing Anne for a fool."

Ellis tilted his head slowly and one eyebrow arched. "*Anne*, is it? But of course it is." He shook his head. "I've been trying to find you two for a while. Since I returned to the island to discover you were gone."

Rook's eyes went wide. So his cousin had come back for her at some point. What would have happened if they'd stayed? Would Anne have gone with Ellis? No...Rook knew the answer to that question. But certainly things would have been different without that long, passionate road trip.

"It seems you and *Anne* became quite close on the road."

Rook set his jaw. "Don't you dare fucking talk to me about her, after what you did."

That hit the mark, and Ellis jerked away. "I know it violated the code we always followed."

"No games with innocents," Rook snapped. "No games with those who don't understand how the world works. Or at least you always chose women who deserved the bitter that went with the sweet."

Ellis glared at the reminder. "You must see how desperate I was. I wouldn't have done it otherwise."

"Oh yes, I can see your desperation. It's written all over you in a way I haven't seen since you were fourteen," Rook said. "What I don't know is *why*. If Leonard were just threatening you, you'd laugh in the face of it. You've done it too many times before. And if he were threatening me, you'd tell me so I'd have my knife ready. So who is it?"

Ellis stared at him, silent. And Rook knew he'd already guessed the truth.

"Gabriel," he breathed.

"I've hidden my connection to my brother for a long time," Ellis said, and his voice cracked with the love he felt for the younger man. The one they'd both watched with pride—from a distance. "To protect the good things he's built for himself with my money. But Leonard found out a few months ago and that has been his final pressure point ever since. He *will* kill Gabriel, you know he will. I had no other choice."

"You *do* have another choice," Rook insisted as he moved toward his cousin. His best friend for most of his life. His blood. His savior. Rook *had* to save him in return. If it were possible, he would do *anything* to save him.

"What's that?" Ellis drawled, and contempt suddenly dripped from his tone. "Are you so enamored with this girl that you would suggest I talk to Harcourt?"

"Yes," Rook said. "He could help us."

"Help me into a hangman's noose. Anyway, I still think that bastard has the treasure squirreled away somewhere."

"Handsome!" Rook said. "You searched this place well enough, it seems, and haven't found a damn thing."

Ellis's eye twitched. "Even if he doesn't, I went after Harcourt's wife. He'd shoot me rather than listen."

Rook bent his head. "You don't know him."

Ellis was silent for a long moment. Long enough that Rook dared to glance up at him at last. His cousin was glaring at him. "Anne Shelley must be awfully sweet when she opens her legs to make you take sides with a toff," he growled.

"Sod off," Rook accentuated each word, fighting to rein in control.

Ellis edged forward. "I have to find that gem, Rook. It's the only thing that matters to me now, do you understand? So I won't stop. I can't stop. I'll do *anything* to protect my own. And my own isn't Anne Shelley or the Earl of fucking Harcourt. They aren't your own either."

"I bloody well know that," Rook said as he turned away from Ellis and the words that burned through his soul. The ones that only spoke the truth he knew down to his core.

"Good. Because it seems like you don't know, but I must be

wrong on that account. So tell me, cousin, are you going to be a villain? Or a victim? Because those are the two choices in life. Pick quickly."

Rook pivoted to speak again, but Ellis was gone, leaving only the open window in his wake. Rook rushed to it and looked down into the darkness of the night. His cousin was gone without a trace. Smoke on the wind.

Rook slammed his hands down on the window sash as he screamed out into the night, "Ellis!"

But of course there was no answer. His cousin was gone, taking his desperation with him. But the danger remained. Ellis would return. He would keep coming back until he had what he desired. Winston Leonard was still in play, as well.

So Anne and her entire family were in desperate danger. To protect her, he knew what he had to do. And it involved the choice his cousin had just asked him to make.

The one he'd been trying to avoid and which was now inevitable.

When Rook stepped into Harcourt's study, he scanned the tall shelves first. Books. So many books. He'd always liked books, actually. Reading penny dreadfuls and novels he'd stolen had been an escape for him when he was a child, one his mother had given him by teaching him the skill.

But those days were over. At least for now.

He moved to the shelves, scanning closer to see if he could find any clues. He was about to take one of the unlabeled tomes when he heard the creak of a footfall in the hall. Quickly he pivoted and watched as Harcourt entered the room.

"Mr. Maitland," Harcourt drawled as he stopped in the doorway and straightened his shoulders. "What a surprise. I thought you were preparing to leave us tomorrow."

"I thought *you* would be with your wife," Rook replied.

Harcourt's jaw tightened. "She and Juliana are comforting Anne."

Rook bent his head at that statement. He hated that he was hurting her. He hated that he would hurt her even more before this was over.

But now it was time to get down to business. Villain or victim.

He straightened up and met Harcourt's gaze evenly. "You realize that the best outcome in all of this is if this gem my cousin and Winston Leonard are obsessed with is found. Then it can be returned and the consequences Ellis and your brother created no longer have to be visited upon your family."

Harcourt arched a brow in his direction. "Yes. That would clearly be the best conclusion for me and those I love."

"Then despite your ill feelings toward me, your mistrust, I need you to tell me what you've found in your own hunt for this item. I don't want to have to repeat searches you've already made."

Harcourt seemed to ponder that for a moment. Then he shrugged as if acquiescing. "We didn't know it was a gem. Ellis kept calling it a treasure at the meeting he arranged with me in Beckfoot the day after you took Anne away. So I had no idea what I was looking for, nor was there any record of it, at least in the diaries here."

"You looked in all of them," Rook asked.

"All of them. Everything my brother ever wrote that is housed in these walls. I reviewed them, and once Thomasina realized what was going on, what I had been hiding from her, she also looked through every line. There was nothing."

"What about a code?" Rook pressed.

Harcourt blinked. "I hadn't thought of that. I suppose those in your…profession…must use codes to protect information."

"It's not a profession," Rook said with a humorless laugh. "I'm not a barrister. And yes, code comes in handy, especially in fraught situations such as this. Did anything stand out as odd? Crude or stilted language, number or letter lines, sketches in margins? Anything?"

Harcourt rubbed his chin and then shook his head. "No. I'm sorry. My brother loved to write about himself. He did so floridly. There was nothing in any of the language that caught my eye."

Rook held back a curse. It would be much easier if Solomon Kincaid had just put a sign up explaining where he'd put them gem. "Your wife said something earlier about finding a hidden statue that you thought was the treasure."

"Yes. I was certain it was because my brother hid it so well. We found it by chance, really."

"May I see the item?" he asked.

Harcourt stared at him a long moment, then nodded and crossed to a painting on the wall. He lifted it away and revealed a safe, which he opened with a key he produced from some hidden pocket. He pulled out a cloth-wrapped item and handed it over.

Rook unwrapped the statue carefully and sucked in a breath. It had a marble base and a terracotta image of a woman was set into the stone. It was lovely, a well-done piece to be sure. And he recognized it for what it was immediately, though he tried to keep his reaction at bay as he nodded toward Harcourt. "Definitely not a gem," he drawled.

"No." Harcourt let out a long breath. "I fear it's just something else my brother stole during his time underground with Ellis Maitland."

"Well, that may be," Rook said softly. "Though I'd say this piece has very little worth if it helps. It's a replica."

The relief that crossed Harcourt's face was palpable. "Oh. Excellent. I wonder why he hid it then."

"Drunken foolishness, perhaps?" Rook said with a shrug to keep the conversation light. "If the item isn't here, then I will think on where else it could be hidden."

"And I'll continue to look once we arrive in London. I haven't searched my home there, and I'm certain my brother had hideaways for mistresses and God knows what other bad deeds." Harcourt sighed and it was a bone-weary sound that Rook felt in his own disappointed and exhausted heart.

"Very good. Well, I should go up now. I'm sure we'll see each other in the morning before we all head our separate ways."

He set the statue down on the edge of the desk and moved toward the door. Before he could exit, Harcourt spoke again. "Will you really walk away from Anne?"

Rook froze, hand extended toward the door. His heart rate jumped and he slowly turned to find the earl staring at him, arms folded across his broad chest, expression unreadable.

"You want to have this conversation with me?" he said through clenched teeth.

"Yes."

Rook shook his head as he took a step back into the room. He could be glib now. But he could also be honest. And he chose to be honest because he knew it was probably the last time he could be so.

"Look at me," he said softly as he motioned his hands up and down his body. "The best thing I can do is walk away. I know where I was born. I know what I did to survive."

"And yet she still loves you," Harcourt said.

That word: love. It felt like he'd been shot in the chest when the earl said it. He had accepted that he was in love with Anne. It had become a comfort, of sorts, to know that he would love her even if she wasn't with him.

But the idea that she loved him? *That* was painful. And he couldn't imagine it was true. She was attracted to him, certainly. He thought she cared for him. But love?

If she felt something akin to that, it would certainly fade when he was gone.

"If I am lucky enough to have even a sliver of her heart, then I must protect her all the more," he said. "The best way I know to do that is to walk away."

Harcourt's expression softened as he stared at Rook across the room. He gave no indication that he agreed or disagreed.

Rook shifted. "When you get to London, I hope you will protect her, regardless of what she did in breaking your engagement."

Harcourt hesitated another few seconds before he nodded. "I would have married Anne if she hadn't run away. I never would have been able to love my wife. So in a way, Anne gave me my heart by leaving," he said softly. "I will protect her with my life in your stead."

Rook had always been good at reading people. It was a necessity on the street. The only way to stay alive sometimes. He looked into this man's eyes and he saw the truth there.

"Good," he said and hated that his voice cracked a little.

Then he walked away without saying anything more. Because if he did he would regret it. Just as he would likely regret the thing he had to do next.

Not for his cousin or to find the gem. But because the truth that he was walking away was very clear now. And he couldn't do that without one last goodbye.

CHAPTER 20

Anne stood at her window, staring out at the stars that glittered above. She was alone for the first time in hours. Her sisters had stayed with her a long time, comforting her, helping her ready for bed, brushing out her hair like they had done for each other when they were young girls.

But it wasn't the same. Too much had changed. Ultimately they had finally left her with hugs and support she knew she didn't truly deserve.

And now she felt the aloneness deep in her bones. She hadn't spent a night without Rook in two weeks. Not since they took to the road in Scotland.

She ached for him as she watched a star streak across the sky and wished with all her might that something would change and allow her to be with him.

There was a light knock at her door, and Anne turned to stare at the barrier. It was from the hallway, rather than Juliana's adjoining chamber. She wrinkled her brow as she crossed to open it.

She expected a servant, or for Thomasina to have returned from her marital chamber down the hall for one more embrace. But instead, as she opened the door, she caught her breath.

Rook stood in the dim light of the hallway, sleeves rolled to his elbows, boots off to muffle his steps to her door, shirt unbuttoned at the collar. He looked so tired as he stared at her.

And then he caught her waist and drew her up against him, pushing her into the room while his mouth crushed down on hers. She opened to him immediately. What else was she to do when she craved him like air or water?

The moment she did so, the kiss slowed. Gentled. His fingers glided into her hair and he cupped her scalp, tilting her head to the side gently to deepen the kiss. She was vaguely aware that he reached behind himself and shut the door.

She wrapped her arms around his neck, ignoring every part of her that wanted to talk to him, to explain to him, to question him. He was here. And he would be hers one more time.

He drew back from the kiss and looked into her eyes as he slid his fingers beneath her nightgown straps and slowly guided one down her shoulder. He left it draped at the elbow and leaned in, pressing his lips first to the side of her neck and then sweeping them down over her collarbone, her shoulder, her arm. She shivered with sensation, dropping her head back as he pulled the other strap down and bared her from the waist up. She tugged at the silky fabric and then she was naked before him.

He stepped away with a ragged breath and stared at her like it was the first time, even though it wasn't. He'd seen her this way so many times that she no longer felt ill at ease about her body. And yet he stared like he was trying to memorize her, a stark reminder that he was going to leave. A stark reminder that whatever happened tonight was very important.

She swallowed past the lump in her throat and stepped up to him. She placed a hand on his chest, feeling the thump of his heart against her fingers before she slid away, across the muscle, and unbuttoned his shirt. He tugged it over his head and threw it across the room.

She stared as he had stared, drinking in every inch of this

amazing man who had captured her interest, her body, her heart. This man who had transformed the reckless choice she made on a desperate night into the best decision of her life. Because it had brought her to him. And he was what she needed, even if it couldn't be permanent.

Tears stung her eyes as she stepped into the warmth of his embrace once more. She lifted her mouth to his as she dragged her fingers around to his back, gliding her nails over his skin until he hissed a sound of deep, dark pleasure.

She smiled against his lips, her fears silenced for a moment by the connection they made with their bodies. She wanted that pure bond now more than ever.

"Please," she whispered against his skin as she pulled her mouth down his throat, letting her hands make a path across the muscles of his chest and stomach, over his hip, around to the thick cock beneath his fall front. "Please."

He nodded against her hair and reached between them to unfasten the breeches. She looked down, smiling at the hard thrust of him, as ready for her as she was for him. She took him in hand, stroking him once, twice, and he made a garbled sound as he pushed harder against her fingers.

Her body ached from wanting, from needing what they shared. All of it. She glanced up at him and smiled, then slowly dropped to her knees before him.

"Anne," he whispered, her name barely carrying in the quiet room.

"Constantine," she murmured in response, and he twitched in her hand before she darted her tongue out and swirled it around his tip.

"Christ." His fingers dug into her hair as she took him into her mouth.

She rolled her tongue around him in a slow circle, reveling in the hard heat of him in her mouth, the taste that was only his. She took him as deep as she could, then a tiny bit deeper as he moaned with pleasure above her. She sucked as she withdrew, then repeated the action, over and over, reveling in the tiny gasps of pleasure coming from his lips.

She looked up at him, watching his neck flex with the sensations. Feeling him tense as she brought him closer and closer to climax.

Clearly that wasn't on his mind, though. He met her gaze as she watched him, and shook his head. "Not like this," he said softly, then crooked his finger for her to come back to her feet.

She sucked one more time and then did as she'd been told, licking a trail as she slowly returned to an upright position. He kissed her, harder this time, and then she was off her feet. He swept her into his arms, kissing her as he carried her to her bed.

He smiled as he set her against the pillows. "This one is a bit more comfortable."

She pressed a finger beneath his chin and pulled him closer. "Only because you're here," she whispered.

His expression softened at that, and he pressed a hand to either side of her head on the pillows as he kissed her once again. She lifted against him, opening her legs wider, reaching between them to stroke his cock and then press it to her entrance.

He swore as she glided him through the soft wetness gathered at her slit, then pushed forward through it to claim her once again. They moaned in unison as he seated himself fully and dropped his forehead against hers. Their breath quickly matched and their sweat mingled.

He held her gaze while he thrust, grinding his hips against hers with every stroke. She lifted to meet him, lost in his eyes and the feel of them as one unit reaching for pleasure. For connection. For a future she feared he would ultimately take away from them both.

She pushed those thoughts aside, focusing on the pleasure building between her legs, spreading through her veins, making her limbs tingle. She reached for it, finding it effortlessly and her back arched as the waves of pleasure crested through her.

He gathered her hips tighter against his with both hands,

denting her flesh with his fingers, bruising her and marking her. He ground harder and deeper as she keened against his mouth. She felt the tension in him increase, the tightening of his very being that meant he was close to release, as well. He grunted her name and just barely pulled from her, pumping himself between them as he crushed his lips to hers.

She clung to him, holding him against her as their kisses gentled, as his fingers smoothed instead of clenched, as his legs tangled with hers. He wanted to pull away, she could feel it, but she held him steady, pouring everything she was and could ever be into this man.

And when he finally pulled back and smiled down at her, she couldn't lie or hide anymore. She stroked her hand along his rough jaw and whispered, "I love you."

He flinched. A brief but powerful moment that she knew she would carry with her for the rest of her life. He *flinched* and her heart shattered even as he leaned in to kiss her briefly once more.

Then he pushed from her bed and gathered up his trousers. He shook them out, his back to her, muscles flexing as he dressed. She reached to cover herself with the rumpled sheets as he did so, no longer safe to be vulnerable.

He turned back to her when he was fixed, staring down at her. His dark gaze rolled over her from head to toe, taking in every inch. And then he sighed.

"I want you to know, whatever happens next, I will never regret walking up that dock to you," he said softly. "I will *never* regret putting you in that boat and taking to my island, or riding home with you, or touching you or being with you. Whatever happens next, you need to know how much all that meant to me. And that it will mean everything to me until the moment I take my last breath."

"Whatever happens next," she repeated, for he had said that phrase twice and it terrified her. "And what is that?"

He shook his head and backed to the door. "What has to happen, Anne. What always had to happen. Goodbye."

He backed from the room with one last look and the door shut between them, and he was gone. She could have raced after him, naked if need be. She could have shouted his name and drawn this goodbye out longer. Made it more painful. Part of her wanted to do just that. The part of her that always went after what she wanted commanded her to make a scene, to make a production, to make him listen.

But in the end, she knew only bad things would come of that. And Rook would still leave. Perhaps because he didn't love her. Perhaps because he did. She didn't know for certain. In the end, the outcome was the same so perhaps it didn't matter.

He was gone. And she couldn't bring him back. So she rolled on her side and let the tears fall.

R ook had to wait in the dark for a couple of hours after he left Anne's bed. With all the excitement of the last few days, the household had remained in an uproar and servants had been preparing for the family's departure long into the night. But at last even Harcourt's butler Willard took to the servant quarters and the house was quiet and still.

Rook stepped from the shadows of one of the parlors where he had been waiting and watching, and slipped down the hallway to Harcourt's study. The room wasn't locked and he stepped inside with no trouble. The statue they had examined together earlier in the day was no longer on the desk, despite Rook's statement that it was a recreation and had no value. Harcourt didn't fully trust him, it seemed.

"Clever man," Rook muttered.

But very few locks had ever stopped him and he had little fear of this one. He stepped behind the huge mahogany desk and grabbed the edges of the painting hung behind it. He lifted and set the price-less heirloom away. The metal of the small safe behind it glinted in the dying firelight. There was no key, of course, but Rook didn't need a key.

He reached into his boot and touched the handle of a lock pick. In the other was a knife, but he didn't need that now. He prayed he wouldn't need it at all. But old habits died hard, which was working in his favor now.

He stretched his shoulders and worked the tip of the lock pick into the hole. It used to be he could strip a lock open in less than a minute. But it had been a while since he practiced the skill, and it took a few clicks of the clock on the mantel to get the safe open.

He shook his head at his rusty skills before he reached in and drew out the cloth-wrapped statue.

He uncovered it and stared at the beautiful clay bust. Recreation or no, it was a shame, really, to do what he was about to do, but there was nothing to it. Sometimes damage had to be done, as he well knew from this entire endeavor.

He wrapped the fabric tight around the clay top of the piece and held the marble base as he whacked it against the desk edge. A second smack against the hard wooden edge and he felt the entire clay portion give. The cloth muffled the sound of shattering terracotta, but he still held perfectly still as he waited for rushing feet in response to the act.

Nothing happened for a moment, two, and he let out his breath in relief that he hadn't been heard. He opened the bag and carefully dumped out the shards on the desktop. What he was looking for wasn't immediately obvious, so he lit a candle and picked through the mess, trying to find what he knew was there. What he hoped was there.

Finally, he found it. A metal vial hidden in the clay dust and shards. He picked it up and opened it to reveal a rolled piece of paper inside. It was a coded message that certainly revealed where Solomon Kincaid had hidden the gem he and Ellis had stolen. The damned fool thing that had caused all this heartbreak and consternation.

Rook didn't recognize the code immediately, but that didn't matter. Ellis had always had the head for these kinds of things, not him. And since Solomon might have written the code for Ellis himself, it was more likely his cousin who could solve it.

Rook rerolled the paper and pressed the vial into his pocket for safekeeping. Then he whipped out a fresh sheet of vellum from the top drawer of Harcourt's desk and wrote a quick note. His words would offer no comfort to Anne, nor any absolution for himself, but he wrote it anyway and left the mess behind so that there would be no mistaking what he'd done.

His heart throbbed as he slipped from the room and down the hall to leave the house. Once outside in the brisk night air, he turned back to look up at the house. He found Anne's window and stared up at it. He had to go. It was the only way to save her.

The only way to save *anyone* in this situation was to fight this evil power at his cousin's side. He and Ellis had always been unstoppable together. They would have to be unstoppable again to make up for everything they had done in the past.

And once it was over? Well, he would disappear. It was obvious that no matter how hard he tried, his past and his nature were what they were. He didn't belong in a house like this with a woman like Anne Shelley. Some dark part of him would always exist. It would always be waiting to threaten her, because even if he pretended his knives were for woodcraft, they weren't. He wasn't.

To save her, he had to embrace what he had once been, and then let her go. So he would.

He turned away from the house with great difficulty and made his way to the stable to take the old horse he had ridden here on beside Anne. He had to find Ellis. Or more likely let his cousin find him.

And then they would end this at last.

CHAPTER 21

Anne walked through the quiet halls of Harcourt Heights, worrying her hands before her. She hadn't slept. How could she after her last night with Rook? She had finally risen early and prepared herself in the hopes she would see him before everyone else was up to get on the road to London.

But he was nowhere to be found. His room was empty, his bed looked as unslept-in as her own had been. His small pile of clothing was still there, though, and his road bag.

She just had to find him.

"Anne?"

She pivoted to find Juliana exiting one of the parlors. Her sister's eyes also looked shadowed and concerned.

"Juliana, what are you doing up?" Anne said as she moved to her. "We have a few hours before we are meant to depart for London and you should sleep."

Juliana arched a brow. "You think I can sleep for worrying about this situation? I can do nothing to help anyone and I feel so useless."

Anne drew back a fraction. Her sister had always been the one who repaired things, smoothed things. And now she was utterly left out in a way. Anne had been gone as Thomasina and Harcourt fell in love. When she returned, she had been so wrapped up in Rook and the madness created by his cousin…

She could see how troubled Juliana was now that she actually looked. She stepped forward and wrapped an arm around her sister. "You help just by being the wonderful, calming force you always are, I promise you. You can do nothing else."

Juliana didn't look appeased by those words, but before she could say anything there was a faint bang from somewhere down the hall. Both women stopped and turned toward it.

"Did that come from Harcourt's study?" Juliana whispered.

Anne nodded. "I think so. Perhaps it's Rook. I've been looking for him all morning."

Her sister shot her a knowing glare but motioned her up the hall. "Let's go see. I promise to leave if you two need to be alone, but I'm not letting you go in there by yourself until we know who it is. Just in case."

"Just in case what?" Anne laughed. "As if a villain would dare to enter Harcourt's hallowed halls."

"Ellis Maitland did, or at least he came onto the grounds." Juliana shivered slightly. "I do not know what to think of such a man. What was he like?"

Anne didn't answer the question because she entered the study in that moment and stared at what she found there. The painting behind Harcourt's desk was leaning against the wall. Broken shards of pottery were spread across his desk.

"Oh my God," Juliana whispered as she stepped forward and surveyed the scene. "There is a letter from Rook."

Anne stepped forward to join her at the desk, her gaze darting over the letter in Rook's even, tight hand.

The moment I saw it, I realized the importance of your statue was within, not the marble or clay. I've taken the coded message I found inside and believe it likely reveals where Solomon hid the gem. I will join Ellis to find it and return it to Leonard. Lord Harcourt, I suggest you take the family to London as planned. Protect Anne for me as you promised you would. Anne is all that matters.

R.M.

She caught her breath at those words. Both the ones that said what he had done and the ones that revealed her worth to him as much as his parting whisper had last night. She could hardly form words to speak.

In the end, she had no time to do so. With a bang, the door behind them closed. When they pivoted, both sisters saw the man who had been hiding behind it. Not Rook. Not Harcourt. Not even Ellis Maitland. Anne recognized the intruder from ballrooms in London. A handsome man, only a handful of years older than Rook was, she would wager. But with a hard glint to his stare, an emptiness that spoke of a predator.

It was Winston Leonard, and he had a gun pointed at Juliana.

"Anne Shelley," he purred. "You are something of a commodity in demand lately."

"That's not Anne," Anne said, maneuvering to put herself in front of Juliana, who was just staring at the gun with utter terror in her eyes. *"I'm* Anne."

He snorted as he looked her up and down. "You're dressed too plainly to be Anne—everyone knows how showy she is. *You* must be that little mouse Thomasina."

Anne looked down at herself. She had dressed in her road clothes because they were the easiest to put on without help. Juliana, on the other hand, was wearing a much prettier and more fashionable frock. Given their reputations, it made sense that he would be confused.

"Lord Winston," Juliana said softly. "There is no need to—"

He lunged forward before she could finish. Anne cried out and tried to push back against him as he reached for Juliana. But he was more prepared and far larger. He hit Anne hard, catching her chin with the tip of his elbow and staggering her to the floor. Stars flashed before her eyes as she watched him catch Juliana's arm, yanking her toward him and pressing the gun to her temple.

"Ellis Maitland *clearly* doesn't care about his brother enough to take this matter seriously, but that means nothing now. According to the note he so kindly left, that cousin of his has what I want, or the means to retrieve it. And it seems Rook Maitland cares about *you*, Miss Anne. So you're coming with me."

"She's not Anne!" Anne insisted, trying to get up even though her head was spinning from the blow. "Please."

"I think I must shoot her," Leonard said with a smile for Juliana before he looked down at Anne. "Don't you? For being so difficult. That ought to keep Harcourt busy at any rate."

"No!" Juliana snapped, grasping for his wrist to keep the gun pointed away from Anne. Her voice was suddenly calm, that appeasing tone she had honed with their father over the years. "Please. We'll stop playing games. I'm Anne Shelley, you are correct."

"No," Anne whispered as she shook her head at her sister.

Juliana ignored her. "But killing my sister won't help you keep anyone busy. That's *Juliana* Shelley, not Thomasina. She has no relationship to either the Maitlands, nor to Harcourt, so no one cares what happens to her. If you leave her be, I'll go with you without fight or trouble."

"She'll go to Harcourt straight away," Leonard argued, and the gun swung toward Anne again. She squeezed her eyes shut.

"That's exactly what you want, my lord," Juliana continued to soothe. "Harcourt will fear his beloved wife is in as much in danger as her sisters. His rush will be to protect Thomasina, for that is all he cares about. Trying to keep her from harm will surely slow him down more than shooting his uninteresting sister-in-law ever would."

Anne's lips parted at Juliana's depreciation of her own worth, even as a means to protect Anne from certain death. More so, she was shocked by her sister's sacrifice in allowing a killer to take her.

Leonard looked at Anne on the floor and then nodded. "I suppose. And it will make it easier if Maitland knows where to find me at any rate. I have my bargaining chip for protection." He glared at Anne. "*You* tell Harcourt and Maitland that they can find me on Donovan Hill. If anyone but Maitland comes or if he doesn't have the message that will allow me to find my damned gem, I will kill her."

Juliana sucked in a breath through her teeth as he tugged her a little closer to him.

Anne nodded slowly. "I-I understand."

"Wait five minutes here and then you do what you're told," he said. He sneered and then dragged Juliana away through the door.

Anne's last glimpse of her beloved sister was her wide and terrified green eyes as she disappeared into the hallway with a villain far worse than Ellis Maitland had ever hoped to be. She waited until she heard the slam of the front door, then rushed to the window. She saw Juliana struggling as she was all but thrown onto a wild-looking stallion. Leonard jumped on behind her, and they rode away down the drive and away from the house.

Immediately Anne raced from the room. She was screaming as she ran, "Help! Someone help!"

But she feared that if Rook was gone, help would not come. Juliana would suffer for it and for her sacrifice if they couldn't find him.

R ook rode along the back roads through the woods behind Harcourt's house. He wasn't certain where Ellis had gone, but he knew he couldn't be too far away since he had insisted upon obtaining Rook's help. His cousin wouldn't ride toward the village, too populated with Harcourt's associates. The main road wasn't safe for Ellis either.

But these back roads were another story, so he'd chosen a direction farther from population and hoped he knew his cousin well enough to guess right.

But now it had been an hour since he started his slow, trotting search, and he was beginning to think he didn't know anything at all anymore. He slowed himself in the path and turned the horse, looking into the trees. Finally he sighed and let out a low series of sharp whistles, the old code he and Ellis had used to find each other when they were separated on jobs. The sound would carry at least.

He was still a moment, and to his shock, he heard Ellis's answering call in the distance. He repeated the call as he pivoted the horse in the direction of the answer and heard it returned louder. He burst through a small group of trees and there Ellis was, on his own fine mount, racing toward Rook with a wild expression.

"Did he show up?" Ellis said as they met in a clearing.

Rook stared at him in confusion and worry over the wildness of Ellis's appearance.

"Who?" Rook asked. "No one showed up. I found a code, Handsome. I think it leads to the gem."

"That doesn't bloody matter right now," Ellis said. "I had some of our old contacts trying to find out where Leonard was. According to them, Leonard got a report from one of his lackeys—Talon, I think his name was."

Rook staggered. "Talon?" he repeated, thinking of the unsavory man he and Anne had encountered on their trip. "Jesus."

"You know the man?"

"Anne and I encountered him on the road through Scotland," Rook said. "The bastard felt foul. I should have listened to my gut."

"That explains a great deal." Ellis looked even more grim. "Once he heard from this person, Leonard disappeared from London a few days ago. Rook, he's headed to Harcourt Heights. He found out about the connection between the broken engagement and me. I think he intends to take what is his."

Rook's heart felt like it had been torn from his chest. "He's a killer," he said, trying to process it. Trying to understand what in God's name it meant for Anne and her family.

"I know," Ellis said. "No one knows that fact better. But right now we have to get back there. Because if he doesn't find what he wants, he might just wipe them all out for spite."

Rook didn't wait for more information. He simply pivoted his horse and nudged him into full speed on the path back to Harcourt Heights. This time he wasn't searching for anyone and he was racing at a much higher speed, but he knew it would likely take him at least half an hour to make it back.

What damage could Leonard do in that time?

Ellis urged his horse faster as the path widened and positioned himself beside Rook as they ran. Rook glared at him. "You did this," he growled.

His cousin flinched. "I know. I know I did it. I have hated myself ever since."

"Some good that will do Anne and her family if we don't reach them in time."

Ellis shook his head. "No. You and I are working together now. You and I *will* fix this."

Rook was happy to be riding because if he hadn't been he knew he would have swung on his cousin for that comment. "You are out of your mind," he snapped instead. "I am not working with you. I would never work with you again. *I'm* trying to save the woman I love. That is what matters to me now. If it happens to save your sorry hide, too, then fine. But hear this, Ellis—you and I are finished. I want nothing to do with you."

He saw that his words hit the mark by the way Ellis's expression collapsed. There was a moment when he saw the same ten-year-old boy who had saved him from certain horror at the hands of his mother's cock bawd. The same boy who had taken him under his wing and treated him like a brother rather than a cousin.

But then Ellis hardened himself. The boy was gone, replaced by a man who had surrendered his scruples for money and power. The one who had gotten in so deep that he had lost who he was. The cocky bastard returned then and he gave Rook a half-smile.

"Then you'll have your wish," he said, and slowed his horse so he was riding behind Rook again.

Rook had no time to analyze that, though. They crested the hill overlooking Harcourt Heights, and Rook pushed his horse to the limit as they careened down the hill and through the gate. When he pulled the horse up short on the drive, he flung himself down and shouldered his way through the door before Willard could open it for him.

The butler looked stunned as he stared at him. "M-Mr. Maitland," he stammered. "Do you have Miss Shelley with you?"

He stared at the man, his mouth dropped open in horror. "Anne? Where is Anne?"

She entered the hall from an adjoining parlor. "Rook!" she cried, and ran toward him. He met her halfway, gathering her against his chest as Lord and Lady Harcourt and Mr. Shelley joined them in the foyer.

He stared at their drawn expressions. "What happened?"

Anne looked up at him, and he saw a bruise on her jawline, dark and purple. He brushed his fingers across it. "Winston Leonard?"

"Yes." Her voice shook. "He…he broke into the house and found your note. He knows you have the code, and he took Juliana thinking that she was me and he could bargain with you using her."

"Jesus," Rook muttered as he ran a hand through his hair. "If only I'd known sooner, I might have been able to stop him."

"Known? Known about Leonard? How?" she asked.

"*I* told him."

Rook had all but forgotten Ellis was behind him in his haste to reach Anne, but now the entire group turned toward his voice. For a moment there was stunned silence, but then all hell broke loose as everyone began shouting at once as they recognized Ellis from their various encounters.

"What the hell are you doing in my house?" Harcourt cried out at last over top of the rest, and his commanding voice silenced the others.

Ellis tipped his hat. "My lord, I apologize for our last meeting. But I think we'd best forget our difficult past because if Juliana Shelley has been taken by that bastard, we have a limited time to get to her before Leonard..." He looked at the other two women with an apologetic expression. "He kills for sport as much as purpose. So I'd suggest we figure out where he's going and get there."

Anne stepped forward. "He said Donovan Hill."

Harcourt pivoted. "I know the place. It's about ten miles from here. An hour's ride on fast mounts."

"Then you best get those mounts up here, my lord," Rook said. "One for me and for my cousin, as well, to replace our tired horses. Because we need to leave right now."

Harcourt nodded and, with a quick glance toward Thomasina, raced from the house. Anne glared at Ellis, but then grabbed Rook's hands. The feel of her touching him filled him with relief once more.

"He wanted to take you," he said, pulling one hand free and pushing a loose curl from her forehead.

She nodded. "He thinks I matter enough to make you do what he wants."

"You do," he said, because he wasn't going to lie when only Juliana's bravery had saved her.

"But he told me only you could come to meet him," she gasped. "Please, he said he'd kill Juliana if he saw anyone other than you."

Rook shot his cousin a look. Ellis had slunk back to the door and was now pretending not to see the icy glares Thomasina was shooting him as she spoke to Willard near the stairs. Mr. Shelley just looked confused, like he wasn't entirely certain what was happening.

"I am the only one he will see," he said. "I swear to you, I'll get your sister back and put an end to this."

Horses thundered to the doorway, servants coming down from two of them as Harcourt called out, "Let's ride."

Rook leaned down and pressed a kiss to Anne's lips before he moved away at last. "I'll see you soon, with your sister by my side."

Anne and Thomasina followed the men out. As Rook and Ellis seated themselves on the fine horses, Harcourt leaned down to kiss Thomasina deeply. "Be careful," she whispered.

Anne looked at Rook. "Yes, please be careful. That man is unhinged. And I don't trust your cousin."

Rook glanced at Ellis again. "You don't have to trust him. Please trust me."

"I do trust you." She lifted her chin and that strength of steel came into her expression again. "And I love you."

Rook held her stare for a beat, and then turned the horse and followed Harcourt and Ellis from the house. As a farewell went, it was not a satisfying one.

He hoped he'd be able to return soon for a better one.

A nne reached back to catch Thomasina's hand as the men exited the gate on their horses, riding hard with dust pluming up behind them.

She didn't look at her sister as she said, "We're following them, aren't we?"

Thomasina laughed and looped an arm around her waist. "Our horses are being brought up now."

"Just a moment," Mr. Shelley said, blinking as he staggered down the stairs toward them. "You two are in no way going to chase after those men on this fool's errand."

Anger lifted in Anne and she was about to retort, but Thomasina shocked her by stepping up to their father. "Everything that has happened is thanks to you, sir. To you and your cruel arrangements that never took your daughters' happiness or comfort or safety into account." She poked a finger against his chest. "And this is *my* house. And *my* decision. You have nothing to do with it. You don't care about any of us. So go drink yourself stupid while you wait to find out if you have any daughters left."

Their father blinked and so did Anne. Thomasina had never been the one to confront anyone. And yet here she was, giving their wretched father the set down he had deserved since the moment their mother left this earth.

Thomasina was stronger now. Because of love, it seemed. As their father staggered off into the house, muttering curses under his breath, Anne tucked her beloved sister closer. She felt Thomasina trembling as they watched two more fine horses being ridden up from the stable.

Everything had changed in a few short weeks. In her life she had always been the bad sister. Thomasina had been the good one. Juliana had been the strong one.

But in that moment she knew she and her sister would have to be strong together now. For Juliana. And Anne would have to be strong for Rook, too, even if he claimed not to want that.

CHAPTER 22

Donovan Hill was a desolate place. There had been a fire in the woods a few years before, and the vegetation was low and scrubby but for a circle of trees on the top of the hill that hadn't been touched. It was an eerie sight to ride toward it.

Rook brought his horse up short. "He chose the place because he'll be able to see an attack. You two will have to walk up, probably even belly crawl."

Harcourt nodded and shot Ellis a dirty look as he dismounted. "Can *he* be trusted?"

Ellis got off his own horse and glanced at Rook. "My cousin feels as darkly about me as you do, my lord. You both have your reasons. But trust that I want to end this with Leonard, if nothing else. I won't fail you."

Harcourt still sent a questioning look toward Rook and shrugged.

"I don't think he's lying." Rook sighed. "We have little choice but to believe him either way, we need all the help we can get."

Ellis hardly reacted to his dismissal except for the slightest tightening of his jaw. But Rook saw it. Knew the pain it represented.

"There's a low scattering of scrub to the north side of the hill,"

Ellis said. "I'll come from that approach. Harcourt, I would suggest the west, as there is similar cover."

As Ellis crept away to find position, Harcourt surprised Rook by squeezing his arm. "Good luck and be careful. We have your back."

"I don't deserve it," Rook said. "But I thank you. Be careful."

Harcourt didn't argue and there was a grim line to his mouth as he crept away to his position. That left Rook to ride closer alone. He took his time to give the men the opportunity to find their places, and also because he thought Leonard would keep his attention on his approach. That might give the other two more cover.

But at last he reached the base of the hill. He swung off his mount and moved up the hill path. As he crested the hill, he saw Winston Leonard in the middle of the clearing. Juliana was tied hand and foot before him, a dirty rag in her mouth. Her eyes widened as Rook neared, and he saw the terror on her tear-streaked face.

"Don't worry, darlin'," he drawled, playing along that she was Anne. "I'm here now."

"See, I told you he'd come," Leonard said with a nudge for Juliana with his foot. "Besotted as he is."

She stared at Rook, holding his gaze. Her eyes were so like Anne's, and all he could think about was if he failed and had to tell the woman he loved that he'd lost her beloved sister. It would break her. So it couldn't happen. It *wouldn't*.

"And I'm here," he said softly. "I want to give you what you want, so why don't you let Anne go?"

"I don't think so," Leonard drawled as he reached down to place a hand on Juliana's head. He smoothed her hair almost gently. "You'll stay in line if she's right here with me. And there must be a price to pay for all the foolishness your cousin has put me through."

Rook stepped closer. "Then let me pay it," he said. "Take me and what I have. You can torture me if you need to count a cost. You can kill me if you must. Just let her go."

"Now that is a fine idea," Leonard said. "Maybe we can get Ellis to come along. Let him watch me kill you like he watched me kill Harcourt's brother. What do you say, gentlemen?"

He called the last question into the air, and Rook flinched. Leonard knew he hadn't come alone.

"Come on out now or I put in bullet in both of them," Leonard said louder.

There were rustlings in the bushes. Ellis came up onto the hill first and shook his head at Rook apologetically. Harcourt came next, his face lined with pain and devastation.

"You murdered my brother," he hissed as he stepped up next to Rook. "I will see you hang."

"I don't think so," Leonard said. "You didn't listen, gentlemen. I told that little girl to make sure only Rook came and that if the rules were broken, Anne Shelley would die. I keep my promises."

"No!"

Rook froze at Anne's voice, coming from the pathway below. He spun around to watch her racing toward him, Thomasina at her heels.

"Thomasina!" Harcourt cried out in anguished horror to see his wife coming into danger. Rook couldn't blame him. He felt much the same way. Though he supposed he should have known Anne wouldn't listen. She did what she did. She protected who she protected. He loved her for that as much as anything else that was wonderful about her.

"Please," Anne begged, her gaze still locked on Leonard. "*I* am Anne Shelley. *That* is Juliana, I vow to you it is true. Take me if you must. Let my sister go."

Leonard stared at her, then down at Juliana. And in that moment if confusion, Ellis looked at Rook.

"I'm sorry," he said softly. Then he lunged forward and hit Leonard at the knees.

∼

Anne screamed as everything on the hilltop seemed to move in slow motion. As Ellis Maitland hit Leonard and toppled the man off kilter, his gun went off with a bang so loud her ears rang from it. She saw Ellis flinch, saw blood expand in an immediate circle from his right shoulder, but before she could fully understand what was happening, Rook had her hand and was hauling her down and covering her body with his.

Harcourt jumped for Thomasina and did almost the same thing, diving on top of her as they watched Ellis and Leonard struggle together, locked in combat. But it was evident Ellis was injured from the gunshot, and Leonard flipped him over, rising up to rain down punches as Ellis tried to fight him off.

"No!" Rook screamed, pain lacing his voice. He pushed Anne behind him and reached into his boot. He withdrew one of those throwing knives he'd shown her on the island what felt like a lifetime ago. He flicked his wrist the same way she'd watched him do so many times, and the knife circled in the air over and over.

It found its mark, hitting Leonard high in the shoulder, near the neck. He let out a howl of pain and Ellis flipped him, sending him rolling off and partway down the hill away from the rest.

"Get him!" Ellis roared. Harcourt and Rook both stumbled to their feet. Harcourt began to look for the gun that had been abandoned in the fight. Rook flatfooted his way toward Leonard, who was yanking the knife from his shoulder with a curse. He flopped onto his back, panting as blood poured from the wound.

Ellis was obviously injured, but he didn't stop there. Anne watched as the man who had tricked her, the man she hated for his lies, inched toward her sister. He cradled Juliana gently, working at the ropes around her wrist as he said something softly that Anne couldn't hear.

Rook was just inches from Leonard when the bastard darted out a foot and caught Rook in the chin.

"No!" Anne cried out as the man she loved staggered slightly, and that gave Leonard enough time to flip to his feet. He lunged forward, slashing the blade he'd tugged from his shoulder toward Ellis and Juliana.

Anne heard her sister's muffled scream of pain and felt the tingle of sensation on her own cheek as the blade found its mark in the side of Juliana's face. Ellis roared and grabbed for the knife, yanking it by the blade as if the knife didn't cut him as he did so. He kicked Leonard hard and twisted the knife away, causing Leonard to fall back as Rook and Harcourt rushed forward toward him.

The bastard got up and ran down the hill, the other men at his heels.

"Juliana!" Anne screamed.

She and Thomasina both rushed for their sister. Her eyes were wide, and she reached her hands up to touch her bloody face as she looked from them to Ellis. He was racing to untie her wrists and ankles now, and then reached up to cover the wound on her cheek.

"There now," he said softly as he applied pressure. "You're fine. Look at me now, angel. You're fine."

Juliana's breath came short as she stared up at him. "It hurts."

He flinched at that statement. "I know it does." He grabbed for Anne's hand and yanked it forward to cover Juliana's cheek. He pressed it hard there, against the warmth and wetness, and glared at her. "Push hard. I have to help Rook and Harcourt."

He rushed away then, leaving the sisters to tend to their wounded. Anne held tight against Juliana's injury, shaking her head as she sobbed. "I'm sorry, it's all my fault. It's my fault."

Thomasina cradled Juliana against her chest, smoothing her hair as she gently rocked her to comfort her. "It's not your fault," she whispered. "It's not your fault."

But as Anne tried to help her sister, she knew that wasn't true. And she also knew it wasn't over.

H arcourt raced back up the hill toward the sisters with Rook
and Ellis close behind. Rook's anger burned within him.
Leonard had escaped. They couldn't catch him, for his horse was
tethered too close by. He had ridden away, finally reaching a wood
in the distance, and vanished.

With Juliana injured, none of them felt they could make chase.
Which left them returning to the women, empty handed and unable
to stop the horror that had taken place.

Ellis stopped as they neared the top of the hill and grasped
Rook's elbow. Rook stared down at his cousin's mangled hand, then
back to his face. Ellis had never looked so drawn, so pale, in his
entire life. "You're injured," Rook said.

"My shoulder," Ellis admitted. "Through and through. It's not
bad."

The pain on his face told a different tale, but Rook didn't say
that. "Come back to the house and we'll get you and Juliana
looked at."

"No," Ellis whispered.

Emotion swelled in Rook as he realized what his cousin was
saying. "Handsome," he murmured, but that wasn't right. It wasn't
enough now. "Ellis."

Ellis stepped away. "I'm a lost cause. Because of me, that girl up
there is maimed. I can only destroy, cousin. And if I stay, I will."

Rook shook his head. "If you stay, maybe you'll become better.
Please. Please don't walk away."

Ellis glanced up the hill, and there was a powerful longing on his
face. For a moment, it felt like he might choose a different path.

But then he looked at Rook again. "Goodbye, Constantine. And
good luck. You were always the better man of us both. I know you'll
find your way."

Rook reached for him, but Ellis backed out of the way, hands
raised. Then he turned and walked down the hill, back toward the

horse he'd ridden in on. Away from their past and whatever future Rook would face now without him.

In the past, he would have followed. Ellis would have been his priority. But right now there was a woman at the top of that hill. A woman who needed him. A woman he loved more than his own life.

And so he went his way and his cousin went his own.

He crested the hill. Thomasina and Harcourt were helping Juliana down the hill toward his horse. He could only imagine the earl would carry her home at top speed to have the slash across her cheek looked at.

Anne stood watching him. When he reached her, she opened her arms and drew him against her briefly. "I thought you wouldn't come back," she said softly.

He shook his head. "Come, we must have your sister tended to. And then we'll talk."

She arched a brow. "I would like to talk."

He nodded, though he wasn't certain she would like to talk when it was all said and done. But it had to happen, so he took her arm and led her down the hill. Toward home. Toward the end.

CHAPTER 23

Anne stepped from Juliana's chamber, wiping her hands on a
fresh towel. It didn't make her feel clean. If anything, she felt
dirty and broken. And when she saw Rook waiting for her in the
hallway, still dusty and bloody from the earlier encounter with the
devil, her exhaustion mounted.

He straightened up and met her gaze. "Juliana?"

She bent her head. "The surgeon stitched the wound." She
pursed her lips. "It wasn't a large cut, but it was deep. She will likely
have a scar."

His mouth tightened and she saw his guilt work across every
feature. "I'm sorry."

She set the towel down on the table near her sister's door and
moved to him. She reached for his hand, taking it, feeling the
roughness of him against her softness. Then she guided him toward
her bedroom. He didn't resist as she took him inside, as she shut the
door. He moved to the chair beside her fire and sank down into the
cushion, staring at his clasped hands.

She leaned against the door for what felt like an eternity. "You
think this is your fault." It wasn't a question, it was a fact, and she
stated it as such.

He glanced up. "It *is* my fault. I tried to protect you by going back to who I am. Instead I let a monster walk into your midst and didn't end up protecting you or your family at all."

She wrinkled her brow. "Who you are," she repeated. "And who is that?"

"Rook Maitland," he said on a shaky breath. "Criminal, Anne. I stole from Harcourt."

"To end all this," she argued. "You cannot blame yourself for that."

He shrugged, and his sigh was long and heavy and pained. "Either way, I went back to my cousin's side. You have to understand, I would have done anything and everything to take care of this. I would have destroyed everything. And it isn't just to save you, Anne. In the end, destroying everything is what I know."

"You *are* Rook Maitland," she said, thinking of the man who had thrown his knife at Winston Leonard. Thinking of the man who had shattered a statue to find a hidden code. One he still had in his pocket, thanks to the confusion of the afternoon.

"I'm glad you understand that," Rook said, pushing to his feet.

"Do you understand that you are also Constantine Maitland?" she asked, tilting her head slightly to catch his gaze when he wouldn't give it to her willingly. "Constantine Maitland is my lover, a man so tender that he made me believe in a future I'd all but given up on. Constantine Maitland walked away from the violence of his past and lived on an island creating beautiful things as he tried to find his peace."

"He also walked away from you," Rook said with a shake of his head.

She let out a long sigh. "You are so convinced you are unworthy. But do you think I lied when I said I loved you?"

His jaw tightened, and it took a moment for him to grind out, "No. You *think* you love me because we spent weeks in close proximity, with an intense physical connection and a dangerous threat looming over us. But all that is gone now. And soon you'll remember who I am. And who you are. You'll understand that we can't be together."

Her heart hurt at that statement, made with such conviction. With such firm belief that it was true. And she was terrified it was. That he would make it so.

"Why?" she asked, wishing her voice didn't tremble.

"Look at your life, Anne." He motioned to the beautiful room around them. "I don't belong here."

She looked at him instead of their surroundings. She looked at the wild, untamed man before her. The one who made her heart race and her body open and put her heart at peace even in the middle of a storm. She looked at him, and she smiled.

"You're right, Rook. You don't."

R ook fought the urge to flinch at her quick acceptance of his words. It was better this way, of course. If she accepted the way things had to be, then she would forget him faster and move on with her life. He would go home. That would be the end of it.

"I'm glad you understand," he said as he edged toward the door she was blocking with her lovely body. "I'll leave tomorrow. As soon as Juliana is able to travel, I'm sure Harcourt will take you to London, because the danger hasn't passed."

"I won't go to London," she declared with a little smile tilting the corners of her lips.

He wrinkled his brow. "Of course you will. You cannot be alone with Leonard still out there, wanting his prize. You must go to London where you will be safe."

"I won't go," she said again, her voice filled with certainty. "Not without you." She moved forward a step, blocking his path to escape. Filling his world.

She took his hand, and some tiny part of his resistance died. "You said you don't belong in my world. But the truth is, Rook, neither do I. Not anymore. I belong in London with the man I love, fighting against an evil that threatens both my family and his."

There was such clarity to her tone and to her gaze that he could almost believe her. "Anne—"

She ignored his interruption and squeezed his hand gently. "I also belong with him on his island in Scotland where I can wonder at all his many talents for the rest of my life."

He shook his head. "You would hate me for taking you away from wealth and privilege, Anne."

Her brow furrowed. "When we reached Gretna Green last week and I didn't want to go home, do you remember what you said to me?"

"Anne—"

She ignored the interruption. "You chastised me. You said you would not accept that I'd live a long, cold life alone. You told me I hadn't earned that, even though my choices had potentially harmed someone I loved. But Rook, I was already living that life. I surrounded myself with frivolity and foolishness and tried to tell myself I was happy. But the first time I'd felt happy in a very long time was when I was with you, digging for clams and throwing knives at targets. It was the first time I felt...real."

His lips parted. "You can't mean that."

"But I do," she said with a tiny laugh. "I want real. I want you. Please don't make me chase you back to your island and ruin all your cast-iron pans until you submit to my whims, as you know you will."

"Perish the thought," he said with a laugh he never thought he'd use again once he lost her.

Only it didn't feel like she would let him lose her now. In a world where he'd fought to merely survive, now this woman stood across from him, fighting for him to be more. To thrive with her.

"I have told you I love you before," she said softly. "And I meant it every time I said those words. But now I need to hear you tell me the same if it's in your heart. Do you love me, Rook?"

He stared at the ground, his throat closing. His heart throbbing with pure terror. If he said those words to her, it would be over. He would be hers and he would never leave her side again. He would drag her down, or so he'd feared all along. But now he wondered if, in the end, she could actually lift him up.

It felt like that was possible. It felt like it could be true. And so he slowly met her gaze and jumped off the highest, most terrifying cliff of his life.

"I love you, Anne," he admitted, and the words felt like honey on his tongue. "I love you with all my heart, even though I know I could never deserve you. Even though I fear you will come to regret me and any life we make together."

Her eyes filled with tears, but they were happy ones. She moved toward him, closing the last distance between them and cupped his cheeks gently. "I love you, Rook. I love Constantine. I love all your facets and I will love them all forever."

He arched a brow. "That sounds like a wedding vow."

She blushed. "I hope it will be."

She said those words, and for the first time in his whole life he pictured a future. He pictured life on the island with her, he pictured laughter and love. He pictured rainy days when they stayed in bed and made love. He pictured children.

A future he had never imagined he could have became crystal clear, and he wanted to protect it, and her, with all his might. There was one way he could do that.

"Marry me," he said. "Marry me, Anne Shelley."

Her face lit with pure joy, pure happiness. And she gathered him closer as she whispered, "I will, I will, I will."

It was only when he kissed her that she stopped saying it. And then she showed him the same long into the night.

EPILOGUE

Ellis Maitland winced as he pushed his wounded shoulder back and felt the blast of pain work through his entire arm. He didn't hate the pain. He deserved it, after all.

He straightened on his horse, lifting his spyglass to watch as the carriage pulled up to the fine townhouse in London. The door opened and people began to pile out. Harcourt and his wife. Rook and Anne Shelley. And then the last.

Juliana Shelley took Rook's hand to be helped from the rig. She turned her face, and Ellis saw the bandage still resting upon her once-perfect cheek. The one that had been marred thanks to his bad deeds and worse decisions.

Ellis had done that to her, the woman he hadn't stopped thinking about for weeks. *She* was why he deserved the pain he felt now. She was why he didn't try to drink it away or take laudanum to numb it. *She* was why he had decided to settle his score with Winston Leonard once and for all, in a way that the bastard couldn't escape. Once the so-called gentleman returned to Town, that was exactly what Ellis would do.

Consequences be damned.

EXCERPT OF A COUNTERFEIT COURTESAN

THE SHELLEY SISTERS, BOOK 3

Preorder Now - Available March 3, 2020

Late Summer 1812

Ellis "Handsome" Maitland leaned back against the long bar, drink balanced in his hand as he scanned the wide, open room before him. It was a room he knew well, for he had hunted here at the Donville Masquerade for years. The notorious underground sex club was the perfect place for a man like Ellis to find lovers, find marks, find trouble.

Trouble had found him here, too. Not the harmless, fun kind. The *real* kind. The kind that had destroyed too many lives. The kind he had to end now in the only way that made sense anymore. There would be consequences, but there always were. This time he wouldn't be able to avoid paying them...and he had accepted that.

He slugged back his drink with a wince. A fissure of pain shot from his shoulder at the movement. He'd been injured there a few weeks before. But it wasn't just physical sensation that made him flinch. *Fear* ripped through his chest. Perhaps he hadn't *fully* accepted the consequences that would come. But he was working on it.

Across the room, the big double doors carved with rutting lovers opened and a woman stepped through. Not all that shocking. After all, ladies made up nearly half the occupants of the room, seeking their pleasure with as much gusto as the men here. Sometimes with more gusto, considering the masks most wore. He wore one too, and lifted his hand to touch the leather edge as he adjusted it.

What made the newcomer stand out was how much she didn't make the effort to do so. The ladies who came here were mostly experienced. Married women seeking what their husbands could not or would not provide, widows who refused to climb into a grave with their lost lovers, courtesans who sought the safety this club and its owner, Marcus Rivers, provided while they sold their wares for pleasure and enormous profit.

Everyone here had their role and their place, and as he looked at the woman who had just entered the room, he realized she did not. It wasn't that she didn't try. She wore a mask, but unlike the other ladies who made a show with feathers and satin and jewels, the disguise was plain. Her gown was daring enough. The neckline dipped down, revealing the upper swell of a truly lovely pair of breasts, but it looked like she had altered an existing gown, perhaps removing some tulle or lace that would offer more modesty. The gown was certainly not designed to attract in this den of sin. It had *butterflies* on the fabric, for God's sake.

And then there was her demeanor. The lady stood stock still just past the entryway and stared into the room, mouth open in just the slightest manner as she stared around her in what appeared to be shock.

Ellis had ceased to be shocked by anything in this world when he was six. Jaded, his cousin always used to call him. Before Rook stopped speaking to Ellis weeks ago.

He shook his head and pushed that troubling thought away. Protecting those he cared about was why he was here. Not pretty ladies who were looking around the big room at couples pawing each other, suggestively dancing, rutting against the wall as others leered.

The woman across the room shifted, looking back toward the door behind her. But she didn't run. She fisted her hands at her sides, and he watched her draw a long breath that lifted her breasts and come farther into the room.

It had been a long time since Ellis had played the libertine. Once upon a time, it had been his greatest pleasure, his way to make a living. Love games were his expertise. He'd carefully chose a mark, one who needed what he provided and little more, or one whose bad behavior made his ultimate abandonment fit the crime.

Then he seduced. He convinced. He fucked. Everyone left satisfied, at least physically, he with a heavier purse. But the last year or so…he'd had no interest in such things. His only attempt at a seduction scheme had started and ended badly…with his cousin's now wife. He winced at the thought.

The only flare of real desire he'd felt in that time had risen at the most inopportune moment, with a woman who surely despised him. The new wife's sister, actually. Juliana. Her very name was a benediction. A prayer Ellis sometimes woke saying in the night, hard as a rock as he remembered a brief moment when he'd held her in the midst of hell on earth.

But as he shook those thoughts away and stared at the woman at the door, he realized he wanted *her*. Just *wanted* her. Not for any ulterior motive, but because she had drawn his eye.

"Why not?" he muttered as he scanned the room another time and found it still devoid of the man he was hunting. "There won't be many chances left for pleasure, after all."

Those maudlin words hung in the air around him as he downed the remainder of his drink, set it behind him and shoved off the edge of the bar to stalk toward her.

She didn't look like she fit here, but certainly she must. Women didn't come to the Donville Masquerade unless they wanted the kind of pleasure innocents couldn't understand. Her darting gaze and shifting body could very well be part of a game. Play the innocent. Bring in the bees through a different kind of sweetness than that of the experienced women who were moaning and pleading around them.

And if she wanted to play games, Ellis Maitland was the perfect man for her.

He edged closer, and she turned at his approach, lifting her gaze to his. He came to a stop as he stared at those eyes. Eyes that he knew. Eyes that had haunted him for nearly a month, dancing into his dreams, digging him further into a hole he would never escape.

He knew those eyes. Knew their owner even though he'd only touched her once, held her once as she trembled in fear that was his fault. They had bled together. He after being shot trying to protect her. She after being sliced with a knife because he had failed. Even now he saw the edge of a scar on her cheek peeking out from under the mask. He flinched at the sight of it and the proof it provided to his mystery woman's identity.

But what was she doing there? What the hell was *she* doing standing in the middle of the Donville Masquerade, looking up at him with an expression of interest and fear, but not recognition?

Well, he was damned well going to figure that out. So he shrugged on a new mask, the one of "Handsome" Ellis Maitland. A persona he had come to hate as much as the physical mask that pinched the bridge of his nose as he smiled at her in false greeting.

Juliana Shelley couldn't breathe. She knew how to breathe, of course. But she couldn't seem to drag in air as the very tall, extremely well-favored man she'd noticed at the bar the moment she entered this place crossed the room toward her.

He couldn't be coming for *her*, of course. Not when all around her far more experienced women offered things she'd been taught all her life to withhold. She was shocked by what she saw, in truth. Men and women grinding together in a titillating display of activities she had only ever read about in a naughty book she found in her father's study months ago.

Being here was far more powerful than looking at those things, dreaming of them while she touched herself.

She swallowed hard because the man coming her way had stopped. He was just an arm's length from her now, and he stared at her, seeking...something. She didn't know what exactly, but she shifted under his regard.

He had a black leather mask covering the top half of his face, but she could see the almost navy blue of his eyes, the fullness of his lips, the harsh line of his jaw. His dark hair was a little too long and slashed across his forehead in a wild wave she somehow wanted to smooth.

Her heart rate increased as he gave her a half smile. Something cocksure and a little smug. She should have been turned away from such an expression, surely she had refused many a man of her class in the past because he had a smirk. But that wasn't what she wanted to do now.

"Good evening," he said, his voice low and rough in the din around them.

She swallowed hard. There went breath again. She could only hope she would remember how to form coherent sentences a bit more easily.

"Good evening," she returned, and hated that her voice cracked a little.

He arched a brow. She saw the movement beneath the leather, and for a moment she felt a sense of familiarity. But that wasn't possible. She didn't know this man. She couldn't.

"I couldn't help but notice your entry into the hall," he purred as he grasped two glasses of wine from a passing footman's tray. He held out one and she took it with shaking hands. When she did so, his fingers brushed against hers. By design, she thought, but that didn't reduce the effect of him touching her.

It was like fire under her skin. She sipped the drink to soothe her dry throat and try to regroup. "Thank you?" she said.

He chuckled at the question in her tone. "But I can't help but wonder if you know what you came for."

She jerked her face toward him. He had a touch of mocking to his tone now. Her spine straightened in response. She had never been the one in her family to fight. That was her sister Anne, but right now Juliana felt like channeling that strength to defend herself.

"I came here for what everyone comes here for," she said, forcing herself to meet his gaze. "Perhaps it is *you* who is confused if you must ask."

She sounded far braver than she felt, and for that she was pleased. He, on the other hand, didn't look as much. His full lips pursed a fraction—was it in annoyance? She couldn't tell without full view of his expression. And in that moment, she realized just what a dangerous position she'd put herself in. She didn't know this man or his intentions or motives. He could be of a cruel bent. He could be the kind of man who didn't accept no as an answer. Or who reacted with violence when challenged as she had just challenged him.

She swallowed hard, waiting for him to say something, do something. Then he cocked his head. "I beg your pardon, my lady. I think I have offended you. I didn't intend it."

"You didn't offend," she said softly, carefully. She glanced around them, the spell broken for a fraction of a moment. There was a couple at a table just to her left who were passionately kissing. The woman was perched in the man's lap, grinding down on him as their tongues tangled.

She darted her gaze away as a gasp left her lips and her body jolted with awareness. Gods, what had she done?

"Do you mind if I ask you a question?" he said.

She turned her attention back to him, wishing she didn't feel so hot and achy when he was standing so near. She nodded. "What is it?"

"Why *are* you here?" He motioned his head to the kissing couple. "Your shocked expression when you see them touch each other, it says to me that you aren't a bawd as you might wish to be seen."

She lifted her hand and touched her mask. It covered the scar that slashed her cheek. She couldn't feel it beneath the fabric, but she knew it was there.

Memories returned to her in a wave. Of a man who'd taken her because he thought she was her sister. As one of a set of triplets, that was a common mistake, but this time it had nearly proved deadly. The man had attacked when he wasn't given what he wanted.

And she was left...*damaged*. She saw it in the mirror every day. She knew what it would do to her future, especially when combined with the shocking actions of her sisters as they found their true loves in the past weeks.

"I'm here because I don't want to..."

She bent her head. This man was a stranger, she owed him no explanation. And yet with the masks, telling him some version of the truth felt easier.

"Want to?" he encouraged, almost gently.

She worried her lip with her teeth. "I want to feel something good," she said. "I want to feel something just for me."

He was silent for a long moment, holding his gaze on hers. It felt like an eternity passed by, like they were suspended in their own bubble amidst the shocking debauchery of the room around them. Then he held out a hand.

"Come with me to the back room. And I can make you feel something. That thing you want to feel."

She stared at the outstretched hand. Ungloved, strong, lean fingers, a scar across the top of the second and third knuckles. She let her stare slide up the man's forearm, hidden under black wool, to the bicep that strained against the same, to broad shoulders that spoke of strength caged beneath propriety.

And finally she let her gaze settle on his lips. This *was* what she'd come for, wasn't it? This moment where a man would choose her, would guide her to some quiet room and take her. Take the thing she had been guarding her whole life, and for what?

She didn't want her innocence anymore. She wanted to feel alive.

Still, those old habits died hard. Politeness, propriety, protection. If she took that hand, everything would change. There was a strong part of her that wanted to pivot and run from this room and its heady air of sex and passion. Run from a man who would crook his fingers and know she'd follow.

"Miss?" he said, his tone gruff.

She let out the breath she'd been holding and took his hand. "Yes."

There was a flicker of something in his eyes as she touched him. Desire, she thought. That emotion had never been pointed at her, but she'd seen such a look in both her sisters' husbands' expressions when the couples thought no one was looking. But there was something else in this man's gaze, too. Respect? Regret? Some combination of the two?

She didn't understand it, but it didn't matter what kind of past or pain brought this man here. It only mattered that he drew her forward, through the milling crowd, back to the entrance to a long hallway. He spoke briefly to a man standing there and then guided her farther from the relative safety of the hall. Into dimness and darkness.

From behind the doors she heard soft sighs, louder moans. Every sound put her further on edge. Made her question her decision, solidified the same decision as excitement grew in her chest. She was going to bed this man. Or let him bed her. She wasn't certain *she* knew how to bed anyone, but certainly not this man who glanced over his shoulder as he opened the last door in the hall.

Their gazes met.

"Still want this, angel?" he asked.

She tensed. Angel. Another man had called her angel once, not that long ago.

She pushed the thought away. She wouldn't think of him. She refused to acknowledge she'd thought of him at all over the weeks since she last saw him. Since an afternoon of blood and pain and confusion that had changed her life forever.

"Yes," she said, a bit too loudly as she tried to make the thoughts go away. "Yes."

He pursed his lips again and stepped inside the room. She entered behind him, passed him, looking around. It was a small room with a big bed in front of a roaring fire. It seemed clean, elegant even, with its fine artwork and silky coverlet. Odd, for she had not pictured a club of ill repute being fine.

The door closed behind her with a click and she pivoted to face it. The masked man was leaning against it now, watching her as she reached out a hand to support herself on the back of a close-by chair.

"Changed your mind?" he pressed. "Now that you're here?"

"Have you?" she asked.

"You know what I'll do, don't you?" he all but purred as he stepped toward her. "I'll strip that gown off you. You'll be naked before me. Then I'm going to touch you all over, until you're arching, until you're begging. And then I'm going to put my cock in you."

She winced at the bold language he used. And yet the soft, sensual tone of those words excited her, too. After living her life without such blunt address, she found she actually *liked* it.

"Tell me you want that," he said.

Her thighs clenched at the order, said in such a gravelly tone. "I-I think my coming with you to the room tells you that."

He shook his head slowly. "No. I need the words. Say the words to me."

Her cheeks felt like they were on fire as she stared at him. He couldn't *really* want her to repeat those wicked things. She'd never said those kinds of statements before. "I can't—"

"Say it," he interrupted.

She squeezed her eyes shut. This was her last out. She could pretend offense and stomp from the room. He was all but daring her to do so. Or she could surrender to exactly what had brought her here tonight. Give herself over to the things this man promised.

"I want—" she whispered.

"Look at me," he interrupted.

She let her eyes open and glared at him. "I want you to strip me naked. I want you to touch me. I want you to put your...your..." She huffed out a breath because her face felt like flames were devouring it. "I want you to put your cock in me. Please."

She added the last bit out of habit. A lady always said please. But his smile fell as she did so. He drew in a long breath and set his shoulders back slightly.

Then he reached up and, without preamble, tugged his mask away. Her eyes went wide and her mouth dropped open as he did so. Because she knew this man. Knew him far too well for her own good.

And he knew her.

"Ellis....Mr. Maitland," she stammered, taking a long step away from him.

He shook his head slowly. "Miss Juliana Shelley," he said softly. "What the hell are you doing?"

Preorder Now - Available March 3, 2020

~

The Shelley Sisters

A Reluctant Bride

A Reckless Runaway

A Counterfeit Courtesan

The Scandal Sheet

The Return of Lady Jane

Stealing the Duke

Lady No Says Yes

My Fair Viscount

Guarding the Countess

The House of Pleasure

The 1797 Club

The Daring Duke

Her Favorite Duke

The Broken Duke

The Silent Duke

The Duke of Nothing

The Undercover Duke

The Duke of Hearts

The Duke Who Lied

The Duke of Desire

The Last Duke

~

Seasons

An Affair in Winter

A Spring Deception

One Summer of Surrender

Adored in Autumn

The Wicked Woodleys

Forbidden

Deceived

Tempted

Ruined

Seduced

Fascinated

The Notorious Flynns

The Other Duke

The Scoundrel's Lover

The Widow Wager

No Gentleman for Georgina

A Marquis for Mary

To see a complete listing of Jess Michaels' titles, please visit:

http://www.authorjessmichaels.com/books

CPSIA information can be obtained
at www.ICGtesting.com
Printed in the USA
BVHW030940060220
571634BV00001B/73

9 781947 770256